CROWN ME DEAD

HEARTSTRING DUET
BOOK ONE

LIV ZANDER

INK HEART PUBLISHING

For my readers...

I know the cold floor where the shattered
things belong,
I was once that wreckage, scattered and
gone.

I was the mosaic, glued blind in the dark,
Put back together wrong, missing the spark.

But I burned down that ruin to build
something new,
A fortress of bone that the dark can't get
through.

Here! Take this fragment of the truth I have
found,
To help you rise whole from the blood on the
ground.

Take it and mend what was broken by
blight,
Until every piece fits you, finally, just right.

CHAPTER I

A WORD OF CAUTION

This is a **dark** fantasy romance, containing situations that might make some readers uncomfortable. You can visit www.livzander.com for details, or reach out to me directly! info@livzander.com

Elara

We wrap the dead with our hands steady and our mouths shut, because the living moan and scream enough for everyone.

Mother and I lift the old man from his pallet. Daron holds the oil lamp in the crook of his arm, his walnut hair mussed from a restless night, pretending he isn't missing the tip of his ring finger. Pretending, because that's how we like to lie to ourselves—if you don't look at rot, then rot can't find you.

It always does.

"He's light," I say, just to cut the silence, dragging my shoulder over that long, brown strand of mine that keeps clinging to my sweaty temple. "Either he starved, or the worms were greedy."

"Quiet, Elara," Mother mutters, but her dark eyes flicker with the shadow of a smile. Grayed, tired, still beautiful in the lamplight. Her wrinkles soften in the orange glow. She shoulders under the corpse's ribs. "Legs."

"I've got them."

The legs are mottled purple and black, marbled like spoiled meat. I carry the weight onto the table, careful not to jostle the man's jaw. We haven't wired it shut yet, and I don't need his tongue falling out like a slab of rotten eel.

Daron coughs behind his teeth—that quiet kind that means pain. Not that he would ever admit it, my little brother, who towers over me like a pine, not yet fifteen.

"Don't faint," I tease. "You'll bring shame to the family business."

"Break my heart." He gives a dramatic pound on his chest and sets the lamp down. "If I pass out, it'll be from boredom."

He leans in to help me strip the old man's shirt off over his stiff arms, his fingers deft, even with the missing tip. Another nail went yesterday. He wrapped the wound with linen and lemon balm on his own, because Mother's hands shook when she touched him and mine shook worse.

Rot found my little brother.

Because we touch the dead every day, some say. Hands in the earth, faces in the grave. And yet I've watched it take a child barely out of the womb. A lord who never once soiled his boots. The oak at the edge of the river that stood for two hundred years. The Henner's entire crops, gone gray-black by morning.

No one can tell us why.

No one can tell us how.

Mother lays out her tools: twine, needle, sponge, copper hook, little spoons for the eyes, and the jaw threader. It matters, the jaw. People don't like when their dead gape. They'll forgive a lot of things, but not an open mouth. Especially not when something climbs out during the Last Watch.

She takes the hook and eases it into the nostril, cracking through delicate bone so the rancid fluids drain. "Bucket, Daron."

My little brother passes it over, nose wrinkled against the gut-turning stench, watching me instead. "You've something in your hair."

"Ah yes, my crown." I tug out what might be a cobweb or a widow-thread and flick it aside. "Do I look royal?"

"You look like a cat that lost to a broom."

"Perfect." I ruffle his hair. He tries to duck, but I grab a handful, anyway. "No one will rob me then."

He sputters, and I giggle because death won't get the last laugh in my life. Not when—

My ears prick.

A small sound, like...like cloth sliding over wood. Not Mother. Not Daron.

I turn my head, but there's nothing in the corner where it came from. Only starched linen, folded tidy as church tongues on a bench.

It's been a long night...

Returning my attention to the man, I stuff the corpse's mouth with rosemary and wormwood. The herbs do nothing for their poor souls, but people believe they do, and belief is worth coin. Used to, anyway. I work some under the old man's tongue and wire his jaw. The thread pulls his lips neat, hiding the pain-choked grimace death had left behind.

Outside, voices rise. Glass breaks. Then silence. A silence thick enough to mean someone stopped breathing over a crumb of bread. The city of Marrowbrae is full of such pauses.

Mother clears her throat. "Eyes."

Flies crawl in a thick tide over the sunken eyes as Daron takes the spoons. He's the best with eyes. Always gentle, always steady. He slides them under the sunken lids with a touch so soft I want to cry, then clips the handles.

"You're good at that," I tell him. "If you weren't falling apart, I'd sell your hands to the king."

"Palace life, huh?" He gives me a cheeky grin. "Do they still pay in gold? Or bones these days?"

"Teeth. Painted to look like gold. Bite one, and it bites back."

He laughs, softly. His fingers shake, but he hides it. I let him.

We wash the body with boiled river water that smells like ash. The floor drinks what drips. Blood. Bile. It always drinks. We shroud him, pin the linen, lay marigolds at his feet so the flies go elsewhere.

Civilized.

We pretend we're still civilized.

When all is done, Daron leans over and washes his hands in the bucket. His breath hisses, the gray creeping along his fingertips getting worse by the day. How long until we have to chop away at him again? How long until the rot finds his heart?

My chest clenches.

I don't want to lose him.

"You'll be fine," I say, lying through my teeth if that sudden pressure behind my eyes is any indicator. His skin has that thin look, like parchment pulled too tight over a frame. I know the look. Seen it on the dying, on the boys who brought their grandmother trussed like meat. "I won't let the worms have you."

He smirks and straightens. "You don't get to decide that."

"Oh, but I do! One word from me, and the—"

"Blasphemy," Mother cuts in. "A disrespect to death."

"If death wants my respect, then he should send food instead of lectures." I kiss the bandage wrapped around my brother's finger, then spit on it. "For good luck."

He laughs. Good. I'll hoard his laughter until death can't find where it's coming from.

"Gutter Lane is next," Mother says when our work is done, ushering us to grab our things so the man's loved ones can cry over him. "I want this last one done with before the sun warms the maggots."

We step out into the city's alley, its foul breath huffing into our faces. Rank. Sweet. A stew of wet stone and boiled bones. Somewhere, a woman sings to a child who doesn't answer. We hurry, but we don't run. No point in that since rot is always faster.

Inside the Gutter Lane house, the boy who came to fetch us earlier sits on the steps, hugging his knees. The corners of his mouth are raw. Probably from screaming.

"Where's your pa?" I ask.

He shakes his head, his blond thatch filthy with months' worth of dirt.

"Sister? Grandma? Uncle?"

Another shake.

My molars clench, but I yawn it away. If I ground my teeth every time I met an orphan in this city, I'd have none left to chew.

"Inside," I say gently. "We'll be quick."

He looks at Mother. Looks at me, his blue eyes wide with expectation. Rumor has it that people used to flinch when the gravediggers came. Now, they look at us like a thirsty man looks at a cup of cool water, eager for us to get rid of the dead that pile in the streets.

His mother lies flat on the floor. Dropped dead from exhaustion is my guess, with how the impact must've popped the pustules on her face. Why else the explosive splatters of pus on the floor, arranged like a halo around her head?

We do the work. Nose, jaw, spoons.

I pack the mouth, pushing the last herbs past her swollen tongue, working them deeper.

Her throat convulses.

All three of us freeze.

The boy whimpers.

Herbs swell against her teeth. My knuckle's still inside the woman's mouth when a wet, gurgling sound rises from the back of her throat, thick and frothy, like a child blowing bubbles in milk.

Then the bile comes.

It trickles out from the corner of her mouth, warm and brown-green. It runs slow and deliberate over my knuckle before dripping between my fingers.

Daron gasps, staggering back, hand clamped to his lips.

Mother's voice is tight. "Sometimes the body remembers to breathe."

I look at the woman's chest. The skin ripples. A sluggish

pulse of air moves beneath her ribs, as though her lungs stir for one last tantrum.

But it isn't air.

A slick, pale wriggle forces its way between her teeth. One maggot. Then another, fat and white, squirming from under her tongue. They drop wetly onto the back of my hand like little pearls of rot that twist and curl.

Daron retches into a bucket. The sound is violent, splashing. His shoulders convulse, and his knees knock against the wooden floor.

Mother curses, jaw tight.

That doesn't stop me.

I just shrug. Wipe the bile off with a rag. Pinch the maggots, flick them to the rushes. One bursts when it hits the ground, spraying that sour milk stink everyone should be used to by now.

Rolling my eyes at how Mother crosses herself, I thread the needle, set it against the woman's lips, and stitch her mouth shut. The thread pulls neat, and whatever wiggles behind isn't my problem anymore.

"It happens," I murmur, mostly for Daron's sake. "Maggots eating someone from the inside out before death finishes the job. Seen it twice."

His only answer is another heave into the bucket. Poor boy.

I knot the final stitch, trim it clean, and wipe my hand on my apron. I look at Mother. She looks back, pale but steady.

After we finish, I wash the dead woman's ooze from my hands and look over at the thin boy. "Payment?"

His bottom lip trembles. He pulls two shiny buttons and a tiny handful of rice from his pocket, reaching it up to me.

"That'll do." Wrapping my fingers around his little

hand and closing it shut around his treasure, I lean down to him. "Take that to the orphanage by the river. Not by the chapel; they'll turn you away. The one by the river. Give them that, and they'll feed you."

At least for a month or two. Still, it's better to starve surrounded by nuns who will hold your hand than alone in this shack. Or worse, out there, where a wild pack of hounds will tear off his spindly limbs.

When we finish, I wash my wrists until my skin stings. The cracked mirror above the basin shows three Elaras. All of them thin. Pale. No rot yet from what I can see, but who knows whether the roil in my stomach is from hunger or maggots.

We leave the shrouded body behind for the Watch before we pick her up later, and step outside. A man is standing there, leaning under the overhang by the rickety stairs as if he belongs, his short black curls too shiny, his leather boot casually crossed over the other too clean.

Mother simply passes him in exhaustion.

Daron doesn't bother looking his way.

But I frown at those cheeks that are too peachy for this street, his silver buttons polished as if he still eats roasted meat. One of those would buy the boy a week at the river orphanage.

"You with the family?"

He drags his olive eyes over my curves like silk that wants to strangle. "I think I can work with that."

My skin skitters from more than just disgust.

"That's not the kind of business I'm in," I say, pushing past him as I look back. "But I'd take that pretty vest of yours for payment to stuff your mouth and sew it shut."

His jaw grinds. "The crown needs to be fed."

My eyes tighten into a squint.

The crown needs to... What?

"Uh...yeah..." A drunk, then. Or a fool. Either way, who can afford that these days? "You better go home and feed it then."

Just as I turn to where Mother and Daron melt into the dark, the man leans down, his breath tingling against the shell of my ear. "I think the crown would love to devour you."

My pulse trips, but I breathe it back into rhythm. Maybe he has a bad case of arrogance because he's noble or something. Clean. Clearly important. Or maybe crown is a euphemism for the palace, and he's been ordered to find a young maid for a night of entertaining our useless king?

I raise my middle finger to his pretty face and hop down the stairs. "Your crown can choke on this."

He chuckles. Low. Amused.

Pleased?

Squinting through the dim light of the city, I turn back once more. The space is empty now. Silent. Only maggots rustle somewhere at my feet. And for a moment, I swear they're chuckling, too.

CHAPTER

THREE

Elara

Dawn breaks like a rotten egg—sickly yellow and with the smell to match.

We come up the alley with our shoulders aching and our eyes full of grit. The graveyard fence crouches like a rib cage, iron spikes crowned in rust. Our house—two rooms and a lean-to—sits just beyond the nearest row of stones. It's quiet in that way that isn't silence.

More like the hush after a shout.

Mother stops so fast that my hip bumps her basket.

11

Daron stumbles into my back and steadies himself on my shoulder, but the pressure is wrong, too light, as if he's there, yet already a step gone.

"What's this?" Mother asks.

Our door hangs open.

I give her shoulder a squeeze and slowly venture forward. Pushing the door with two fingers, I listen to the room breathe.

Oh no...

Chairs tipped. The small chest overturned. Bowls on the floor, one smashed, one left whole by accident. The peg where Mother's shawl should be is bare. The nail where Father keeps his shaving knife hangs empty and splintered, as if someone yanked the steel and took the wood for spite.

Daron scoffs, the sound half amusement and half shock. "They robbed the house."

"Not only the house," Mother whispers as she jerks her chin at the lean-to door at the back that stands ajar, her shadow cutting the slant of early light.

I walk over and peek in. No spades on the hooks. No mattock under the bench. Rope coils stripped. Linen gone. Even the pitch we use to seal seams pried out of its pot with a spoon.

"I'll fucking bury you," I ground out as if the thieves might be waiting in the bushes to be corrected. "Of all the people out there, they come and steal from *us?*"

Mother runs her fingers down my strands as if combing out my rage. "We are all hungry," she says in a voice that holds no excuse. "Hunger makes thieves of the gentle and beasts of the rest."

"We deal in death," Daron says. "Since there's plenty of that going around, they think that means coin."

"They think wrong," I say. "If death were coin, then Father would be king."

As if the word tugged a string, Father coughs inside.

No, not a cough. A tearing.

We run inside.

He lies where we left him, propped with pillows that were once fluffy goose down but are now tired sacks. His beard is gray at the corners and dark where the sweat clings. Beside the bed sits the bucket they didn't bother to take. The surface is pink, flowered with bubbles. A clot slides down the inside as if it's trying to leave without troubling anyone.

Mother takes his hand. "Husband."

He blinks. For a moment, his eyes are young and bright, and offended by the dust in the morning sun. Then the fog floats back and settles. He reaches for the bucket by instinct...and fails. Daron lifts it with reverent hands, and Father spits a string of blood into the rim, gasps, and falls back into the narrow world of damp sheet wrinkles.

"Sleep," he breathes into a room that smells like pennies and soggy wool. "Let me sleep."

After a pat on Father's hand and a nod that straightens the useless worry from her mouth, Mother goes to the hearth and takes stock of what the thieves left us. A carrot so old it's wrinkly. Two onions, one moldy. A nub of lard. No salt, because of course not.

She sets the pot anyway. That's the kind of woman she is—building a fire even when the thatch is wet, lighting the flame with determination alone.

"It's not so bad," Daron says with a slow, tired swat of his hand. "We can—"

His voice turns to coughing so violent his knees bend to

sit on the stool. But the wood shifts, and his shins hit the floor, ripping another heave from his caving lungs.

I reach him too late, but I stay with him, one hand on the nape of his neck until the fit passes. "What did I say? That you should stay home, right?"

"It's fine," he says when he gets enough air to lie. He wipes his lips with the back of his wrist, a gray smear left behind. Gray, not red. Somehow that feels worse. "Someone has to step in for Father. Two women can't carry a big man."

"Well, you shouldn't be carrying anything at all," I snap, because if I say it gently, I'll break. "Lie down."

"For once, I shall obey the queen of the broom," he murmurs, but when he tries to stand, his hand slips on the stool's seat.

I shoulder his weight the way I did last winter when he woke with his fingers numb as stones. He's too light. Young men should feel like carved wood when you lift them, not like empty baskets.

I put him to bed in the corner where the light doesn't reach. He turns his face into the pillow the way he did when he was small, afraid of thunder but pretended he wasn't. Half his hand stays outside the blanket where the bandage sits. I tuck it in. I stand there and pretend that what I'm doing matters. That it will somehow save him.

That clench in my chest worsens.

It won't.

"We should eat," Mother says, stirring the pot as if she were stoking a miracle. "Then we right the shack."

Shaking my head as though it might distract from the mounting pressure beneath my ribs, I head for the door. "You eat. I'll set the shack now."

Outside, the graveyard hisses with slow heat, dew

rising from the grass in a breath you can see. The sun lifts itself over the palace hill to the right, smoke coming from chimneys smearing the sky. The city says it's their cooking fires, that King Kael is feeding the poor with it and will soon bring an end to this pestilence that starves the kingdom.

The city says many things.

The city lies to itself like a lovesick drunk.

I pass between headstones I know better than faces on the street, the dirt littered with broken trinkets dragged from graves. A brooch with its stone cracked out. A handful of glass beads, sticky with soil.

That's how deep we've fallen.

We steal from the dead now.

I sweep the mess with a branch because the broom is gone, too. *Who steals a broom?*

What remains, I put into a broken crate. Not because anyone will come put them back, but because I have the feeling they'll sink if I leave them in the dirt. Iron does that.

Grief, too.

When my hands slow, I let them. No one to watch. I squat between graves with my elbows on my knees and the hem of my dress in the dirt. There's a place in me that aches exactly the size of Daron's palm. It has for weeks now.

Today, the ache has claws.

I press my forehead against my palms and let the air leave me, slow enough not to sob. If Daron dies—no...*when* Daron dies, how will I ever smile again? How could I possibly?

The light changes.

Boot leather whispers on dust.

My pulse drums against my throat, but I don't flinch. If it's a thief, I want him to see a woman who doesn't bend to fear.

"Long night," a man says conversationally, his voice somewhat familiar. "Death kept you busy."

I look up...

...and frown.

The same man from Gutter Lane sits on the gravestone across, his long leather-clad legs stretched out, his starchy, white-ruffled sleeves crossed in front of polished vest buttons. His black curls are cut ordinarily, but the shine defies the dullness of the world around us.

"You again," I say, unsweet. "Have you come to steal what's left?"

Eyes like moss assess the trinkets strewn about, the crooked lean-to, the footprints in the dirt. "I'm not in the trade of stealing shovels."

"What's your trade then?" Sitting back on my heels, I let my hands dangle between my legs in all their heaviness. "If it's forcing conversation on bored young women, then I suggest you should learn a new one."

A scoff tumbles past his lips before he shakes his head. "My trade is as old as breath." He glances over the field of stones before his eyes lock with mine. A beat suspends the moment before he says, "As is yours."

"Death work isn't a trade." If one has the stomach and the nerves, it takes little to dig a grave and drop a body into it. "It's a heavy shovel you get handed when the wolves come."

"A shovel you carry, oh so well."

"Commendations are for the dead," I say and brush the dust from my fingers. "Save your compliments for obituaries; they need it."

His mouth curves up, a line so perfectly even it seems studied, mocking. "And what do the living need?"

"Bread." I stand slowly because my knees are a debate

I'm tired of losing. "And for men in pretty vests to say what they came to say."

"Very well…" His lips straighten. "I brought you a choice."

Because life isn't cruel enough already, we definitely need more of those. "Humor me."

A curt nod. "Turn me away and watch your kin die while rot hasn't claimed your eyes yet. Or…" His gaze flicks to the palace roof far away, then back to me. "Help me and sacrifice your own life to save those of your loved ones."

I don't flinch at sacrificing myself. I flinch at the audacity of the word *save*, the most casual delusion when we all know there's no cure for the rot. No hope for us. "Did you bring bread with that choice? Might make it easier to swallow."

"The crown needs to be fed."

"Does it?" I lift a brow. "Do I need to take you back to the head doctor? Is he missing one of his patients?"

He takes the rebuke like wine—pleased it stings. "Insolent. He will like that. As will the crown."

"Listen, I have no idea what you're talking about, but I'm sure the crown has teeth enough to feed itself."

"The crown has no teeth." He rises from the headstone. "The king does. For now."

My gaze trails to the faraway roof of the palace, its spires like spindly fingers. The Reign of Rot, the city calls King Kael's tenure. Each year since his ascension has been nothing but a step deeper into pestilence.

"You're from the palace." It's pretty clear now, beyond his health and the meat on his bones. They're suffering neither rot nor hunger there, are they? "Are you working for the king? Is that your age-old profession? Pulling strings in the background to distract the common folk from a king's incompetence?"

His jaw clenches for a second, muscles jumping beneath skin as flawless as polished stone. "That sums it up well."

"So you're what?" Dressed and fed like this, moving about with such certainty, he had to be consequential. "His...steward?"

He hesitates for a second. "Indeed."

"And what do you want of me?" The words come out flat so they cannot shake. Not even the palace rats ever make it down to the city, so why is this peacock strutting between my graves? I don't trust him. "What does it mean? The crown needs to be fed?"

"The kingdom is rotting, and the people rot with it. As does everything else, turning the realm into an endless field of death the likes of which existence has never seen before." His mouth slants, something like exhaustion carving into its line. "This will not stop. Not until everyone is dead. Or until the crown on the king's head is fed as its curse demands."

"Curse?" That word alone braids cautious dismissal through my rumbling stomach. "What do you mean, curse?"

"The crown gives certain powers to the king who wears it. But the cost is..." A solemn nod, gaze sinking to a torn ribbon trampled into the dirt. "Blood is what the crown demands. Your blood might do."

My blood.

I turn that over once, the way you'd investigate a gold coin looking for rust. A gravedigger's blood, smelling of lye and river water and other people's rot. Sure. That'll do it. That'll save the world.

"There's no such thing as curses." Nothing but superstitious nonsense mumbled into empty ale jugs. "I've never heard of this. Not even from the drunks in the tavern."

"Because the royal families did a fine job of keeping the curse a secret. Rightfully so." He meets my eyes, the way the rising sun casts over them, bringing out specks of gold in his mottle-green irises. "Simple folk love to trade in gossip. Gossip breeds fear, and fear makes kings look very mortal, and that cannot be allowed. Only the bloodline, the priest, and those who clean the bloodstains are permitted to know what the crown truly costs. The rest of the world sleeps better believing it's just a crown."

That clench in my throat, I swallow down. "What a load of drivel."

"King Merrick, Kael's father, reigned for nearly five decades," he says with more force in his voice. "Fifty years of fat harvests and flowing wine. Have you ever wondered why his three queens all died?"

I can only tilt my head at his ridiculous question because I didn't even know he had three queens. "Not a single damn time."

A scoff tumbles from his lips, but his mouth carries no bemusement as he turns away. "Right." His slender fingers rake through his short black curls, straightening some of them before they twist again. "Peasants don't ask what happens at the palace. They ask if the baker has any bread left."

"Take your silly stories and get off our land," I grind out. "I don't believe any of it."

"Belief is a lantern." He leans close, too close, cooling the air between us. "Dusk comes either way."

I laugh because I am not made to show fear with my mouth shut and turn back toward the house. "Get off the graves before I bury you in one."

"Very well." He gives a tug at his white cravat. "Should curiosity change your mind, find me after sunset. The copse behind the graveyard," he calls after me. "Come alone. Bring no light."

Back at the door to our house, Father drags at the air. Daron coughs until his ribs creak. I stop in the doorway with my fists full of nothing and glance back over the empty graveyard. Behind it, the palace roofs swim in the rising heat like marrow under the steam of broth.

I don't believe him.

I count the hours to dusk, anyway.

FOUR

Elara

The evening porridge lies to us. It steams as if it's rich, smells as if it remembers milk. But milk isn't gray, and certainly not specked with black grit to give it weight.

Mother sets two bowls.

"We'll need a third." I rise from the chair by the table and turn toward Daron's bed. "I'll get him."

"Don't." Mother's voice is a thread pulled tight.

"He has to eat; he needs strength. He can't keep sleeping through meals and expect—"

"Elara!" My name snaps, brittle as dead twigs. "Let him rest."

I turn. The rebuke prickles, and for a beat, I'm ready to sling mine back. Until I see it, the wet glint she swipes from her pallid cheek with the heel of her hand, quick and secret, the way a strong woman hides her sorrows.

I swallow, put my ass back on the chair, and pick up my wooden spoon as I watch Mother fill two bowls. Then she sits without sitting, her spine like a spear that won't bend, and stares into her porridge.

"Daron will eat when he wakes," she says, softer now, and scoots her bowl toward me. "Take half."

"I'm not that hung—"

"Take half." No more argument in it than gravity. "It will only be the two of us tonight. Best fuel your strength."

I split the porridge and push the rest back. She nods once and lifts the spoon. Our roof pops. Father coughs in the back, and the bucket answers him.

I keep my eyes on the window so they don't run to Daron and turn damp. The sun's begun to slide behind the yew, stripping the color from things as it goes. The graveyard is a page going blank, line by line.

A pulse starts along my ribs, a little drum counting down each annoying second. If there's a curse—*there's not*—then where did it come from? Who put it on the crown? Why? And if the rot will leave when the crown gets fed—*which sounds so ridiculous*—then why hasn't King Kael done it already? Is he cruel? Stupid?

I could've asked that stranger.

I should have...along with his name.

Sighing, I dip my spoon into the porridge, scalding my tongue with a steaming mouthful. He was right about one thing: the palace keeps its stories close, always has. That's how they like it: quiet halls, quiet people. Births, coronations, heirs, funerals—always a whisper, never a word. Privacy for holy rites, the priests say.

Now it smells more like secrets...

"Mother," I say, not looking away from the window. "What do you know of the palace and King Kael?"

She makes a sound that might be a laugh or might be the spoon knocking her teeth. "Is this the hour for gossip?"

"Not gossip. Just wondering."

"He was kind once." She nods into the steam. "Lowered the city tax the year the barley turned yellow. Opened the granary when the river climbed the wharf. Men do not forget kindness from a king. They forget everything else."

"And then?"

"Then the harvests halved, fifth year. Halved again. Bread went dear. Rats fattened on the dead." She stirs, even though the spoon has nothing left to do. "Perhaps he fattened with them, hiding in his palace, not showing his gut to those who starve. Perhaps the palace stinks like the river by now." Her mouth twists the way it does when she threads a needle into tough cloth. "What should a woman whose roof leaks care why it leaks? She sets out buckets."

"What of King Kael's father?"

"King Merrick?" Her eyes focus on nothing, spoon hovering. "Times were good. The poor grew round. Festivals were honest. Even when the rain fell, it fell politely."

"And his queens?" I keep my tone flat, curious but not too curious. "He had many, didn't he?"

"Three." A frown, spoon pausing mid-air. "Or four, maybe. The priests change their songs so often, who bothers to keep count? One of them—Queen Ophelia, I think—gave him the heir. Or maybe it was the one before her?" She shakes her head. "Doesn't matter. Stories change like bed linens. Deathcloth doesn't."

"How did they die?"

She lifts one shoulder. "Birthing, fever, sorrow. A slip on the steps. A cough that did not stop. Depends who you ask. The palace gives no reason. The reason is that women die. Elara, I don't care why queens fade if the ovens are hot and the winters tolerable."

"You've never wondered?" I press, impatient for answers, for a thread of hope that the stranger's story is true. That there is a curse. A *solution*. "Ever?"

"I have wondered if the butcher would forgive our debt," she says. "I haven't wondered about palaces, or queens, or kings."

A soft thud on the window.

I look back at it.

A moth kisses the glass and leaves the powder of its wings. Behind it, the sun rubs itself smaller on the hill, and the palace roofs catch the last light, holding it like a secret you cannot force from a mouth.

After sunset, he said. At the copse behind the graveyard. Come alone. Bring no light. What sensible girl ventures into the night—to meet a stranger, no less—without bringing a light?

"What will you do?" Mother asks when I rise.

I carry my bowl and spoon to the washbasin. "Walk the grounds. See if the thieves dropped anything of use when they hurried off."

"Do not go far. Night will set soon."

"I won't."

She hears and doesn't believe me, folding her hands over her knee until her knuckles pale. "Do not be brave."

"I don't know how."

FIVE

Elara

The sky is already the color of prunes when I step outside and fetch the good lamp. I trim the wick clean. Oil is dear, but so is getting stabbed by a lunatic I don't see coming. I take a rusty knife from an old milking bucket and tuck it into my belt, more for the comfort of the weight than any hope it could cut and kill.

The graveyard leans toward night as I walk along the headstones. Names sink, rise, stretch, and narrow as my lamplight washes over them. I pick my way between stones, lamp low, the light puddled around my boots.

Moths come to drown and leave their lace on the glass, following me into the trees.

They sit where the fence fails into brambles. No path. Only a suggestion where others have passed—boys to dare each other, men to piss, lovers to ruin each other gently. I hold the lamp higher, and the trees answer by knitting closer, leaves whispering above my head.

"He said after sunset," I mutter. "Of course he's not here. Men who speak in riddles can't be trusted with punctuality...or anything, really."

The ground dips, slick with leaf rot. The lamp throws more shadow than comfort now. Then, the air cools.

"Fine," I call out. "Steward? Court rat? Pretty vest? If you've dragged me out to be murdered in a romantic setting, I'm charging—"

A hand seals over my mouth.

Another clamps my wrist.

"Saints blind you," the man hisses against my temple, angry and close. "Bring no light, I said. Dusk, I said. Not beacon."

His hand slides off my mouth. A breath brushes my cheek as he yanks the lamp from my grip, flame roaring up for a fight until it sighs out with a pop. Dark slams shut.

My eyes see nothing.

My pounding heart imagines too much.

"I like to see the blade pointed at my belly." I shove at a chest as hard as a slab of iron. "Or do you prefer women to stumble into your knife so you can feel gallant when you catch them on the steel?"

"If I wanted you gone," he mutters, low and furious, tossing my lamp into the shrubs, "then you'd be waking up in a cell with your name written wrong on the door."

"Such an important man you are," I shoot back, because if I don't argue, I will notice that we are still close enough to share a damn heartbeat. "If you expected me to arrive like an obedient fool, then perhaps you asked the wrong girl to come."

"I asked exactly the right girl," he says. "After all, you came."

He shifts, and his shoulder brushes mine. Now that my eyes have adjusted to the darkness, I can see the line of his cheekbones sharpen inches from my face. Hints of moonlight filter faintly through a canopy of a thousand leaves that rustle above, bringing out the fine curvature of his dark brows, that thin shadow around his full lips. Annoyingly handsome.

"Don't enjoy that too much," I mutter, which is bravado dressed as wit. "I came for answers. Haven't decided a thing."

He lets out an annoyed breath. "Very well, Elara. Answers, then."

"Stop saying my name like you own it just because you heard my mother hiss it at the Gutter Lane house." Heat slips under my words. "What's yours, anyway?"

He hesitates the smallest half-beat. "Vale."

"That's a place, not a name."

He shrugs, unbothered.

"Fine, Vale." I fold my arms. "Where does this cursed crown come from?"

He smacks his tongue. "It is from Death."

A laugh climbs my throat and thinks better of it when it finds no air. "From death," I repeat flatly. "As in...what? Grave dirt climbed onto a throne one morning?"

"As in...*Death*," he says, capital in his tone like a bellstrike. "A king tricked him a very long time ago."

"Him?" I blink at Vale. "Death isn't a person. It's sickness, rot, a sermon, and a shovel."

"And life is birth, breath, a prayer, and a miracle." He doesn't flinch. "Language cheats. Death is a man, and he bargains like one: keeps ledgers, honors debts, takes what's owed. And what is owed is blood."

When the wind howls through the canopy above, he looks up and leans us both deeper into the shadow under a branch, steering me with a hand at the small of my back. The touch is warm, precise. Infuriatingly gentle.

I huff against the frustration in my chest. "Cheated Death, how?"

"That hardly matters at this point, unless you came for history lessons."

"Fine," I drawl. "Let's say Death is a man, and a king cheated him. What's that got to do with the crown?"

"A very long time ago," Vale says, "a king demanded a crown that held every grace greedy men beg for: prosperity for his realm, health for himself, and protection for his rule."

"Protection for his rule?"

"Aside from the sand of life running out on him eventually, our kings cannot die. Not of sickness, disease, or injury," he says. "Not while he wears the crown, which is fused to his skull unless he decides to lift it."

"And Death gave away such a crown?" I ask before I can help myself.

"Death doesn't break the law," Vale says softly. "Nor does he forgive what it cost him to keep it. He tore a string from his heart and tempered gold around it. That string sits inside the circlet even now, humming like a nerve. The crown does what was wished, but the heartstring grows hungry for blood, about every fifteen years. Sometimes much sooner."

"And then?"

"Then it must be fed." His breath moves the hair near my ear. "Fed on a king's wife—a queen. Her life poured into the gold to quiet the string."

"And if not?"

"Sickness. Rot." He lifts his arm, gesturing into the blackness of the night. "Death."

I taste unease and the porridge that lied. "You expect me to believe this? That Death—an actual person, no less— plucked himself like a harp."

"Believe it or don't. The fact stands whether peasants accept it or not."

"Ridiculous." But what if it's not? What if it's true, and there's an end to this rot? A chance for Father and Daron to recover? To live! "Alright," I venture carefully. "Assuming that I believe you, why hasn't King Kael fed it then? If this is all so neat? Marry a girl, bleed her out, make a sacrifice. Why no wedding? Why no funeral?"

"Because our king is selfish." That last word carries a sharpness to cut. "He thinks if he denies the crown, denies the blood, then it will starve the curse. Break it."

"What if he's right?" The words come too quick, too defensive, like I've taken the king's part without even fully believing this story. "What if starving it works? What if the curse shatters and we all dance with bellies full and pockets heavy?"

"Then you will have buried half the realm to get there." Vale's voice is too calm, too certain. "If it breaks at all," he adds, "which it will not."

"You speak like a man who knows the end of every story."

"I know the end of your brother's story." His words are like a blade pressed against a wound already weeping. "How much longer does he have, you'd wager? Enough time for the king to condemn hundreds, *thousands* of lives... where only one will do?"

My throat thickens with whatever tears I swallowed earlier. I hate that he knows where I hurt. Hate that he puts his finger in, swirls it around in my sorrow.

Taking a deep breath, I run his tale through my head like a length of rope, testing for integrity. If it holds, my life buys that of Father and Daron. If it frays, nothing changes but the manner of my death: quickly, inside a palace instead of slowly out here.

"If this heart thing is real, then one life saves the rest. One." I hold up a finger I'm glad I can't see. "In trade for my family."

"An entire realm," he says with a reverence that doesn't quite match the lack of heroism in my blood. "What is one life weighed against the realm of Issoria?"

"My life. So you'll forgive me if I argue the scale."

"Argue," he says. "But argue with the numbers, not the story. How many houses boiled filthy water for soup this week? Ask the gravedigger's daughter how many maggots fit into a woman's mouth."

"I *am* the gravedigger's daughter."

"I know," he says quietly. "That is why I asked *you* to come."

I swallow around a dry stone of anger. Anger that I could've saved so many sooner. Anger that I might still end up saving none.

"Say I'm a fool and do what you ask," I venture. "The king hasn't wed anyone yet. Why would he start with me? A gravedigging peasant."

"Because…" His gaze slips to my lips, and that shouldn't cause my stomach to squeeze the way it does. "You have something the other didn't have."

Words that would have just about any girl giggly, if not for how my wit catches on his mention of *other*. "You tried this before? Getting him to marry someone? To feed the curse?"

"Once. Obviously with no success."

"Why not? What's so complicated about killing a girl when there are plenty to be found in ditches each morning?"

"Because love is a troublesome thing," he says with a shrug, letting the delicate silver strings embroidered onto his tailored vest shine here and there. "It has to ache his heart when he sacrifices his queen—the crown will accept no less. But he keeps his heart well-guarded, opening it to none."

"Love?" I all but breathe. "You expect me to walk into a palace and…what? Make a king fall in love with me? By when? Supper? I don't know the first thing about…" The word sticks, ridiculous and huge in my mouth. "Love."

"You know more than you think." The back of his knuckles find my jaw in the dark, just a graze to remind my skin of our closeness. "You turn down payment so a boy can live for another day. You hold your father's bucket with steady hands. You make jokes for your brother, giving the rot in his lungs the sound of laughter."

"You've certainly paid attention from the shadows." A realization that has me go still for a moment. "I'd say what you're doing is treason, plotting behind the king's back. If King Kael can't even trust you, then why would I? What else is in this for you?"

"You mean, aside from not having to smell rot wherever

I go?" He arches a brow. "Do not let my presentation fool you into thinking that I don't suffer this curse alongside everyone else."

"Well, *you* look very healthy. Fed. Groomed." I make the mistake of flaring my nostrils in jest, only for his scent of carnations and dew to climb into my nose. "Insultingly clean."

"At dawn, a carriage will wait for you down by the eastern bridge," he says. "It will take you to the palace, where you will fill the position of caretaker. Everything has been arranged."

"Caretaker? Of the grounds?"

He dares to roll his eyes. "The king."

"I comb his hair, help him into his breeches, button his shirts?"

Vale's head wavers as though it doesn't know in which direction to move, but eventually nods. "Among other things."

"I've only ever cared for corpses."

A strange sound stirs in his chest, like a subdued laugh, his torso shifting to leave. "At dawn, Elara. Assure your family that coin and bread will be sent in lieu of your presence."

"Wait!" I grab his shoulder, strongly enough I hope I don't look like I need the answer, but... "What is it I have that the other didn't?"

His mouth is close enough now that I feel the shape of the words before I hear them. "You'll see."

SIX

Elara

The carriage waits where the eastern bridge sags over the river, a relic that barely remembers being beautiful. The gilded trim? Dulled by weather. Those carved dragons along the frame? Gnawed to toothless lizards. The crest on the door? Gouged to a smear, as if the city took its knife to pride and kept cutting when it bled.

I stand with my hand on the latch and look back.

Our house makes itself small in the distance the way animals do when they're shrinking from a predator. Mother is not in the doorway. No, she's at the stove, pretending that I hadn't announced that I would leave to work at the palace.

It would be a lie to say it didn't break my heart to leave them behind, with little excuse beyond the coin we needed for useless medicine and even more useless healers. It's not fair how I'll get to sleep on starched linen tonight with my belly full of bread while my family beds down with rats, their stomachs twisting.

I climb into the carriage.

Vale sits inside, wearing the same clothes as…well, always: clean boots meant for better floors, a fine vest that refuses to stain, white ruffle at his throat, bright as a dove held too tight.

He taps the seat beside him. "Close the door."

I do. The driver clucks his tongue, and the carriage lurches. The curtains shiver and fall still.

Vale leans over, unspooling the tie on the nearest curtain, drawing it shut. "Privacy."

"For what?" I settle knee to knee with him because the carriage is stingy with space. "Whispered treason? Riddle lessons?"

"For your education," he says. "And because I dislike the way light invents me when I'm not paying attention."

Arrogant peacock. "Is that a joke?"

"Almost."

The wheels strike a pothole deep enough to bury a child. I bounce and catch myself on the curtain pole. Vale's hand comes to my knee—steadying, supportive, too warm. He leaves it there until the road turns less evil, then takes it back with a rubbing of his fingers as though he touched dirt.

"First," he says, businesslike, "you will not pity him."

"Pity him?" I echo. "Why would I? I lost neighbors that I

knew and relatives that I didn't, all because he's being stubborn."

But that's not entirely true, is it? The king is trying to break a curse. I just don't know if that's stupid, or valiant, or both.

"Second, and perhaps more importantly." Vale shifts to sit a little slantwise, thigh resting against mine in that practical way people have when they ride and pretend they aren't touching. "Breathe with me. Deeply. Into your chest."

"Pardon me?"

"Elara..."

"Vale." I smile with too many teeth. "You want me to pant in a box with you at dawn? At least buy me supper first."

"Miss?" A voice comes through the window from the driver's box along with the *ca-lop* of the horses. "Are you quite alright?"

My molars dig down on the fleshy inside of my cheeks for a moment before I shout, "Just bored with the company."

"Breathe," Vale repeats, unamused and very patient. He touches two fingers to the soft place just under my ribs. "Not here." He moves his hand up, flat over my sternum. "Here. Quiet. Fill the top of your lungs. Deeper. Less"—he flicks a glance at my throat—"less apologetic."

"I never apologize." But I do as he asks because the carriage is small and my bravado can't stand up in it without hitting its head. "Why are we doing this?"

"Like this, the king will notice that you're not strangling your breath," he says. "That you're not flinching."

"From his...authority?"

"Precisely," he mumbles as he retrieves his hand. "He's notoriously difficult, rejecting any aid offered. When you speak to him, never say that you wish to help. No. You want to...to...*stay*."

"Help makes men smaller." Mother told me that a hundred times whenever Father refused her holding his bucket. "Stay makes them feel—"

"Wanted," he finishes. "He has not felt wanted for a long time."

"Hard to believe," I say with a scoff. "Rotting kingdom or not, he's still a king. Surely, girls line up on the palace gravel for a chance to exchange plums for potatoes."

His jaw grinds. "Power does not quicken every pulse the way songs promise."

The road takes a long breath and exhales on its own, rocking us. A village slides past the narrow slit of light where the curtain doesn't quite meet the frame: black windows, a goat on the stoop chewing cloth as if it were hay, two boys playing at knucklebones with teeth.

A woman darts from a doorway, thin legs flashing pale in the rutted dust. She runs after the carriage, hands out, like the air might drop bread into them if she just reaches far enough. I watch her shrink to nothing and bite my tongue, because what's the point of a king trying to starve a curse if it starves all of us first? Maybe he *is* selfish.

"There will be staff," Vale eventually says. "Not many. The sensible ones left when the smell started."

"Smell?"

"Vinegar, myrrh, and the like," he says with a dismissive swat of his hand. "To keep the rot away."

"What do I call him? The king?"

"Your Majesty, until he tells you not to," Vale says. "Ideally, he forgets he *has* a name whenever he's speaking to you."

"You want me to be flirtatious."

"I want you to be true." He tips his head. "Speak your opinions the way you do. Be blunt, don't sugarcoat. Do not curtsy too low."

"I wasn't planning on throwing myself onto the floor. I do that only for death and spilled soup."

A strange kind of focus settles around his green gaze, but it's gone with a quick shake of his head. "You will bring no flowers. Ever."

"Tragedy. I look gorgeous behind lilies."

"Never open the curtains." He flicks his eyes toward the slit, where the morning sun fails miserably against the gray haze that lingers over the countryside. "Light is unkind."

"Why not just say that the king is hideous?" That Vale doesn't correct me only confirms what generations of royal inbreeding can do to a face. "How do I get him to sacrifice me? Gaining his love first seems pretty counter-intuitive to that."

"It is a challenge we will see to once it presents itself. At first, his refusal to take a queen was sheer stubbornness." Vale rubs his thumb over his lower lip, his gaze getting lost in the world behind the curtain for a moment. "But the determination to break the curse he developed in the last year..."

The last year? That's quite recent. So, that begs the question: what changed? Someone or something must've planted the thought of trying to get one over on Death yet again. A dream. A priest. A memory. Something.

"Do you know where it came from?" I ask. "The idea to break the curse?"

"At this point, I believe it must have been a fever dream." Vale's gaze lifts, unreadable in the half-light. "He won't say, and I found no recordings, no witnesses of anything that suggests otherwise."

"Well, this is quite the lover's list. The king sounds about as pleasant and personable as a porcupine for wiping your ass after a stew of beans. And you want me to seduce him? Tie into his soul? With long, dull hair? Eyes of the most ordinary brown? And not a single clue about the few female graces I possess." To make a point, I hold my hands out. "I'm a gravedigger's daughter."

He studies my hands—my calloused, practical hands—and takes one. He turns it, thumb finding the center of my palm as if he means to press a coin into it. Instead, he traces small circles there, light enough that heat climbs my neck in a wave that wishes it were anger.

"Never reach for him first; you will let him reach. You stay if he retreats; you do not chase." He moves closer, knee touching mine once again. "That is the seduction."

"And words." I pull my hand back, because if he keeps caressing it, the carriage will run out of air with how fast I'm breathing. "What do I say?"

"Nothing sweet," Vale says. "He would hear mockery. Nothing cruel; he is already cruel to himself most the time." He tilts his head, studying my mouth like a craftsman measuring a seam. "Let him hear that he is good."

"Good," I repeat. "As in...you're doing so well, Your Majesty?"

"As in," he says, and the words drop heavy and certain between us, "you are not a thing I fear."

The carriage hits a rut that should have been a grave, and I pitch forward. Vale catches me at the waist, one hand braced at the small of my back, the other sliding to my arm. The curtains slap the windows and sulk. His breath is right there.

"See?" he murmurs. "Let the man reach. He will."

"I hate you," I say, if only to release some of this damned heat trapped under my collar.

"Excellent." Vale sets me back exactly where I was, but with more distance. "Hate is a clean line. Love is all spills."

"Oh, I know spills." That nonchalance in my tone brings some bravado back because I need it. "Sounds like you have this all figured out."

"I do not, actually." Giving his long legs a stretch as far as the cabin will let him—which is not very—he folds one over the other. "Like I said, love is a troublesome thing. Much will be improvised as we get closer to our goal."

We rattle on. Noon comes. Noon goes. The driver stops once to water the horses. Vale stays inside, curtains closed, and passes me a heel of bread and a shard of hard cheese from a little cloth bag as if I'm on a picnic and not being carried to my death.

If I succeed.

And I have to. Fast.

"Don't forget the coin for my mother," I say around a chew that would break weaker teeth. "And bread."

"You have my word," he says. "Someone will knock with it. They can say that you like the palace if she needs the story to be kind."

"She doesn't need kind," I say, and that old ache that fits Daron's hand yawns open. "She needs food."

"She'll have it," he says, and for all his many words, he doesn't make that one into a riddle.

By the time the light outside the curtains turns sullen, my bones know the jolt of this road by heart. The carriage slows, then slows some more before it lurches into a careful crawl like a person trying not to wake a dog.

"Look." Vale shifts the curtain with two fingers, barely enough to make a blade of early evening slide in.

The palace rises out of the hill, ugly and tender to look at, not at all what I saw from our home. The roofs are crumbling slate, the color of wet ravens; the windows squint through cobwebs and cracks. No banners. The stone around the servant's gate has a rash of black where torches once spat smoke. The air smells of vinegar, tallow, and old water.

"It's quite the eyesore up close." Unexpectedly so, though it makes sense, I guess. No coin, no taxes. "Sad."

"It's exactly what it is, and no better," Vale says when we draw up at the low gate. Two boys with lanterns stand shoulder to shoulder, both thin as fence pickets, and the carriage stops. "Only some souls inside the palace know about the power the crown holds. Fewer are those who know its cost. Toward the king, you will pretend to be one of the latter, else he may grow suspicious."

"Makes sense."

"You will not speak of me. To anyone."

I frown at him. "Why not?"

"The fewer things that connect us, the safer," he says. "My work takes place in the background. If the realm knew the king isn't the one keeping them breathing—even if barely—he'd become what every starving man already suspects."

"Incompetent? Ripe to be overthrown?"

One corner of his mouth twitches. "Our king ensures I get no credit because credit grows into loyalty, and loyalty grows into power. But make no mistake, he can tolerate my work so long as I remain invisible."

"And if I need to seek you out?"

"I will be the one seeking you out." His brows lift. "Do you understand?"

It's not a question of understanding.

It's a demand for quiet compliance.

"I'm plain," I say, "not stupid."

The coachman climbs down with a groan and knocks on the side door with the butt of his whip. Behind him, where palace stone meets rugged oak, the servants' door opens. What comes out, I presume, is the head of staff.

I expected crisp linen, tidy shoes.

At least the performance of order.

Instead, I get a woman who has starched the same black dress so often it cracked into white at the seams. The skin at her temple gleams with a wetness I dare not name, and her cap is a dirty gray.

As are the few fingers she has left.

A sudden wave of dizziness washes through my head, drowning my bravery under cresting dread. They would never hire a sick, infected servant to work so close to the king, inviting rot into the palace.

Unless it's already here...

"Caretaker?" The woman's smile is a line a knife drew once when she opens the carriage door. "At last. Come, then."

I barely remember I have legs. Still, somehow, I gather my brown cotton skirts, step down, land on stones, and stare at the fat, shiny pustule above the woman's right brow. Something squirms inside it.

Maggots.

Behind me, reins snap.

"Coin!" I quickly turn back to the carriage, to the storyteller who lured me into yet another graveyard. "For my family. Tod—"

The carriage jolts away with a hungry lurch. The curtain flutters once, just enough for me to catch the dark shape of a sleeve inside. And then the carriage is already sliding down the lane, shrinking into the haze.

I swallow whatever curse my mother wouldn't forgive and breathe past my dread.

Breathe. Deep.

Again. Deeper.

The palace is rotting, too. So what?

I'll feel right at home.

I turn and face the woman. "Elara. That's my name."

"You may call me Miss Hampshire." She reaches for me with nubs instead of fingers. "Your chamber, girl. I will show you the way."

Her palm is warm, damp.

The missing digits make a cradle for my hand that I cannot wiggle out of without insulting the kindness it offers. I count: one, two, gone, gone, three. More fingers missing than my brother.

I let the half-hand lead me along stone that sweats with disease and death, telling myself that's not an omen.

CHAPTER
SEVEN

Elara

The gray dress they gave me looks like deathcloth.

A quiet girl brought it before dawn, a shawl over half her face to hide the rash of red welts across her cheek. She didn't speak. She laid the folded gray on my cot, bobbed a little, and fled, leaving the air smelling like lye.

I pulled it on. It's clean, which feels indecent in a place that sweats rot with the same enthusiasm as the whorehouses down in the city. The hem has been let down and let down again. The apron ties twice around my waist. I tuck my hair into a plain coil that takes me an annoying eternity to get right.

A knock on the door. "Girl."

Miss Hampshire.

I open the door.

She takes me in with a long look, smelling faintly of vinegar and whatever putrid things vinegar fails to hide. "Are you ready, child?"

I nod.

Another moment passes where she musters me, but she eventually nods. "Follow."

She doesn't waste the word on me so much as spend it on the corridor as she turns into it, leading me deeper into a palace that is no longer a place—just a sickness with rooms.

Along the walls, rushes turn brown and then surrender. Bowls of something sharp sit under window slits, pretending to cleanse the air. Tapestries hang with mildew halos around useless saints. A boy with a lantern blinks past us, his left eye white with film.

Miss Hampshire walks like someone who doesn't remember what it's like to stand still. Her half-hand taps the other when she talks, the nubs a metronome.

"You will go when you're called, and you will leave when you're told." *Tap.* "No unnecessary noise; no talking to yourself." *Tap.* "No flowers. Never open the curtains." She glances at me to be certain that I understand. "And mind who you speak too freely around. Fine cloth does not mean clean intentions."

There's a chance she means Vale, so I nod, but not as desperately as someone who's conspiring with the man. "Yes, Miss Hampshire."

"On most days, our king will refuse food." She says it

like a fact and not like the confusing sin it is. "If he does, inform the maids so they may arrange for it to be taken to the nearest orphanage. That is how he wishes it."

A runner catches my toe as if to ask whether I heard her right, slowing my pace. Did I? I came ready to loathe a glutton with grease on his lips and crumbs in his beard, all while the city gnaws its own bones. Instead, meals refused are sent to feed small, hollow mouths? *Really?*

"Come," Miss Hampshire urges, half-hand at my elbow, tapping me forward before I can decide what to make of this.

We pass servants' chambers, where pots hold what bowls can't hold anymore. Where men with cloths tied over their mouths sit and stare at walls.

Gutter Lane. Sweat Alley.

All of it, here.

Only with stone instead of mud.

We turn down a corridor colder than the rest, where the light seems to shy from the walls. To our right, a set of double doors loom: taller, finer, their brass handles dulled by disuse. Miss Hampshire doesn't even glance that way as we pass.

"Oils." She lifts her chin at a narrow table nailed to the wall under a drooping flag. Dark glass bottles stand in a line, each with a scrap of parchment tied around its neck. The handwriting is neat and tired.

"Camphor when his joints ache," she recites. "Myrrh for...well, surely you know what myrrh is for."

"For preventing rot," I say, when what I wanted to say was for *pretending* we can keep it away.

Miss Hampshire offers a pleased smile, half her teeth gone and the other half graying toward the same fate. "Then there is pine pitch—"

"Pine pitch?" My ears prick at that. "Isn't that only used for mending split wounds?"

"Wonderful!" she says with a nod that's too fast. "The staff who wrote your recommendation did not promise too much when she said you know your trade."

Which has to be the lie Vale used to get me into this position, making it clear that I'm not his only accomplice here. "How kind."

"Read the labels." A nubby point toward the end of the line of bottles. "No rose extract. He hates the smell."

She stops at a low door banded in iron, the paint bubbled from a fire that didn't take. "Of course you have been made aware of…" She turns, looks me over again as if I might have added—or subtracted—parts since the last corridor. "The crown's…restorative powers?"

That must be the health part that Vale mentioned. "Yes, Miss Hampshire."

"The punishment for gossiping about the royal household, for airing *anything* that happens within these walls, is death by flogging for you, your kin, and whoever you've infected with it. That is how it has always been." The way she lifts a brow lets the pustule above it stretch white-taut. "Yes?"

"I understand," I say, though her stare pins me until I add, "completely."

She sniffs, satisfied, and leans closer. "It is not for the lower folk to know the nature of royal afflictions. The peasants would only invent songs and prayers to meddle in what none of them can mend."

She opens the door and waves me inside.

The room beyond is not grand.

Not even a little.

A long chamber made small by screens and folded

panels. Windows blinded with layered cloth that wants to be white but fails. The smell is what cadavers smell like twice warmed by the sun. Candles sit in clusters, short and wide, so their smoke drifts low and gets tired before it can grow black.

And him.

At first, he is nothing but a shape. A man on a low couch behind two screens, one of carved wood and one of gauze. Why? He can't possibly be sick with rot. Not a king. Not with that crown.

Miss Hampshire goes ahead and bows, not with her back, but with her chin. "Your Majesty. The new caretaker."

He shifts.

His voice stirs low, worn at the edges like a grindstone in an old mill. "Send her away."

It's not cruel when he says it; it's tired.

"Your Majesty." Miss Hampshire clears her throat. Then, more gently, she says, "She has traveled far. And of high recommendation."

"I will see her." His voice comes after a while. "Then send her away."

Miss Hampshire looks at me without turning. Her half-hand flicks forward.

I go.

The gauze reeks of pus, and the tulip pattern blurs when I pass close enough to touch. I stop where the edge of the screen tells me to stop and lower my head.

"Your Majesty." My voice is low. Even. Not sweet. I practiced it all morning.

Silence breathes between us before he says, "Look at me."

I lift my gaze...

...and my stomach drops.

I have seen rot. I've seen men drowned in their own lungs, women eaten from the inside, and boys with half their faces wasted to something that had the poor taste to smile, anyway.

Never have I seen *this*. Not alive.

Shuddering, I bite back a gag.

The king's face is a map of battles no one won. Whole provinces of him are stitched into borders and then torn open again. The crown sits on his head, dull, and the place where it touches the skin looks soft and new at the edges, pink and wet, as if the flesh keeps healing to meet it, only to die anew. His blond hair grows where it can and fails where it can't, cropped close around matted, crusty wounds, not for fashion but for mercy. Eyes once blue shift behind a film of slime, drowning under its coldness.

Bile licks at the back of my throat, sharp and burning. Yes, I have seen rot.

Never did I have to seduce it!

The king lifts an arm that sits higher to protect something in his shoulder, the knuckles on the hand he waves thickened and two nails blackened. "Closer."

I want to vomit. At Vale, most of all, for luring me into the arms of a corpse. This man would cough maggots into my mouth with a simple kiss!

For one white-hot beat, I want to turn and run. But I grind my heel into the floor and pull my breath where that jerk taught me to keep it. Told right, Daron would faint from laughing at this story.

I have every intention of telling him.

"Closer," the king repeats, so I step up, keeping my face the way Mother taught me to keep it when visitors brought bad news and needed you to be a wall to lean against. His pale gaze musters me, precise, factual. "Name?"

"Elara."

"Why are you here?"

It's not a question, and we both hear it. What then? Maybe he suspects what his steward is up to and is waiting to watch me flicker out. Maybe he doesn't, and this is simply how he sands everyone down until they leave him to rot.

"Because Miss Hampshire promised a warm meal, a roof over my head, and coin." I pull his stench into my lungs without even a flinch and walk over to the table that holds cups and a carafe. "And because your throat sounds like it's chewing gravel."

I pour water. Put the carafe down with an unapologetic *clank*. Turn around and reach him the cup.

"No." The word falls sharp as a coin on stone. "You will leave."

"Just as soon as you empty this." Stretching my arm further to where he sits on the low couch, I hold his rot-smeared gaze. "Until later, that is. The crusts on your scalp...they need wetting so we can open up the wound for healing."

"I will not be tended." His eyes—storm-quiet—slide to the cup and back to me. "You have come here for naught."

"I've been promised a bowl, a bed, and coin for keeping you well," I say in the gravedigger's voice I brought with me. "If you collapse, I'll be the one who gets blamed. So be well, and do it properly."

He huffs, bemused surprise rather than a laugh. "You have a mouth for the gutters."

"And you have a mouth for drinking." Another shove of the cup toward him, bringing me close enough to the rash that runs along his neck and disappears under gauze that radiates heat. "If you wanted honeyed lies, then maybe you shouldn't have scared off whoever was before me. From me, the best you'll get is salted truths."

"Truths." His hand lifts, not to grab the cup, but to reach for the gauze along his clavicle. "If you insist on truth, then let me give you the whole draught."

He doesn't pull his yellowed shirt; he unbuttons. He peels the gauze back with the care of a man folding a flag. The linen loosens. Moisture glistens. The wound beneath the edge shines raw and gleaming, strewn with angry-red pustules.

It's a test.

He wants the breath-flinch, the eyelid blink, the heel that leans toward the door. He's made a study of disgust, and I'm the sum he's measuring.

I give a nod. "I'll tend to them next."

From the low table beside him, he takes a thin steel lancet and rests its tip on the swell of a shiny white pustule. He looks at me while he presses. The skin yields. A bead blossoms—yellow-white, with a thread of pink—gathers fat, then breaks in a swell of pus that bubbles with maggots. He catches them neatly in one hand. Scoops them up. Drops them into the cup.

"I said…" He doesn't blink. "Leave!"

His hand moves—no warning, no flourish.

A clean backhand to the cup's rim.

Water arcs into the air, the faint pink smear of pus diluting as it flies. The cup slaps my knuckles. Warm, sour, iron-sweet wetness breaks over my face and open mouth. A maggot hits the back of my throat like a flick of rice.

A sound tears out of me as I gag. My hands stupidly slap at my face, one maggot sticking to my lower lip, another wiggling into my nostril.

Before I can command my feet to stay put, they spin me

around. Then I run—no, storm—past the screen. Past the curtains. Past Miss Hampshire, who presses nubs to her forehead as I flee through the door and into the corridor.

Vinegar reeks. Stone sweats.

I rake my nails down my cheeks and flick and flick. *Off me! Off me!* When I think there are no maggots left, another wriggles free from some seam, dropping onto the latch of the door to my room.

I push against it.

The room coughs me in.

I slam the door.

Water. Basin. I upend the pitcher so fast that the lip chips the bowl. I scrub my face with a rag until my cheeks burn and my eyes water.

Straw crunches behind me.

"You stayed longer than the last. Good." The words drift from behind me, the familiar aloofness in the bastard's tone making my skin itch with heat. "On a side note, how would you rate the room?"

Elara

I spin around, breath catching when I find Vale comfortably stretched out on my bed, and stab a finger toward the door, wishing it were a knife. "Get out!"

He folds his arms behind his head and crosses his ankles, very pleased with the comfort he's trying to make of my self-control. "What did he do? What did you two speak of?"

"What did he do?!" I slap what might be the last

clinging creature from my jaw. "He baptized me with a splash of maggots carved from his festering chest!"

He studies my face the way men study shades of yarn. Bored. "Ah."

"He's rotting alive, Vale," I yell. "And he's an asshole—albeit one only half the size that you are because you mentioned *none* of this!"

He shrugs, infuriatingly calm. "I mentioned enough."

I stomp toward him. "Winning the heart of a man who is decomposing at the speed of his manners is not what I signed up for!"

"Whenever was there a story told about someone who saved a realm, and it was easy?" he asks mildly, tilting his head, almost as if he'd woken from a nap beneath a tree and is now studying me with ardency. "Hard is why I chose you."

"Oh, now we arrive at that hymn." My laugh is a desperate thing, more high-pitched than I'm used to. "You didn't come to my door because I'm beautiful, or brave, and certainly not because I'm smart. Oh no, you came because I'm the gravedigger's daughter. Because I've got a high tolerance for rot, and you thought, *'Perfect, she's made for kissing a corpse that still remembers how to talk.'"*

He sits up, swinging his legs off the bed to squish a maggot that failed to wiggle away. "Kissing will not be enough, Elara."

A pang in my stomach. "Pardon me?"

"Obviously there has to be a wedding," he says. "Followed by a proper bedding."

The picture arrives uninvited—my body under the king's, wet gauze sticking to my nipple, pus dripping down my neck. Something claws up my throat so fast I taste iron, nearly making me gag on the saliva that pools sour beneath my tongue.

My stomach pitches, but it's not only disgust. "W-with…with *him?*"

"How else does a woman become a wife? A queen?" He arches a brow at me. "Surely you know how heirs are produced? Obviously, we need your sacrifice to come quick. Kael's next queen can bother with producing an heir after he's had some practice with you."

I lash before I can think, kicking Vale's boot with such force it makes him pitch sideways. "You could have led with that!"

He straightens and fluffs his white cravat, as though a wrong wrinkle is his most dire concern. "Touching him where his skin still feels like a man's will do wonders, given how deprived he kept himself. Simply do not put your mouth where the rot smells worst."

"You're disgusting," I spit with all the fury my voice can carry.

"I'm practical." He takes my outburst like a wave that simply breaks over him before it trickles away. "And I'm trying to save your brother."

"Don't talk as if you care about my brother."

"I do not, but the rot does. Very much so." He stands, closing the small room until the shrinking walls seem complicit. "Every minute you fight me on circumstances not of my making, the rot climbs an inch higher on his fingers."

His words land like a stone would in Father's bucket—heavy, gulping, drowning in the bloody truth. I drag breath to the top of my lungs, the heat thinning to something less biting. The bastard is right. And between burying Daron and fucking a living corpse?

Well, I choose the latter.

"I know," I say slowly, forcing my breath to calm alongside my heart. "It's just..."

Vale arches a brow. "If the possibility of falling pregnant is a con—"

"I haven't bled in a year, maybe longer." Hard to grow a babe when you can't even grow enough blood, so that's not a pressing worry. "The thing is..." There's a tremble in my voice I wish was still anger instead of nerves. Instead of dread. Instead of old, undiluted, righteous fear. "The only men I've ever touched were cold."

His gaze lifts, interest catching like a hook. "You are..." A beat. "A virgin?"

My hands flatten on my skirt. My eyes study anything that isn't him. I don't answer. Don't tell him that it just never happened, and the longer it didn't happen, the more terrifying it grew in my head.

He reads it anyway.

"We'll cross that river when we must," he says, stepping back the smallest inch, as if to give me air. "Not before. For now, do not let him scare you off. Stay put. Get close to him."

"But he's revolting." Even my voice shudders, the tone melting into a whiny puddle at the end. "He's a...a monster."

"He is not a monster." There's a subtle quiver in Vale's voice that surprises me more than how his usual nonchalance makes room for it. "He is a man rotting alive who still tries—badly, stupidly—to undo a curse. He is selfish, but he is also starving for connection."

"Connection." I taste the word like something bitter. "He is vile."

"Forgive me for being so blunt, but you are not exactly a

mouthful of…of…"—he draws elegant circles in the air with his hand as his mossy eyes search the room for words—"charm."

"Oh, shut up." I pace, because if I don't, I'll lose my temper once more, and that won't help anyone. "He put me to the test and I…I failed. I ran."

"To your room, not off the grounds." He flicks up a finger. "Different animals."

Wrapping my arms around myself, I sigh, a brown strand tickling the back of my neck where it must've escaped my disheveled coil. "What now?"

Eyes narrowing, he studies me for long seconds. "Wash, change, then go back to do it all over again. Fewer maggots, more success."

"As if Miss Hampshire isn't already preparing my first and final wages before she sends me off with no letter. He tried to dismiss me the moment I stepped into the room."

"Ah, and yet he has never dismissed any of his caretakers, maids, or healers." He crosses his arms in front of his chest, letting the silver and dark blue brocade of his vest stretch taut. "Why do you think that is?"

"Because he doesn't need to." Isn't that obvious? "Because he knows full well that they'll all run just fine on their own."

There's a pause as he sucks in his upper lip, biting down before he releases it with a pop. "Imagine what a shock it must be for him…the one woman who stays."

That has me hesitating for half a second. "And when he plays butcher and carves himself up?"

"Then you will watch him with the excitement of a sloth," Vale says. "Or, better yet, help him set the blade. Your unwavering touch will be a miracle to him."

"I don't want to touch him," I say more to myself than

him, knowing full well that what I want matters little. There's no way around any of this—not if I want my family to live...

Vale turns toward the window and leans his forehead against the pane with a sigh. "Trust when I say that I know how difficult it is...to look at something so revolting, and still find beauty within."

I watch how his gaze loses itself somewhere behind the glass, somewhere far off. "You speak from experience?"

A mother he lost? A wife? A lover?

I shouldn't care. Maybe I do in this moment out of sheer desperation, searching for courage in ridiculous places.

"Aside from his selfishness regarding the curse," Vale says, offering me nothing on my question, "he's not an unkind man, Elara."

Nodding slowly, I release myself from my hug and wipe my palms down my face. I think...I think I know that. The king has a foul mood and a temper, yes, but there are also specks of kindness, aren't there?

"He's starving himself." Because as much as he can hunger, he can't die from it. "Looks like the streets didn't lie after all. He *is* feeding the poor."

"Like I said, not unkind."

"Still stupid, though." Trying to outwit Death instead of spilling a bride and being done with it. No one grows that kind of haughty on his own. So who planted the idea?

"He's clearly sick with rot, but his wounds look... strange," I say. "The crown is healing them?"

"Only for the pestilence to bleed them anew." Vale nods. "Endless suffering. Never death."

"All kings die eventually," I point out. "And then the curse gets passed down, I assume? How?"

"Those are circumstances that do not pertain to our

cause." He clears his throat. "So long as he rightfully wears the crown, he cannot be killed before the sand runs out in his hourglass. And if he were to give up this foolishness and feed the curse, then he would still have many years to live. He is, after all, still young."

"He doesn't look it." Not with his posture of a gout-ridden priest. "He looks ancient."

"Twenty-nine is hardly ancient."

"Twenty-nine," I repeat, half in disbelief, half in awe. "You should have told me all of this, so I could've come prepared."

Vale gives one of his mild shrugs and turns back to the window. "Apprehensive as you were about even the curse, I couldn't risk your rejection by making the task less appealing than it already was."

"Right."

I drag in a breath, steady myself, and head for the small mirror on the wall. Great. My hair's fallen out of its coil during the chaos, hanging in limp, uneven curls around my face. I unpin the rest, refusing to wear my defeat once I step out there again.

Except the damn thing refuses to cooperate. The strands slide out of my grip, snarl around the comb, and puff where I want smoothness. I try again. And again. But the mess grows.

Behind me, Vale watches, arms crossed, amusement softening the sharp line of his jaw. "You're making it worse."

"I'm aware." I stab at a knot with the comb. "The dead never cared what I looked like. Now my hair won't listen. It's stubborn."

"Like its owner," he murmurs before a pause. "May I?"

I glance at him through the mirror. "What, you plan to do it better?"

His mouth quirks. "I might. You're *plainly* not built for vanity."

It's meant as a jest, I know, but it stings in some small, traitorous place. "Plainly?"

He lifts a hand in mock surrender, an almost-smile tugging at the corner of his mouth. "Poor choice of words. I meant it kindly."

I should refuse out of pride alone, but pride won't hold that damn hair in place. "Fine," I mutter. "Make it quick."

He steps in behind me, his reflection close enough in the mirror that I can see the faint pulse in his throat. His fingers slip through my hair, slow and deliberate, dividing the strands into three neat parts. The comb's teeth rake gently across my scalp, sending tiny prickles down my neck. It feels far too intimate, and far too steadying all at once.

"You've done this before," I say, trying to sound unimpressed, though my voice comes out softer than I'd like. "Sisters perhaps? A wife?"

"No sisters. No wife," he answers, tone unreadable. "Just...observation." When he finishes, he ties the end with a black ribbon from my table and lets the braid fall over my shoulder. "There. Presentable."

I face the mirror, fingers brushing the neat plait. "You've missed your calling as a lady's maid."

"And you did not at all miss your calling as a gravedigger," he says, stepping back. "Are you hungry?"

"Yes." I point to the door, desperate to end the strange heat crawling under my skin. "For you to leave."

He inclines his head, bows a sliver. "Very well."

I let out a breath when the latch clicks behind him. I

stand a moment longer, staring at my reflection, at the braid too neat to belong to me. Then I square my shoulders. Once I gather my courage, I'll go back to the king.

This time, I won't fail.

I was never afraid of corpses.

I won't start with this one.

CHAPTER

NINE

The Prince
...long ago

The rose is red, like my blood.

The spiky thorns tried to bite me as I picked it from the bush in the greenhouse. One of them did, but I don't care. Maybe she'll say I'm brave.

"Mother?" My voice is always so small in the big greenhouse. Maybe that's why she's standing at the glass, not looking at me.

I walk closer, holding the rose up so she can see. "Look what I got you!"

She doesn't turn.

My hand starts to shake. I hold the stem tighter so that—

Ouch! My finger hurts. Blood runs down. It doesn't matter. She likes roses.

"I love you." The words come out so fast. "I love you, Mother."

She looks down at me then: at the rose, at my hand, at the drop of blood running down my wrist. Her mouth moves, but no sound comes.

I hold it out higher.

Her eyes get shiny, her lips pressed tight. Then she turns away. Just turns.

I don't understand. The rose is still in my hand. Doesn't she like it?

"Do not love me," she whispers, the words shaking like her hands. "Where there is love, there will be grief." She makes a sound, like a cough, then she looks at the door. "Maribel! Take the prince to his chamber."

CHAPTER

TEN

Elara

Vinegar. Wormwood. Witch hazel.

Only the first came easily this morning. Still, I balance all of it on a slat of wood that used to be a shelf but is now a tray, because I say so. Balls of boiled sheep's wool ride my belt in a linen pouch Miss Hampshire let me borrow, and a rag sleeps in my collar in case I have to wipe maggots off my face again.

"His wounds would heal faster than they can decay with some salt," I say. "A good soak."

"The kitchens are short on salt. The king's tolerance for soaking in it is shorter." Miss Hampshire half-hand-taps our steps toward the king's chamber. "Neither does he need an incident like yesterday. Too much excitement wears on his lungs."

I'm not here to argue about stupid rules that clearly keep failing them. "Yes, Miss Hampshire."

The low door is still an ugly tongue of bubbled paint and iron. Still that same stench of vinegar and wound-breath leaking from the seam. I set my tray's edge to the latch, shoulder the weight, and enter.

The chamber is a lung that forgot how to exhale, trapping stale air and the sicknesses that cling to it. Even the candles struggle under its weight, barely flickering as I approach the screens, where he sits in the same place I left him on the low couch—a sick man learning his chair too well.

"Leave," he says in greeting.

I set the tray down on a nearby stool and head for the carafe on the table. "Good morning to you, too, Your Majesty."

Miss Hampshire shifts uncomfortably in the doorway, but then steps back into the corridor. "I will not be far..."

The door closes.

For once, she leaves me be.

"You again..." The king tips his head, unbothered by how the crown digs into fresh pink skin that had the audacity to heal overnight. "Are you deaf?"

"Only when it suits me."

A sound tries to be a scoff and pays for the attempt. Pain wrinkles his mouth. He hides the wince the way men hide all weaknesses: by being louder. "Who coached your bluntness?"

"The lesson that rich and poor wind up in graves the same size." I pour. Raise the cup. Hold it without plea. "How are you feeling on this fine day?"

He exhales, loud, annoyed, almost theatrical.

His shoulder draws in minutely—as yesterday—guarding the right side, then he reaches. Not for the cup, but for the gauze over his breastbone, peeling it away from the pustule he lanced. It's damp and shiny, angry red where maggots devour flesh straining to heal.

He lifts a sparse brow that still carries some nobility. His voice wobbles with pain and contempt in equal shares. "Rotten."

"There's only so much healing a body can do in a day, and it clearly focused on your face." I bridge the wasted distance and shove the cup into his hand. "What's with your shoulder? Pain?"

His fingers, swollen at the knuckles, twitch around the cup. He could throw it. He did yesterday.

Instead, he studies me from those cold eyes, like a once-beautiful lake of blue trapped under ice. "Stiffness."

The word is seamed with embarrassment, as if admitting it were a ridiculous luxury amid all this obvious ruin.

"You sit like a corpse; you ache like one." I fish a sheep's-wool ball from the pouch and drown it in witch hazel. It comes up dripping, sting already parting the air. I sit beside him, wool clasped between my fingers. "You sit, you sweat, you rot. When was the last time you left this room? Moved about the gardens? Visited the sea?"

He sidesteps the question because answering it would probably admit that he's lost track. "Are you lecturing me?"

"Someone should, since your staff swaddles you like a babe, only to leave you to stew." I lift the tired gauze higher. No rip. No speed. Let it unstick with its own awful sound.

The skin comes with it for a breath before surrendering, slick threads snapping like sinew pulled too far. Three more swollen hills show themselves, skin stretched so tight a breath might split them. "Gauze is a blanket for rot. These need air, not pity. Sun, if we dare. For now, this."

He sniffs at the soaked wool. "It reeks bitter."

"Rot likes sweetness. I mean to disappoint it."

Edge work first. Always the edges. I swipe around the pink rings where new healing fights old offense, circling until the skin glistens. The center can sulk.

At another swipe, he jerks his head in protest. The crown doesn't move, not even a tilt. It sits there, seemingly welded to him by the curse. Only when he anchors his fingers on the gold does it shift, leaving two pale crescents pressed into his temples.

"It burns," he mutters, lips curling in pain.

"It has to sting." The light is so thin, I might as well be working with my eyes closed. The skin wavers at the edge of my sight like heat on the horizon. "Witch hazel dries without a blade. No need to lance and invite—"

"I said, it burns!"

His hand clamps my wrist with a strength I didn't think he'd kept. He drags my palm lower, over the worst of it, heat radiating like coal under his skin.

Then he presses down.

The pustules give with a wet, obscene *pop*, the sound bursting against the silence like a scream drowned in muck. A spatter leaps—warm, thick, vile—hitting his throat, my chin, the front of my dress. The smell hits next: sharp, metallic, rancid. Like meat left in milk and forgotten.

Bile climbs. My throat cinches around it. Because, all night, I practiced not gagging.

The pustules deflate in a sluggish collapse, oozing a

yellow slick threaded with white. Then movement. Tiny, pale ropes push out, twisting, writhing, greedy for air. A maggot drops onto my knee and splits. Another wriggles down the edge of my wrist, leaving a gleaming track.

He watches me, calm and expectant, like a butcher watching to see if the apprentice will faint at the smell. His other hand trembles faintly from rage or pain, or both.

"Leave...me...to...rot," he grinds out. "My entire body is foul."

Bile sears the back of my throat. My eyes sting. Every breath is curdled with the stink of him. I want to flinch, gag, scrub my skin raw.

I don't.

I pin the bitter saliva under my tongue until it scalds my teeth. He wants the disgust to drive me off? To condemn Daron to death?

Not today.

I hold his stare. Rip my hand free. Reach for the bowl again. The wool hits the witch hazel first, then his chest to the sound of his hiss.

"I've seen fouler." I bathe the wound, voice steady. "Your mood, for example."

The witch hazel bites worse now that he carries open wounds, his mouth twisting around the burn until it becomes rage. "I could have you hanged for speaking to me like this!"

My scoff carries too much amusement and not nearly enough concern. "As the king of a rotting kingdom, you really have to be more creative with the punishments you threaten," I say. "Of all the deaths I've seen this year, none of them was as kind as hanging."

Another one of those sounds that could be a scoff, maybe even a laugh, but it turns into a rasp as his mouth pinches. He snatches the cup—not to sip, but to upend. The water goes down in greedy glugs, as if he's praying it's liquor hot enough to cauterize a life. The last swallow is smaller, defiant. He places the cup aside with a *clink,* as if to say he's still king over something.

It's a small victory that's supposed to lift something inside my chest. Instead, a shadow falls over it. No man endures this kind of pain, this burning agony, this undiluted suffering for the sake of stubbornness alone. Something gave him the strength to endure, dangling the promise of breaking a curse.

Not a mere fever dream, that's for sure. But then what? What's the point in making him fall in love with me—which already seems impossible—if he refuses to feed the curse? How am I supposed to undo a belief I can't even name?

"This should do." I let the wool drop into the bowl and move to the wormwood.

But the room is all dusk.

My eyes find the exhausted curtains that smother what little day exists, the gauze levees stuffed into cracks where day might seep through. My mood would be sour if I sat in an oversized grave all day, too.

I rise, slip around the screen, and fetch a weeping candle—careful, because the flame is a nervous animal—and set it on my tray.

"The flame," the king all but whimpers, eyes clenching into slits, lifting his arm against the stiffness in his shoulder to ward off the brightness. "It hurts my eyes."

"Of course it hurts. Drag anything into the light after letting it fester in the dark, and it'll complain." I angle the candle so its flicker grazes the wounds but spares his face. Shadow does most of the work; the flame only suggests. "A midnight walk in the gardens will help. Moonlight first. And the sun...eventually."

"I am heat under my skin, fire in my joints, flame in my marrow." His voice slips into a hiss. "And you expect me to go for *walks*?"

"You're all that because you haven't moved from this couch in weeks—months, likely. Sit in darkness, never shift, and you rot from the inside out." Wormwood pinched between my fingers, I press it along the edges, then the center. The sharp green scent claws its way over the vinegar in the air. "Seems as though rotting quietly is our king's most pressing ambition."

He mumbles something no priest would forgive, then swerves, grasping for a different battle. "This herb will stick to the pus and embed itself in the wound."

"No, it won't," I say. "It'll dry out nicely. Maggots only go where it's wet."

"You speak with the confidence of a healer, rather than a caretaker."

"Experience." The city is a hard tutor. And while I usually care for the dead, he's not far from that if it wasn't for his crown. "Swaddle anything wet and it turns to soup. Give it air and it crisps. Bread, grain, wounds—same rules."

He sinks his head beneath the weight of his crown, the gold as dull as his eyes. "Credentials?"

"Two eyes that don't faint, ten fingers that don't shake, and a nose that's smelled worse than you," I say, proud. "If I'm wrong, you may declare me an idiot after you stand, walk, and remain upright."

From a stool beside the couch, I fetch fresh gauze, which I set on his shoulder. My palm lingers there a moment longer, fingers sensing for the tendons beneath.

His head shifts toward my touch—just an inch, barely

visible. His gaze conquers the rest of the distance, settling on my hand. "You are tiresome."

"You're not the first to say so."

"Insufferable."

"Also heard that one before." I ease off and layer his chest in a vented lattice, not smothering, not bare—lines of breath between lines of restraint. "I'll be back in the afternoon."

"Leave," he answers. "Do not return."

I rise. My curtsy is a crime against grace, but I commit it anyway because it makes him scowl and me smile. "I'll be back tonight to replace the wormwood."

Because if he truly wants me to go away, he'll have to slit my throat and bleed me over his stupid crown.

ELEVEN

Elara

That evening, the king sleeps like a man trying to be a corpse and failing at both, and not even in the bed that stands in the far rear. Instead, he's slumped sideways on his beloved couch, mouth parted just enough to catch a breath he seems reluctant to keep.

No drama tonight.

Almost disappointed, I lift the gauze, edge first, the wounds beneath dry, the maggots curled into tiny brittle twigs. If even the palace is short on salt, a soak in the sea might serve better—though I can't imagine him agreeing to leave this tomb of a room.

Still, a bit of sun might do what the salves can't. Fresh air could chase the rot from his skin. Maybe even from his mood.

After a new layer of wormwood, I vent the gauze again, pulling—

"Mother." My fingers freeze at the king's whimper, a sound so desperate it makes my heart shudder. "...have to... break it."

Mother. *Ophelia?*

If a man bleeds such a thing in his sleep, it has to be meaningful. Was it her? The one who gave him this undying determination to undo the curse? When? With what words? What proof?

The candle gutters low, its light catching on the gold of the crown where it rests crooked against his temple. Curiosity rises like a tide in me. I reach out slowly, carefully. Fingers meet metal that feels almost warm, as though it borrows his pulse. I give it the smallest tug.

Not an inch of give.

The gold clings to him like an extension of bone. I know I've seen *him* lift it. What happens if he takes it off? Can he be killed? Is that how the curse gets passed down? Did his father put this thing on his head, then fade at last while his son was burdened to carry this fate?

I finish the wrap slowly, so as not to wake him, and turn away. "Goodnight, Your Majesty."

The candles flicker as I pass them. The door sighs shut behind me. I hurry back into the corridor, the stones finally quiet enough I can take in my surroundings without hurry. The rooms lining each side. The windows overlooking ponds, or stables, or woods.

The pair of fine double doors left ajar by either carelessness or nostalgia. I glance left, then right. With the thin staffing, reckon I can dare a peek...

I glance into the room. Moonlight has more courage than candles here, spilling in through a high window. A bed stands in the middle like a ship at anchor, draped and draped again under rich velvet. A mirror watches the bed, its face veiled, the cloth secured with a single pin that catches a breath of moon and gives it back shyly. The air tastes like old perfume that stopped being alluring. A bowl sits on a low table, dried rose petals catching dust in layers.

This is no ordinary chamber.

After a glance over my shoulder, I step inside and run a finger along the edge of a carved chest. Time sleeps there, deep and forgiving. Under it, the wood is smooth and proud. On the night table, a ring-mark says a cup often rested here ages ago, lifted by a hand that held authority.

Like a king's.

Then why doesn't he sleep here, choosing that pitiful excuse of a chamber instead? What did the pillows hear whispered in this room? What did the mirror see that the king doesn't want to look at?

Outside, boots hush over stone.

I quickly retreat. I shut the doors to a breath's width and turn into the corridor. Vale walks with the practiced indifference of a man who knows the halls better than their builders, hands clasped behind his back, his boots too clean to confess where they've been.

I walk up to him. "You move like a traitor."

"Then you best keep up, following quickly like an accomplice before someone sees us." He turns, eyes pale green and unreadable. "I figured I might find you with the king."

"I just finished."

"And even with your hair intact," he says with a smirk. "Hungry for food at last? The kitchens are long abandoned."

"In fact, I am." This place has enough corridors to work a body dead. "Feed me before I do something reckless, like be agreeable."

TWELVE

Elara

The kitchens at night aren't kitchens.

They're a chapel after mass: everything clean and tidy, chairs pushed in, the congregation gone, as is their gossip. The hearth has been banked to an obedient glow. A cooling pot sighs beside it.

"I smelled cabbage earlier." It's a funny sight, how Vale lifts lid after lid from pots, layered cuffs fighting him at each attempt, frowning into whatever contents he finds. "Where on earth did they…"

A girl comes through the larder door with a cloth over her arms and startles to a dead stop. She's pretty in the way hunger makes women pretty—small wrists, blonde curls framing a slender face, big eyes that grow even bigger as she looks at me, Vale, then me again, as if she's assessing the order of danger.

"Whatever food remains," Vale says, voice soft as a secret, "if you please."

The girl blinks and stumbles into action. "Yes, of course."

She scurries to the sideboard and returns with a loaf end, a heel of cheese as white as fear, a spoonful of tiny onions only brushed by mold, and a pot that holds remnants of broth.

She sets it all down and curtsies so low that the cloth on her arm nearly tumbles. "It's all they have."

"It's plenty," I say so she'll stop apologizing with her body. "Thank you."

"Take what you need," Vale tells her, and there's nothing cruel in it, but there's no space, either. "Then go and be silent."

She shakes her head as if relieved he didn't ask for anything she can't afford to give, then vanishes like smoke through the door. Vale's sustained calm makes it clear that he isn't at all concerned about her having seen us together. Does she know about Vale's scheming?

"You terrify her," I say when we sit at a scrubbed table that holds the scratches of a thousand knives. "Whatever have you done to her, Vale?" I keep my head still, letting my eyes slide his way in a playful, taunting way. "Threatened her family? Ruined her in some dark corridor?"

"No need to go through such efforts," he says. "Fear is

often a byproduct of failure. She was the previous one I had sent to seduce the king. Pretty enough to catch his eye, employed long enough to make herself unassuming, yet entirely incompetent at everything else. Retched on the floor the moment a pustule split open on his bottom lip."

So, she probably figured out right away why I'm here, newly arrived, sitting in the kitchens beside the treacherous steward at the hour of the wolf. That dampens my hunger for a second.

"What if she tattles?"

"And add having known about treason brewing inside the palace on top of her failure when she tried to partake in it?" He shakes his head. "Silence is not so much a command she obeys for me, Elara. She obeys it to keep her head."

"Who else knows?"

"As few as possible."

"Miss Hampshire?"

"Saints, no." Before I can object, Vale hands me the entire end of bread. "Not even rot speckles that woman's loyalty to the crown. I avoid her just as she avoids me."

"Won't you eat?" I ask. "There's plenty of food for both of us."

Shaking his head, he pours water from a clay jug that sweats like stone in summer and sets the cup by my hand. "Eat your food, Elara."

I eat in the kind of silence that knows how to sit without fidgeting. The onions are dull. The cheese is hard. The bread? Stale, of course.

"Why no wife?" I ask after a while, curiosity getting the best of me. "You don't long for one?"

His jaw twitches once, twice. "I have longed for a wife longer than I have had a name for longing."

"Dramatic," I say, because if he wants me to be gentle with his sadness, then he should've asked someone else to supper. My eyes go to those barely-there wrinkles at the corners of his eyes—the only thing betraying age against the virility that seems to seep off him in waves. "You can't be much older than the king."

"He is slightly younger, to be certain."

I weigh my next words like coin I can't spare but spend them anyway. "Then you're still young. Healthy. And"—I make a vague, irritated circle at his face as if that might smudge the truth—"handsome."

Heat climbs my neck right then. I pretend it's the stove, and not the fact that he truly is an attractive man. How wrong is it that I notice?

Vale inclines his head as if staring at a gift brought to the wrong door. "How superficial, coming from a woman as pragmatic as you."

His unfazed rebuke stings more than I would ever admit. "Right, well, if it isn't the wrapping, then I presume there's something wrong with the contents."

He takes a breath and lets it out tunneled. "What about you, Elara?"

"What about me?"

"Why no husband?"

I shrug and scrape the tough crust through the broth. "Like you said, death keeps me busy."

There's a twitch on his lips before he says, "Yes, yes, we settled that already."

"It might come as a shock to you, but gravedigging girls aren't the most sought-after during times of pestilence. Or ever, really." I take another bite, because bitter truth still tastes better when your mouth is full. "Every night, I carry disease on my dress. Every morning, I come home smelling of rot. Few men find it anything other than appalling."

"I find it to be honest work." Those full lips of his soften some before he asks, "Still hungry?"

I shake my head as I empty the last string of overcooked vegetable from the pot. "How bloody was Queen Ophelia's sacrifice?"

Vale's gaze finds mine. "I beg your pardon?"

"O-phee-li-aaa." I stretch it out extra-long just to pretend he's slow. "King called her name in his sleep. His mother?"

"Indeed."

"Clearly, her memory is working on him."

His eyes search my face as though he's chasing it for answers to questions he doesn't dare voice. "How does this tie into your goal of being bedded, wedded, and killed?"

"Just wondering if his mother somehow planted the idea of breaking the curse in his head." If I know where the thread started, then maybe I can unspool it where it's still thin. "Besides, it's easier to win a heart if you understand how it beats, don't you agree?"

"Hm..." His lips pout. Flatten. Shove around. "He loved her dearly. Her coronation was...traumatic."

"Coronation?"

"It is what the kings call the sacrifice." His thumb finds my forehead before I can think to shift back, tracing a slow, deliberate path along my hairline. Something in it makes my breath go shallow. "Kael will lift his crown," Vale says, almost gently, "and place it upon your head. The Queen's Coronation. Then he will slit your throat."

My esophagus bobs once at that. "How was Ophelia's coronation traumatic?"

"She had no vision of dying." His eyes focus on a knot in

the wood for long seconds before he shrugs. "From the little I know, I believe she wasn't...*informed* of the fate that awaited her. Have you spoken to him about his mother?"

"I can barely speak to him about the weather without him spitting his foul mood at me. His body might forever be rotting, but his soul seems rather dead already."

There's a scrape of something sharp in his tone. "Difficult man."

"How long have you been his steward?"

"Too long if measured by my exhaustion," he says on an exhale. "Not long enough, given how far the previous steward allowed the realm to deteriorate before the man hung himself three years ago."

"What if the curse got passed on to someone less difficult?" I ask, too mild to be innocent. "Someone more... willing to kill a queen."

His brow lifts. "Are you plotting a king's death in front of his steward?"

"Oh, so deceit, treason, and marching me to a blade sit fine on your conscience, but the king's throat is sacred? Convenient."

A laugh cracks out of him like flint on steel, which is a startling experience given his usual indifference. Then he shakes his head. "For that, the king will have to lift his crown. And trust me when I say that he has no ambition to do so, passing on a curse he's determined to end."

"How do you know all this?"

"Books," he says, and the word is almost a flinch. "Coronation annals. Ledgers no one reads unless they are paid to be lonely. Margins priests wrote in the years heirs were birthed. Letters inked by queens in the years before they died."

Letters.

That word strikes a chord somewhere inside me. Perhaps even diary entries? If anyone ever recorded how this madness started—how the king got the idea that the curse could be broken—it might be buried there. Maybe a sermon, maybe a journal. Whatever it is, it's more talkative than the king is, and a damn sight easier to reason with.

"Can I read them?"

Vale stares at me for a moment before he says, "Stewards and bloodline only."

"Um, you *are* the steward. Take me?"

"And risk my position, along with my head?" He tortures his upper lip for a moment. "Rules are strict, always have been. Too many secrets hiding in the library."

"Secrets?"

"The kind that the priests fear will be the end of all kings," he says, voice low and almost amused. "The royal family line itself is..."—his head tilts left, right, left again—"no longer intact."

"Intact?"

"At least once in the past, the curse went to someone not meant to carry it. The incident was hidden under words, stories rewritten and birth ledgers burned, may the crown reign long and prosper." He chuckles, but it holds no humor. "Even a whisper from the wrong mouth can turn faith into doubt—and doubt topples thrones faster than pestilence ever could. Hence why there's no getting past the scribe with you in tow, and not enough coin left to motivate me into slogging through the recordings of some king's bowel movements again."

In other words...

No books, no annals, no letters.

No way to pry open the past and find what got us into this mess. And it's not as though I can ask the king. *Pfft...*

Even getting him to drink a sip of water is like wading barefoot through nests of thorns. The idea of asking about things that might flare his already volatile temper seems like suicide. Premature suicide.

What else then? What?

"There's a grand room with a veiled mirror," I all but mumble, grasping at straws, but what are my alternatives? "Drapes on a large bed. Perfume in the air that went sour."

"The royal chamber," he says. "Yes."

"He doesn't sleep there."

"No."

"Because it reminds him of something?"

Vale looks at my hands instead of my face. "This curse left no inch of this place untouched by grim memories."

"What happened in that room?"

His teeth grind just as the hearth pops, as if the fire were deciding it would rather be a tree again. "I cannot say. I was not there."

He rises and reaches forward. Sets a bit of wood at the right angle. Tucks in the coal. Makes a small order out of heat and habit.

Is he...is he evading me?

"I find it interesting," I say, "how you seem to know everything...except that."

"And I find it interesting how you seem to want gruesome details on events that are horrendous even in the mere state of the concept. Whatever it was that happened in that room, it is older, from a time before Ophelia's coronation, and therefore irrelevant. Now come." Waving me off the stool, he juts toward the kitchen door. "The hour is late, and we don't want to be found here once the kitchen staff starts on the morning porridge."

We walk the dark corridors, the ghosts of laughter

suffocating in the still air as we pass cold fireplaces, thread-bare chairs, planters with nothing left but dirt. When we turn into a long gallery, walled with glass that extends into a room I haven't seen before, something inside me sits up.

"A greenhouse!"

Behind a glass door, moonlight makes ribs of the iron that crowns it, paints the panes silver, and lets the night sky sink down on it in all its glory. Within, a geometry of tables and trellises holds what was once abundance: leaves like the ears of starving hounds, stems gone black at the joints, rose bushes cut down to stalks, soil caved in where something gave up in the night.

"It's beautiful," I say, because it still is. "Even dead things manage it sometimes. Can I go in?"

"Forbidden." The word is quick and unadorned. "King's order. The lock is Miss Hampshire's. She only brings a gardener at first light on odd days."

"Hmm."

My nose squeaks when I press it against a pane, trying to get a better look against the mist my breath leaves on the glass. I rub it clear with my sleeve and blink. A small bronze plaque blinks back—oval, riveted into the column like a law.

～

A GIFT TO THE QUEEN
ON THE BIRTH OF HIS MAJESTY,
THE PRINCE,
KING MERRICK'S SON AND HEIR.

～

The letters catch the moonlight, clean and proud despite the corrosion around them. My breath fogs the glass again before I even realize I'm staring. If this was his mother's, then why lock it away? If he loved her so dearly, then why let the place she likely enjoyed rot to bone?

Maybe *because* he loved her.

Maybe he couldn't stand the sight of her touch living on when she didn't. The roses that dared to bloom would've bled red like her last day. Easier to cut them all down than let them remind him of what he lost. Reminders of what the curse took from him.

"It's cruel," I say. "Not only having to kill the person you love, but also the mother of your child."

Vale is quiet for a moment. "Presume it is."

Beyond the plaque, the gardens open: paths silvered with light, hedges trimmed by someone who appreciates order, even in ruin. A fountain glimmers in the distance, its hooded statue looming over the spill of water.

It's pretty. It's...perfect?

A flicker stirs low in my chest. If I can bring him here—let the king breathe air, feel light—then maybe his mood will ease. Maybe he'll talk. Maybe I can trace the thread of his madness back to its source and cut it clean.

"On the next clear night, I'll bring him here," I say more to myself than Vale. "The moon's not bright enough to hurt his eyes."

Vale's spine snaps straight. "Don't."

I peel my face off the pane and look at him. "Why not? He's listless, grumpy, and impossible to reason with. His mood would be easier to stomach if something as simple as the moon touched his soul once in a while."

"And what if he uses that improved mood to strengthen his resolve further? Have you thought of that?" His voice cools to stone. "Besides, you're rushing this, which might very well ruin this plan of mine for good."

"Without him opening up, it's ruined already," I snap. "I need—"

"What you need, Elara, is patience."

"Patience?" The word bursts sharper than I mean it to. "Daron rots a little more with every day that I waste time tiptoeing around the king's mood. You want me to sit on my hands while the king broods my brother into the grave?"

Vale exhales through his nose, slow and deliberate. "You don't understand the mechanics at play. You've known the king for days; I've known him for years."

"And what did all those years earn you?" I throw back before I can stop myself. "Failure. That's how you ended up at my door, remember?" The air between us crackles with anger, defiance. With something hotter tangled between us that I don't dare name, so I just turn away. "I'm not going to sit around here, waiting for—"

His hand finds my forearm, fast, firm. "Elara."

The world tilts.

I pivot straight into him, shoulder striking his chest, breath knocked from both of us. The cold pane kisses my spine. He's close enough that I catch his scent again, dew and carnations, the greenhouse glass humming with the night. Between us, heat threads taut and bright, a wire drawn through silence and sparked at both ends.

My palm finds his vest to steady what pride refuses to call a stagger. "You're hurting me."

His fingers loosen, but don't leave. His green gaze slides to my mouth, then climbs back to meet my eyes. "Follow the rules," he murmurs, voice low enough to make the air shiver. "Do as I say."

When he sidesteps around a gleam of moon, giving me room, giving me an opening, I rip my arm from his grasp and stomp back into the familiar corridor. "Keep your stupid rules."

I'll keep my plan, even if it kills me.

Especially if it kills me.

THIRTEEN

Elara

*S*queak-squeak-squeal.

Blessed saints, the wheelchair I found in the infirmary sounds like a nest of frantic mice when I push it through the chamber's threshold. Getting this thing past Miss Hampshire without her noticing wasn't the easiest task by any stretch of the imagination. Vale was much easier, namely because he's been blessedly absent ever since our greenhouse disagreement.

Time to get the king out.

Out of the room, out of the gloom, out of the habit of

listening to his own decay. If he moves, he might talk. And if he talks, he might show me the man under the ruin. And if I can find that man, then I might find his heart. And if I have his heart...then maybe I can learn who taught him to fight the curse instead of feed it.

I set my foot against the rear axle, test the wobble, lean on the handles until the right wheel groans instead of screams. "Good evening, Your Majesty."

He sits where he always sits: half-turned on that low couch, as if lying down costs too much effort. "Come to pester me at such a dark hour? You ought to—what...what is that?"

"A chair," I say, likely with a bit too much cheer in my voice. "With wheels."

Two lines cut between his eyes, tightening the pink skin I coaxed smooth yesterday. "Miss Hampshire would never have consented to this."

"That's why I snuck this thing past her room."

"I refuse."

"It's either the chair," I tell him, nudging the cushion so it huffs dust like an old man clearing his throat, "or I light every candle in this mausoleum, line them all in front of you, and lash your lids open with gauze. Choose your miracle."

His lungs almost remember a laugh, then abandon the attempt when his chest rattles. "You know nothing of miracles."

"I know they rarely attend the lazy." I move beside him. "Lean forward. Heel under. One. Two. Th—"

"Do not count at me."

"Then move at one."

He grumbles a word that would start wars if spoken in court before he gets his foot under himself—bare, cold, old grace in the way he tests the floor before weight—hands braced at either side. For a moment, he's heavier with flesh than pride. Then pride lifts and flesh follows. He drops into the chair like a king refusing to concede even to gravity.

"Blanket." I tuck it over his lap.

His gaze falls to my hands, lingering for a beat. "I should dismiss you."

"Sure. After our walk."

We squeal into the corridor, stone growing damper the closer we come to the gardens. Two footmen argue in whispers about what they ought to do at the sight of their rotting king, if anything. They do what men often do best: nothing.

The side door sticks like old doors do, but my shoulder makes quick work of it. Cold breath spills in. The king flinches at the first bite, then holds still as if listening to something he hasn't heard in a long time.

"Wind," I inform him.

He lets out a grunt. "It stings."

"It reminds you that you have lungs."

The garden keeps itself alive as best it can. Water worries a stone somewhere. Dew sets tiny greedy teeth into the edges of my old shoes. I push off the flagstones and onto a seam of black-green moss, the wheels going quiet in the moon's half mercy.

"Did you come here often?" A question that's innocent enough, if not for the fact that his mother clearly appreciated plants. Why else the greenhouse gift? "I mean, in the past. Before the rot climbed these trees."

He lifts one foot from the rest, baring his pale toes, and lets the ball skim damp grass. "Once," he says. Then, more reluctantly. "Often."

His head maps the sky like a man embarrassed to be

caught marveling at the stars. Then, a cough rattles his chest.

"Does the cold air pain you?" I ask.

"It reminds me I have lungs, like you suggested." He watches his breath rise and vanish. "Pain is a cartographer...it draws boundaries."

"That's useful. Boundaries keep fools out."

"I am more concerned with fools kept in."

My giggle jumps out before I can warn it not to. He looks up, startled by my amusement, as if he dropped a small jest by accident and isn't sure whether to pick it up again.

Then his mouth tilts—almost a smile.

Moonlight is a liar with good intentions in that moment. It smooths the angry reds to salt-pale, inks his eyes blue, lays a clean edge along high cheekbone and jaw where royalty survived. Close-cropped gold looks like wheat in frost. Come to think of it, his mouth is a fine, decisive line. Even his hand on the blanket reads handsome work: signet knuckles, long fingers, and—

His gaze cuts through my stare.

For a heartbeat, something sharp flickers behind his eyes—shame, maybe, or anger at being seen as anything less than a ruin. "Focus on the path," he says, too low, too fast, his gaze shooting forward again.

"I'm sorry." The words scrape out, brittle, heat gnawing my nape.

Silence follows, stretching long enough that I think I've lost him. Then a slow shift—his shoulders easing, his breath exhaling long and slow.

"I used to study on the east lawn," he ventures carefully, almost like a peace offering for a battle we're both growing tired of fighting. "Scrolls. A blanket. My mother at the windows, thudding them shut when her eyes and nose would not stop itching." A breath, softer. "Occasionally, she would venture out and indulge me with a game of chess beneath a tree."

Something unclenches under my ribs that I must've braced against since stepping out here. This is the first time he's shared anything personal with me.

A tingle of hope.

"Did she let you win?"

"Never. Losing teaches an even temper, she said." The corners of his mouth trudge up. He smiles, truly smiles. Then the smile wobbles, folds, and dies. "Clearly, the lesson was lost on me."

And there it is again, that little vise under my ribs, tightening at the sadness in his voice, the tension clawing the air. I could prod, ask what else she taught him besides losing—like how to break a curse, for example—but the last thing I need is for my impatience to kill a decent minute.

"Your chest is healing up well," I say, picking a softer lever as I angle us toward the water's whisper. "Your eyes seem to be clearing up, and nothing has torn on your face today." Even the bald spots on his scalp seem to carry a newborn fluff of gold. "The crown was generous."

"Yes, we are surrounded by its charity. Let us kneel in gratitude." A muscle jumps beneath his ear. "I do not care for any of its offerings."

"I noticed." I slow the wheelchair, almost as if navigating around potential pitfalls in this conversation is a physical hurdle. "Some days, it mends only slightly quicker than you can undo it. As if it's a race you mean to win by losing." A breath for courage. "Another lesson from someone?"

His head turns as if he wants to look back at me, only to pause halfway through a breath before his attention sinks to his toes. "I am bored with talking about myself. Tell me something about you."

My tongue presses against the roof of my mouth. I got close, didn't I? But that's neither here nor there, now that he's changing the subject, putting up a wall against my efforts.

"What would you like to know?"

"Tell me about your family. About something that your thoughts drift back to when you're alone in your chamber at night."

My fingers tighten around the handles as my mind strains to find a cheerful memory that can maintain the mood. Most of them lie so far back, but...maybe this one? Daron at seven, with flour in his hair, sword fighting with a stale crust, swearing he'd make a meal laugh before it was eaten. Something warm enough to hold the moment steady, but—

"Is your family well?" the king cuts through my thoughts. "Healthy? Or are they...ill?"

The question tightens like wire around my knuckles. Be true, Vale had said. But what if the truth makes the night fold back on itself?

"My brother..." I gather breath to the top of my lungs where it won't shake, taste the metal of it, and feel the answer splinter against my teeth. "Rot chews his nails. The missing knuckle wakes him. He's silly. He's too thin. He is... loved."

Silence.

Heart-rending silence.

"Reign of Rot." The king's jaw knots on the words until it grates, the little warmth we'd gathered draining out of him with them. "I know full well it is what the streets say."

"Streets aren't meant for saying kind things, and alleys even less so." I turn us toward the water. Maybe it's a distraction cleaner than memory. "Look. It's the fountain I discovered yesterday."

From a distance, the statue at the center could be a man. Nearer, the differences assert themselves. Cloak thrown over shoulders, mostly made of sinew. The left hand lifted, palm up, offering a heart that is not a heart, not really—too smooth, too perfect, a symbol dressed in veins. The right hand is hidden deeper in the folds. You could call the face beautiful if you were a poet. You could call it a skull if you were drunk and honest.

Somehow, it's both.

"What is it?"

"Death." He all but spits that name, looking at the statue like it's a relative he barely tolerates. "To remind us of what is owed to this unfeeling monster. It was erected by my *father*."

That last word drips with enough disdain that it might leave puddles on the ground. "You didn't care for him."

"The crown demanded that I slit his throat." His hands tighten on the blanket, the tendons showing white. "Did you know? Did someone tell you how the crown gets passed on?"

I shake my head. "Miss Hampshire wouldn't approve of such talk."

"That's how it goes. Father crowns son, and son ends father. That's the mercy of it." His voice sharpens. "But mercy wasn't what I wanted."

Silence takes care to step out of the way when I say, "What did you want?"

"To put my blade in his eye," he says. "And then the other. He screamed like an animal, and I didn't mind it. I opened his neck; I stabbed his groin. I ripped up into the belly he filled while he lectured me about goodness—stabbed, stabbed, stabbed—until even the crown was bored and counted it done." His mouth pulls tight. "Many years, I'd waited for the opportunity to kill him."

My tongue turns to iron, unmoving. Every clever sentence I brought dies in my mouth like a fly in milk. I've collected men butchered like that in alleys, but there's a difference between arranging the pieces and listening to the hand that broke them say it liked the sound.

My next swallow goes down like dust as I cling to this raw truth between us, the anchor it could be into vulnerability. "You were—"

"Enough." The word stabs the cold air like an ice shard. "Back."

"We could—"

"Back." The old, clean cruelty returns to his voice. "Do you hear me?! Take me back! Now!"

It's not a roar. Roars need breath.

It's a lash.

It cracks me into motion, my steps wobbly as though I'm barefoot on the shards of my miserable defeat. There's no more prying anything out of him anytime soon. It's locked behind temper and tenacity, every word a door I don't have a damn key for.

But maybe keys aren't what I need.

Not if I have a lockpick.

If I can't lure clues from the king's mouth, then I'll steal them from ink and parchment. Lies. Distractions. *Something* has to get me into the library, or to some lesser recordings, even if it takes feigning curiosity over bowel movements.

The chair shrieks, and the hedge behind me answers with a small, precise rustle. I don't turn. If it's staff, then I better get close to the annals before Miss Hampshire hears of this incident and throws me out with or without the king's urging. And if it's Vale?

Pfft... He'll be chuckling in the dark, counting my mistakes like beads.

FOURTEEN

Elara

"Lineage and stewards only." *Bam.* The scribe slams his book shut, letting a whirl of dust cough into my face.

"All I need are the annals of the late queen." I step closer to the scribe's worm-eaten lectern because cowardice is a disease, and I wasn't born with that affliction. "Diary entries pertaining to the king. Notes on health."

"What you need is the door behind you." The old, bald-headed scribe looks up just long enough to cough into his rag and stain it the color of old cherries. Spots freckle his cuff where blood and pus didn't quite make it to the rag. "Maids look at linen ledgers, not royal annals."

"I'm not a maid," I say. "I'm the king's personal caretaker. The more I understand about his upbringing, the better I can serve His Majesty."

He dips his quill, and the tremor that rakes the length of his hand makes the ink stutter across the page. A wet rattle stops the spill. He leans aside and spits into a chipped basin without shame, threads of red webbing the porcelain.

"Lineage." He taps a bone-thin finger against the cover of the nearest tome. The knuckle clicks. "Stewards." His gaze lifts to me, one eye brown, the other a dry, wrinkly plum rotting away in its socket. "Leave."

I turn on my heel hard enough to scold the floorboards and storm back into the corridor, fury as biting as lye under my tongue. It's bad enough that the king slammed himself shut again in the garden after he'd finally started to talk. Now the books won't open, either! How am I meant to pry at the hinge of this curse when every hand in this place teaches doors to stay closed?

It's impossible! "Ugh!"

The library is truly off-limits. Vale talks only when he wants to. For the past few days, not once. How else can I—

Something in my belly tips.

A small whirl. A shift in gravity.

My feet falter to a halt right where an alcove of shadow opens to my right. My eyes lift uninvited, landing on the double doors of the unused royal chamber.

That whirl in my belly intensifies.

It's older than Ophelia, Vale had said. But if that's true, then why would the king care? It makes no sense. And if neither Vale nor the library will speak to me about it, well, then perhaps the room will!

I lay my palm against the latch and wiggle it a little. The doors are closed today, but unlike the greenhouse, they aren't locked. I listen for a breath on the other side. Nothing. I press.

The handle yields, and the door swings on a sigh, as if it's been holding it in for years. Inside, the room still has that tidy loneliness, the mirror veiled, the bed draped.

A glance over my shoulder.

Nobody there.

I slip inside. Close the door. There has to be something in here. A letter. A journal entry. A long-forgotten secret. Anything that can tell me why the king avoids this room, and how it might relate to the avoidance of his duty of feeding the crown.

So I start.

Drawers: lined in paper gone brittle, but nothing inside that holds as much as a single stroke of ink. Wardrobe: gowns asleep on their hangers, stitched for festivals that turned into funerals. A chest in the corner: cedar breath, clean blanketing, nothing anybody would bother to hide. I dip my fingers into the seam under the mantel. It gives me nothing but soot.

Footsteps creak.

I step behind the bed drapes and make myself flat. Four counts, high in the chest. The sound passes.

I move slower. Rooms give up their secrets to people who stop hurrying. The mirror asks to be unveiled, but I refuse. Mirrors are far too good at making people believe that what they see is true. Wood, however...

Wood doesn't flatter.

It keeps score.

The shine on a chest lid tells you how often a hand sought it for comfort. You can smell whether a board was fed beeswax or lye; hear if a floor is lying about rot by the way it sighs under your knee. Joints confess the craftsman; splinters confess neglect.

Mirrors are opinions.

Wood is evidence.

Kneeling, I palm the boards and let the grain talk—knuckle taps for hollows, fingertip presses for give, a slow pry where a seam looks sullen. Only dust answers. No loose tongue of plank, no hidden graves for secret notes. I crawl the perimeter, knees drinking the cold, cheek near the wood to hear if it lies. Nothing. Nothing. Nothi—

There! A freckle in the plank, close to the rug.

Not dust, not a beetle. Too uniform for dirt, too flat to be sap. Brown the way dried things become.

Like old blood.

I hook my fingers under the rug and peel it back slowly. The weave clings like a scab, then lets go with a rip...

...and the stain blooms.

It starts as a wrong shine, a circle polished by a hundred frantic scrubs that shaved it smaller and drove it deeper in a way that makes my stomach turn. Saliva pools under my tongue as I lift the rug more, making the stain grow and swell like—

"What are you doing?"

I jerk, rug slapping down on the floor in crumpled folds, my breath pinned too close to my heart. My head snaps toward the door.

Vale leans against the jamb as if the wood has been built around him. Sunlight from the corridor draws a seam over his shoulder, giving his face a warm glow.

"Breaking rules," I say, because I don't like being caught, and I like being scolded even less. "What's your excuse?"

"I heard a complaint from the scribe. A maid asked to gain access to the library." His mouth almost smiles. "Obstinate, he said she was. I decided not to argue with his talent for adjectives."

Neither do I, shifting from my knees to my rear as if to convey that I have no intention of leaving this situation behind. "So you hunted me down."

"I looked for you," he corrects. "You were not in your chamber. Not with the king. Not prying at the greenhouse lock. That left…" He tilts his head at the room. "Here."

"To do what?" I throw the words in his direction, low and dangerous. "Keep me from figuring out what you're not telling me?"

He's quiet for a heartbeat before he closes the door behind him—does not latch it, but shuts it enough that the hall will have to work to overhear. He steps in and lowers to the rug beside the blood, as if kneeling were something he rarely practices.

His gaze sinks to what's still visible of the stain. "You found it."

His tone is unimpressed, unsurprised.

"It's old."

"There's older." The words scrape out like he wishes they didn't. "The palace has stains in its bones. In the kitchens. Under the chapel. On the privy floors." His mouth tightens. "This one isn't even the worst of them."

"Why did you keep this from me?"

"Because you're going down a rabbit hole," he says softly. "And there is nothing at the bottom of this one but splinters." A scoff. "So much about you not wanting to waste time."

That last part lands heavier in my stomach than I want it to. "Whose is it?" I ask. "Ophelia's?"

He exhales through his nose. "No. Before her."

"So a queen died in this room."

"Queens have died in many rooms."

I look back down, peeling the rug another inch to expose the jagged edge of the discoloration. "Who bled here?"

"Elara, this palace is a butcher's block wrapped in velvet." He glances at the stain with a boredom that feels studied. "You found a spot. Congratulations. If we peeled back every rug in this wing, we'd find a dozen more just like it."

"Goddamn it, Vale, who—"

"Queen Maeryn." He reaches out and flips the corner of the rug back over the wood, extinguishing the stain from sight. "King Merrick's second wife and sacrifice."

I frown at the rug, unconvinced. "Then why does Kael refuse this room?"

"Merrick's bed. Merrick's mirror. Merrick's chamber pot. Presume he avoids it because it reeks of a father he *loathed*." His voice edges into something sharper. "Every night, that massive blood stain would remind him of what ought to happen to his future wife, what his father had done to a mother he adored."

My fingers curl away from the rug as if they want to believe him. And it makes sense. Given how Kael spoke of his father in the gardens? Yes, it makes sense...but then why does something keep murmuring in the back of my head?

I shake it away for now because there's no way I'm getting a different story out of Vale, anyway. "Why did you come?"

"To apologize."

I bark a small laugh and stare at the rug. "Of course."

"For the greenhouse," he says, the words leaving him

like shards. "For...raising my voice. For putting my hand on you. Rather roughly." He doesn't even pretend it had been anything else. "I am sorry."

I keep my eyes on the speck of blood, because if I look at his face, I might forget to be upset. "It changes nothing."

"Look at me..." His hand comes up slow—heel of palm first at my jaw. Warmth settles, thumb resting just under my cheekbone. He doesn't turn my face. He waits, asking with skin what strength would bruise. "Will you look at me, please?"

Not a command.

A plea.

I tell myself I don't lean into the cradle of his palm as my gaze finds his. God forbid I notice the clean heat of him, the faint scent of carnations, the way my stupid pulse steps too obediently into his touch.

What is it about this infuriating man?

"The more the king drowns in determination and disease, the more work finds me," he says on a slow exhale, heavy enough it turns the air between us thick. "Moving bread from where it rots to where it won't. Seeing to taxes no one can pay. Signing decrees that no longer change anything. Filling the silences he leaves behind. Burying the truth before it festers into rumor. Elara, I am..." His voice trips, tangles, then finds itself again. "I am tired."

His words sit bare and vulnerable between us, and something loosens under my collarbone—a small, soft give like dough rising under steady warmth. Compassion slides in before I can bar the door. Because I know what it feels like, being tired of a million efforts that lead to nothing.

"I need this to stop." His palm shifts along my cheekbone, not even pretending it's anything else but a caress. "Not for the sake of the realm, for I will not pretend to be that valiant. For me." His thumb drifts, slow as thought, tracing the edge of my jaw before stopping at the corner of my mouth. "If I put my desperation over yours, then I'm sorry."

My pulse flutters against his touch, shy and sharp. He's so close. So warm, making me want to press my face deeper into his touch.

I don't, though.

Maybe I don't know how, with my skin trained for the cold of death, for weight that does not answer back. So I twist away, letting his hand fall, trying not to shiver at the cool air settling across my cheek.

"He...he opened up to me," I say, quickly swallowing the thickness that somehow gathered in my throat. "A little. He made a joke in the gardens. He smiled. He spoke about his mother. Asked about my brother." I feel the betrayingly soft edge on my tongue at the mention of Daron and sharpen it. "But it isn't enough. Every second counts. I need to understand him faster without having to pester him about things that darken his mood. A view into his past will not only do that, but it might even give me a hint about how to convince him to feed the crown."

Vale's jaw tightens the way men tighten a belt when the work is about to be ugly. "If the library held an answer to that, don't you think I would have found it by now?"

"Men can stare straight at a thing and still not see it."

"Some things you claim to know about men..." He sits in silence just long enough for me to realize I'm listening to his breath like a fool. When he speaks again, it is with resignation wearing good manners. "In five nights, I will try to take you to the library."

"Five?" The word comes out too fast. "That might as

well be the number of fingers my brother loses in that span of time."

"Well, the scribe coughs more on Thursdays, and the sound will give us cover," he says sarcastically. "Lineage and stewards, Elara, and that rule is tighter than the gauze on a leper's hand. I am one, but you are neither, which means that this excursion requires...finesse."

"Alright." My eyes go to the speck of blood that peeks out from the edges of the rug. It's old, yes, but not ancient. "In five nights."

FIFTEEN

Elara

"Un-acc-epta-ble!" Miss Hampshire's half-hand taps each syllable with scolding force, matching her angry steps toward the king's chamber. "Taking His Majesty to the gardens without my approval. And not just anywhere in the gardens... Oh no, but the fountain of all places!"

I keep my eyes on the floor, counting the cracks in the stone as I take the scolding I saw coming from leagues away. "He needed air."

"*He needs rest*," she snaps, the tips of her words sharp enough to peel paint. "The man's constitution is delicate, and his temper"—she exhales through her nose like steam escaping a kettle—"is hardly improved by this!"

I weigh my options: argue and lose, or apologize and lose slower. "I meant no harm. How was I supposed to know that the statue would upset him so?"

"That statue marks the place of Queen Ophelia's coronation, girl!" She turns sharply, skirts whispering against the wall as we take the corner toward the king's door. "You dragged him to the very spot where she bled—" Her words stumble, half-hand freezing mid-tap as if the syllables caught on a boulder in her throat. Then her mouth shuts so hard her jaw clicks.

My stomach knots together.

So Vale didn't lie...

For a heartbeat, the only sounds in the corridor are our footsteps and the faint hiss of torches fighting damp air. "Bled by the healers' counsel," Miss Hampshire finishes tightly, as if she can stitch the lie over the gaping hole in her story. Her gaze darts to me, sharp and assessing. "In her... final days. When she was sick."

I lift my brow a little, just to pretend she spilled gossip rather than a secret about a curse I already know everything about. "It won't happen again, Miss Hampshire."

Interesting. Whatever happened in the royal chamber, whoever bled out on the wood... It truly wasn't Ophelia, wasn't Kael's mother. Perhaps Vale is right, and this *is* a dead end, leaving me flailing for answers once more.

"Miss Hampshire!" The kitchen girl runs up the corridor, flushed and panting, hands wringing the hem of her apron. "You must come. The flour delivery."

Miss Hampshire's sigh carries the weariness of a thousand similar interruptions. "By all the saints, the flour will still be flour when I arrive. What now?"

"Thomas says he needs you right away," the girl heaves, glancing at me, then lowering her voice. "There are people everywhere holding it up. Walls. Gate. Everywhere."

Miss Hampshire pales to the same shade as her cap. She turns to me, caught between irritation and duty. "You'll wait outside the chamber. Do not go in until I return."

I nod, hands folded so she doesn't see how tightly I've fisted them. "Yes, Miss Hampshire."

And then she's gone, her steps slapping sharp against the stone as she hurries after the girl. The sound fades fast, leaving me alone in a corridor too still for comfort. As things stand, I'd best do as told for once and wait. I don't need—

Noise leaks through the silence.

A dull scrape.

A shuffle.

Another, louder this time, followed by a violent crash of something toppling inside the king's chamber. Wood? Metal?

Pulse thudding against the bottom of my throat, I look at the door. What's going on? He's never that animated. No, that would require him to get up from that damn couch, and—

The king's shout shatters my thoughts, bellowing with a strength I've never heard before. It sets me into urgent motion, feet stumbling toward the noisy chaos. He's in trouble...

A hurried knock, then the latch gives way under my palm. Nervous candles dodge and duck the draft I let in. That, and how the king rises from the chair by the darkened window with an angry whirl. He grips the table in front of him before he hurls it into the room.

Wood splinters.

Ivory clanks.

Chess pieces scatter.

"Know your place, you bastard!" he roars, that last word thrown like a blade at the figure sitting quietly on the chair across. "Get out! Crawl back into the shadows where you belong."

Vale rises from the chair with the silence of a grave. He doesn't look at how the king whirls around to kick a splintered chair. Doesn't say *Majesty*. He simply stands, smooths his cuff, and turns toward the door. Toward me.

A chill numbs my fingertips.

What is all this about?

Vale passes me without looking. His sleeve brushes the edge of my knuckles. His hand finds mine—one quick, treacherously warm squeeze. Then he is gone, the door's sighing breath stealing him into the corridor.

The king doesn't see.

He's too busy spending himself.

"I won't be outwitted," he mumbles to the room, to the window he keeps blind, to the bishop rolling on the ground as he paces back and forth, back and forth, back and forth. "I won't be—" He stops. Breath jerks. Starts again. Another kick sends the broken chair leg hurtling across the room. "Not by a filthy snake in a clean coat!"

His roar trembles the air clear into my quivering lungs. This is insanity. Pure madness!

"Majesty!" I rush toward him like a hare toward a wolf. "Please calm down!"

"Do you think me cruel!?" he snaps, rounding on me as if I'm a chess piece that dared remain upright. His face is winter-stung and too thin for the rage that's raising veins along his cheeks.

"Tell me. Do you think me inept?" When I only shake my head, he shouts, "Use your damn voice!"

"N-no." A startle squeezes that out of me before I lift my hands in an appeasing manner. "I think you're angry."

"Angry." He laughs. It's a cracked thing, the sound of cartilage trying to remember humor before it collapses into a whimper small enough to be ashamed of itself. "Reign of Rot," he pants, as if the phrase were climbing him from the inside and cutting its way out through his teeth. "Reign of Rot. They say it. They carve it into doors. They mutter it at the market with mouths...full...of... *nothing!*"

My breath stutters along my spine with how he stalks around me, the crown on his head far straighter than the state of his mind. "Please, Your Majesty, you have to calm down."

"Every day..." he says, softer. Quieter. More dangerous. "Every day the poor knock at the gate with stubbed wrists. Coin. Food. Salvation." He grips his crown, pulling it down on his skull as if he means the gold to crack through the bone. "And I turn them away."

"You're doing what you think is right." I carefully wrap my trembling fingers around his arm. "Why don't you sit on your couch? Then we can—"

"Leave!" He rips his arm from my clasp, hissing at the pain it causes his shoulder. "Get out! Go practice patience on some other carcass."

Against the caution tensing my muscles and the anxiety stirring my guts, I don't step back. I won't let him chase me off.

"Camphor." I grab the flask of oil from the nearby table.

Uncork it. Carry it toward him. "It'll help with the pain. If you would just—"

He swats the flask.

Not a throw, a slap.

The arc is small and petty, but it still manages to paint the floor between us in a glistening sheet as the glass shatters. "Get out!"

"Majesty."

I step toward him. My heel slips on the oil, leg flying out from underneath me. The room tilts. A hit against my temple. *Thud.* The room turns away from me and disappears into the dark.

CHAPTER

SIXTEEN

Elara

I wake to the smell of clean gauze and the tired sweetness honey leaves when it has done what it can.

Where am I?

The light is low and not ambitious. The ceiling above me is the same cracked plaster as always, but the angle is wrong. I'm higher, my blanket heavier. The pillows under my head are good ones, not straw.

The king's bed?

The moment I move my arms, trying to sit up, a voice stops me.

"Not yet." The king is seated beside me on the red blanket, elbows on his knees, head braced in his palms. "Rest a while longer."

My tongue presses up against my gums at the sight of his posture that reads awfully close to despair. How did I get up here? Surely he didn't heave my body this far and this high when he struggles to even lift his bad arm.

I glance around.

It's only us.

His shirt is open at the throat, the angry rash there paled to something I wouldn't call beautiful, but I would no longer call it ugly, either. A line of old muscle still lives beneath his skin, stretching taut with each of his slow inhales.

He lifts his face. The fog over his eyes has cleared some over the last few days, revealing a deeper shade of blue. Red-rimmed, though, like a man who's held his breath too long. Or had an angry outburst...

"This is not at all how I have been raised to act. How I ought to treat a woman." Clenching his eyes shut, he releases a slow breath, shaking his head before his gaze returns to the room—only to lose itself somewhere on a wrinkle within the red velvet. "Or perhaps I have been raised to treat them far worse..."

My ribs are all but counting my breaths. Something changed about his air. It's denser, yet more open at the same time. Like a door of heavy oak left ajar.

I don't trust it. What if it swings back on my fingers?

His gaze lifts and finds mine. "Why are you here?"

There's no anger in his voice, no curiosity. Only factual blandness, making it impossible to gauge the renewed question. It could be the kind a king asks when he has caught on to his steward's treachery. What did Vale and he talk about before I came into the room? What has that man done to rile the king up like this?

"My family needs coin." It's true enough an answer as I tiptoe around this strangely calm energy that floats in the air between us. "For my father's lungs. My brother's fingers."

"Your brother. Loved." He's turning that last word over in his mouth as if tasting if it's something he might swallow. "How far would you go to save him?"

"Your Majesty?"

"What would you give, Miss Elara...to save him?" His gaze is very plain; plain enough that I can't tell whether he means to test me or warn me or bless me with a choice I already made even before coming here.

A knot swells in my throat at the sound of my name from his lips, so thick it aches when I gulp it down and carefully venture, "All that I have."

He bows his head—a little involuntary tilt that I can't read, that I can't keep from driving up my pulse. Did his resolve to break the curse crack alongside the marble figurines? Or did my answer just confirm his steward's scheming? Is he measuring me for the crown or the noose?

He takes a cloth from the bowl on the stool beside him and touches it to my burning temple. Cool. Damp. Smelling faintly of honey. Honey he must've used to tend to the obvious cut there while I was unconscious?

"I owe you a king's apology," he says, and his voice is court again—not the cruel court, but the one that learned manners and didn't always forget them. "For the shouting. The yanking. My ill temper. For...all of it."

For a breath, I just watch him, this man who only ever comes in nasty storms now sitting in still water. No vileness, no biting words.

There's just quiet and the glimmer of regret in his eyes. It's strange seeing him like this...stranger still that he looks younger. The ruin is asleep, and for the first time, I glimpse the man beneath it.

How do I meet him, this version I've never seen before?

"You upended a chessboard," I say carefully, because humor is cheaper than righteousness. "The pawns will never forgive you."

A very small smile disobeys the rest of his face, if only for a second. "I have endured worse censure from men in better positions."

"Men in better positions still don't know the weight of a crown," I say quietly. "It's easy to judge when you're not the one bearing the weight."

An old shadow returns to his face, but it somehow fails to age him the way it has before. "I've brought my people nothing but ruin. Every day, this kingdom rots a little more under my hand." His head lowers, as if readying itself for the executioner. "The weight of that kind of failure was...too much to bear earlier. It is not an excuse; merely serving as an explanation that begs your forgiveness."

I should hate him for the suffering he's causing, but there's something disarming about the way he says sorry—like a man unused to the word, yet meaning every letter.

He moves the cloth again, slower now, his touch almost reverent. The damp edge drags cool across my temple, down to the hollow beneath my cheekbone, careful not to press too hard. His thumb follows, barely there, brushing away a stray drop, and for one disarming heartbeat, I forget which one of us is meant to be healing the other.

When his eyes find mine, he clears his throat. "I shall make amends." He drops the rag into a shallow bowl that stands on a stool beside the bed, then returns his attention to me. "Tell me how, Miss Elara."

Tell me how.

Those words bring a tingle to my core. An apology from a king alone is likely a treasure, but this feels like something much bigger entirely: like an opening.

A rare, fragile chance.

The library. I could ask him for access to the queens' annals, to a hint, a clue about his determination.

No. He would question my reasons. Might grow suspicious. Besides, Vale already said he'd take me.

My eyes drift to the curtains, to those heavy drapes that choke the room in shadow. I could ask him to open them; to let the light touch his room, his mood, his very soul. Too simple, too...still very much bound to this damn room.

It needs to be something deeper. Something that brings me closer to him once more. Something that breeds intimacy. Something like—

My eyes go to the rash at his throat, much improved but still refusing to leave altogether.

That's it.

"Yes, you shall make amends." Because he offered, and I'm not a woman who wastes opportunities. "Salt water. You'll agree to take a long soak while I tend to your skin. It'll do more than all the wormwood and witch hazel in the realm."

There's a faint tilt of his head, a subdued moment of surprise as his eyes narrow for a fraction of a second. "The kitchens are—"

"Short, yes. Everyone is short," I answer. "Except for the sea."

"The sea is far. Dangerous at night, and painfully bright during the day."

I lift a taunting brow. "Sounds as if the king's desire to make amends ends where his comfort does."

He gives a bemused scoff.

Then he leans back enough that the open part of his shirt shifts, letting a nearby flame flicker soft and warm over the lean muscles on his stomach. He had to be strong once, with soft skin raised by the most fragrant oils, and muscles honed with the help of the best sword masters. With his hair long, perhaps a bit curled, framing those blue eyes?

He had to be regal once.

Handsome, even.

"There is a spring," he eventually says. "On the far side of the grounds. It broke into the old salt mine many years ago. It's a cave's mouth now, where the air is wet enough that lanterns sputter. No one uses it. The smell...persuades people that they do not need to discover it." He pulls a breath deep into his chest and lets it go slowly. "If I am to make amends, let it be there."

"A soak it is," I say, and no small sense of victory lifts inside my core. "We can go at night, when there's enough moonlight and no clouds to make us slip on rocks and break our skulls."

He considers me, then he nods once. "At the next clear moonlit night."

SEVENTEEN

Elara

"Do not get your hopes up." Vale walks the way men who've made a habit of going unnoticed do—hands behind his back, pace unhurried, the exact speed of nonchalance. "The scribe may yet refuse us and inform the king, and then we'll have a problem."

"A problem," I say, because repeating stupid words sometimes makes them less so. "Such as the fit the king threw a few days ago, thanks to whatever you said to stir his rage? Whatever was that about?"

"Insults are a currency he spends freely with me." Vale

turns down a narrow run of corridor. "I mentioned a nearby granary where guards got killed and the grain plundered. He disliked hearing it. He also dislikes losing to me at chess." A sigh. "The two together offended him."

"That's all you said?"

"That is all he heard, and nothing more once he threw the table."

The library door waits for us around the next corner. Vale raps once—not a knock so much as a courtesy. Then, he pushes in.

The smell of paper meets us.

And blood. Lots of it.

The scribe hangs slumped over his lectern, cheek pressed to the margin, jaw slack against the red-stained paper. His quill has drawn a last thin river and dried in mid-stutter. The rag in his stiff hand is stubborn with red threads, and the basin beneath his desk shows a dried sunburst where the last cough tried to wash itself away and failed.

"Saints," I whisper as I step to the old man and lay two fingers to his throat where a pulse would be if he were alive. He's not. "Rot took his lungs for good."

Vale frowns for a second before he simply shrugs. "Let's go."

I'm not exactly shocked by his aloofness, though I don't feel comfortable with it, either. "Shouldn't we...report it? See to it he gets his grave?"

"Plenty of men die quietly here. Graves are patient." He lifts the ring of keys from the hook on the side of the lectern and holds them like an apology. "However, time is not patient, and ours is sprinting. At some point, someone else will find the scribe. Come on."

With a jut of his head that puts me into motion, he

turns toward the door behind the lectern. The key slides into the lock and whines, then relents with an effortful *click*. Hinges complain like tired knees.

"Ophelia," I say when we enter, the stacks holding up a ceiling that looks like it would rather fall on us and be done. "I want to read up on her coronation. Actually, I want to look through her life."

Vale slowly shakes his head. "The king's mother has been dead for many years now. If she gave him the idea, then why has his stubbornness only now turned into nothing short of obsession?"

"Maybe something changed," I say. "A new discovery of evidence. A new piece to the puzzle."

Vale only huffs, making it clear he's not so much helping me out of conviction, but to shut me up and keep me compliant. Which works for me.

Lanterns squat in high niches, their light made shy by the draft coming from windows barely big enough to let a cat in, let alone much brightness. The air is exhaustedly sweet—glue and leather and a hint of old milk in the paste.

Vale moves, the keys barely speaking in his hand, and steers me to a ceiling-high case with a brass label smudged by many thumbs: *Household Annals*. "If memory serves, then these are of a more personal sort. Perhaps if you started—"

"I got it from here." The strap that keeps the book I reach for lifts without argument. I pull it out, place it on the table, and flatten it to a random page. Ink, tidy and smaller than it ought to be, looks up at me. "Light the table."

Vale lifts a nearby lantern from the hook. Puts it on the table, where a handful of scrolls lie strewn about. His gaze flicks to my temple; the bruise must be blooming ugly under my hair. "That wound is bad for seduction."

"I'll wear it." I let my pointer trace a line in the book.

Something boring about indigestion. "Because it bought me a shame-ridden king who's trying to make amends. I have a feeling things will be different between us now, allowing me to try for his heart."

Vale's mouth doesn't move, yet it manages to sharpen somehow. "Oh?"

"The salt spring," I say. "He agreed to go with me."

"Hmm." Vale's silence stretches—long enough that I want to mistake it for quiet disapproval. Then his voice breaks it, soft and deliberate, the kind that slides under skin before it pricks. "Perhaps I was mistaken in my approach. Saints, maybe I should have let you lead from the start." Words like warm oil on skin, if not for how he adds, "A fine rehearsal for the bedding."

The word lands like a slap of cold water, making my fingers jerk up from the book. "What do you mean?"

"A spring is made of water, Elara." He doesn't rush to elaborate. He leans against the table beside me, rolling his cuffs once, slowly, thoughtfully. "And water, by its nature, doesn't like cloth. It clings, reveals. People rarely enter it dressed." His gaze drifts, almost lazily, over my face before settling on my throat. "And if His Majesty's weak balance fails him on wet stone? Well, he'll need help. Steady hands. *Your* hands." He lets the weight of it hang there. "Imagine it—skin on skin. His breath, close. His naked body, *closer*."

My stomach pitches, twisting so hard it feels like the floor gives under me. Heat crawls up my neck, licking behind my ears and down my collar. God, I haven't thought that far. Not really. What if he strips down to nothing? What if...what I have to do the same?

Breathe. Fucking breathe.

The panic hammers once more, twice. Then it dulls. I knew this would come. It's part of the plan, the price, the inevitable deal. Just...not yet. Not here, not in this room full of too many pages and not enough eyes to read them.

"Shut up," I snap, louder than I mean to. Or maybe not loud enough, given how Vale smirks, faint and merciless. "I'll deal with it once it arrives."

"Of course," Vale murmurs, the edge of amusement softening to something quieter, almost pity. "After years of loneliness, it'll be *hard* for him to hide his...natural desires. His body—"

"Here's something!" I tap on the page. "On the third hour of the fifth day in Harvest," I read out loud, "the Lady Ophelia stood with the young prince in the painter's chamber. The child showed reluctance to take her hand, even though the painter requested it for a pose. Lady Ophelia bade him wait, then produced from her sleeve a small toy— a boxwood horse with a blue thread at the mane. The prince brightened and consented to the pose, clasping Lady Ophelia's fingers with his left hand and the horse with his right. The painter noted dimples, which Lady Ophelia had encouraged with a smile. The session proceeded without further upset."

"Ophelia doted. All the old, mostly retired staff know." Vale touches the open page lightly with the back of his knuckles, as if pointing without having to be impious about it. "It's all here. Boring things: favorite soups, a gown with lace she favored, how the boy had a talent for numbers. Lovely, domestic nonsense. Tell me, why are we here again?"

"Anything written here that the king refuses to share could be helpful," I say, turning pages with a thumb that's feeling for worn seams. Most entries are mundane. A story of how the king broke his arm once. A note on a cough. "Where is what lit the match?"

"Lit the match?"

"Somewhere, there's a spark. Something that made a prince grow into a king who decided to break the curse." Men who feed the poor and tend to their caretakers don't just get up one day and decide to starve a kingdom. "If I can find the first thought that said *break it*, then I can follow its footprints to whatever still listens to reason."

Even Vale doesn't argue that logic, and he half-sits, half-leans on the table. "Presume it will suit once the time comes to—why are you smiling? What is it?"

"Listen to this." I clear my throat. "By request of Lady Ophelia: the chessboard in the schoolroom is to be fixed to the table; pieces weighted. The tutor is to stand two paces out of reach when delivering mate, sugared pawns sent after to sweeten tempers." A chuckle rumbles loose before I can rein it in, and I angle the page toward Vale. "He hated losing so much his mother bolted the game to the furniture."

He leans in and touches the margin, his warm breath ghosting my cheek and sending a flurry through my core. "Kings have an uneasy pact with checkmate."

"Maybe I should teach him how to resign with grace."

The corner of his mouth curves into a true smile, more sincere than I've ever seen on him before. "I would pay to see that."

His finger lingers in the margin, brushing mine. Our eyes lock. For a breath, neither one of us moves. Time slows. That flurry in my core slows with it, turning into a sensuous swell of heat that sinks low into my belly, deeper than anything ever before.

Before it can reach my groin, I breathe it away and nod at the nearby ladder. "Maybe I'll get luckier up there."

Vale grabs the rail, steadying the wood. "Careful."

I test the first rung. It holds.

I climb the ladder that leans into the heavy shelf with more faith than my quivering knees possess. "Heights were never my strength."

He smirks up at me. "Presume that's why you prefer to shovel down into graves instead."

"Probably."

I climb two more rungs, the hem of my dress whispering along my calves. The lantern's breath makes the book titles shine. Inventories. Chapel Receipts. Sermons.

Boring. Boring. Boring.

I step higher. The ladder complains just as the light shifts, making the spines go pitch black.

I swat at a cobweb that tickles my ear. "I need light up here."

"Coming." Vale's hand leaves the rail, reaching for the—

Snap.

The wood turns to powder under my sole.

Gravity makes a claim, and I drop. Air flees my lungs with a sharp squeal, the room blurring into a rush of shelves and shadows. I brace for the floor, but I never hit it.

I hit him.

It's a collision of ribs and panic, my body sliding down the hard length of his until his boots take my weight. His arms lock around me instantly—one banding my ribs, the other clamping low on my waist, fingers digging into my hip with a force that has nothing to do with saving me and everything to do with keeping me.

I gasp, my fingers fisting into his vest, gripping leather and thread, waiting for the room to stop tilting. "Oh my god."

"Are you hurt?" The rumble of his voice is right there, in the sensitive hollow where my neck meets my shoulder.

I unclench his vest, feeling the rapid, violent expand and contract of his lungs beneath my palm. "No. No, I…"

The words die in a throat suddenly too tight to hold them.

I look up.

The lantern's hiss, paper dust, and the smell of him—carnations and heat—flood my senses. He doesn't let go; if anything, his grip tightens, pulling my hips flush against his. His gaze is dark, blown wide, dropping to my mouth with the kind of hunger that usually ends in ruin.

My breath turns shallow, trapped high in my chest. His does the same, uneven, a jagged rhythm against my own.

His hand moves first. Not to release me, but to map me. His thumb drags, slow and heavy, along the curve of my waist, pressing into the soft dip of my side with a possessiveness that makes my knees tremble more than the fall ever did.

My hand stutters up the line of his lapel, intending to push. It forgets the command halfway there and curls into his shirt instead.

"Elara," he breathes, and it sounds like a warning he's too weak to heed.

We hover there as the air between us pulls taut. He leans in, a fraction of an inch, testing the gravity. I don't retreat. I can't. My chin tips up, a silent, damning invitation.

Then, he sinks in.

There is nothing shy about it. His mouth crashes onto mine, hot and desperate and tasting of secrets. A moan vibrates in his chest against my palms as he devours the gasp I try to take. His lower lip drags roughly against mine, prying me open, and then his tongue is there—a flick, a stroke, a deep, sweeping claim that wrecks me.

Heat floods my veins, liquid and heavy. I melt into him, my body curving to fit the hard lines of his, my hands sliding up to tangle in the black curls at the nape of his neck.

Vale groans, a low, ruined sound, and hauls me closer until the only things left in the world are pressure, friction, and the taste of him chasing my mouth and catching it with—

He gasps. It's sharp and wrong, as if something pinched him, sending a tremor through his entire body.

He pulls away from me, hands leaving my body, green eyes chasing something on the floor that I can't seem to see.

"I shouldn't have... I don't know why I did that." The words scrape out at first, but then his voice recovers quicker than my pride can handle as he tugs the wrinkled proof of us from his sleeves. "Best forget that I did, and trust it will never happen again."

"Right." Heat climbs my neck, and I step away from him and back into purpose. Purpose is easier to look at than the ugly maw of rejection.

Anger flares. At him, at me.

Mostly at me.

I don't get to feel rejected by a man I don't even want. I don't get to ache over the *wrong* mouth. What am I doing, letting heat climb this far with the steward who walks me toward a blade? Vale is a means, an accomplice to my ending—nothing more—and I've just kissed him like I'm allowed to live.

Fool!

I pull the word over myself like a wet cloak, turn, and face the shelf instead. Gold shifts on the spine of one of the books, writhing under the flicker of candlelight. *Household Annals—Ophelia.*

"Let's finish what we came for." I pull the book out, flatten it open on the table, and flip to a random ledger. Fevers reported, then another. Walks taken. Menses reported. Useless. Useless. Useless. "Maybe you were right. Maybe there's nothing helpful here."

Another page flip...

...and then a tug.

A page catches, thick where the corner has been folded under. It must've been stuck to its neighbor for years, maybe longer, the edges faintly glued together by age and dampness. I pry it loose. The sound is small, papery, but Vale's head lifts at it, anyway.

"There's something here," I murmur, smoothing the brittle leaf flat. The handwriting runs close to the spine, half-faded where it's been pressed shut so long.

Vale goes still behind me. "Likely an inventory of prayers or some other domestic triviality."

"Maybe..." I lean closer, squinting at the script. "It's about her coronation. Per the date, the king must've been around...fifteen at the time?"

His silence sharpens before he exhales softly. "Then read."

Upon the third toll of the bell, Her Majesty, Queen Ophelia, displayed agitation unseemly of the rite. The chaplain urged calm, though Her Majesty continued to protest.

Witnesses report she struck one attendant across the face and attempted to flee the fountain, during which she tore her gown and lacerated her forehead upon the paving stones. Her speech thereafter grew incoherent—weeping mingling with laughter. The chaplain deemed her seized by hysteria as Her Majesty, Queen Ophelia, accused His Majesty, the king, of having "slaughtered the last queen in the royal chamber," and of having "made his son, the prince, watch."

When His Majesty brought forth the blade, Her Majesty fell to her knees before the dais, pleading that Prince Kael be taken away, shouting that she would not be bled before his eyes.

The prince, overcome by distress, broke from the dais and attempted to reach his mother. Two guards were dispatched to restrain him and were injured in the effort. When he could not be subdued, Death appeared in His divine form. His touch stilled the prince, who fell senseless and silent until four additional guards arrived to remove him by royal order.

Her Majesty's cries subsided only after the chaplain completed the anointing. The rite concluded under ecclesiastical supervision. Chalice received.

—Marginal note (Chaplain S.): I have counseled His Majesty to place the prince under lock and key. For his safety and survival, his chamber has been stripped of unnecessary items; windows to be barred.

I read the words again.

Then once more.

The ink looks steady, measured—written by a hand

untouched by the chaos it describes. But the meaning beneath it begins to pulse, faint and awful.

"Slaughtered the last queen in the royal chamber." The second queen. The bloodstain beneath the rug. "She said King Merrick made his son watch. The prince." The phrasing gnaws at me like a rat behind the walls. "Why accuse him of having made Kael watch the death of a former queen when—"

The thought halts halfway out of my mouth. Something's wrong here...

"When what?" Vale asks.

"When Kael wasn't even born yet." My eyes go back to the entry. *Slaughtered the last queen in the royal chamber and made his son the prince watch.* "Did King Merrick have another son prior to Kael? An older heir?"

Vale scoffs. "No."

Those faraway murmurs echo through my skull again, faint and unintelligible. "But then why else would she have said something like that?"

Vale's hand comes to rest beside me on the table as he leans over the page. "Hysteria," he says, smooth and steady. "You see it plainly right here. The chaplain wrote of delirium. She struck attendants, split her brow, likely concussed. Her words were nonsense."

I want to agree, and god, I almost do. But the thought won't die. It lingers, quiet and stubborn, like a half-buried seed that refuses to rot.

"What if they weren't?"

Vale's mouth curves into something polite but firm. "If there had been an older heir, I would know."

I turn to face him. "You've only been steward for three years."

"Her panic found words, Elara, that is all. Nothing else is mentioned of another son here. Or anywhere."

Vale's logic holds, neat as fresh stitching. And yet...

"Fine," I say. "Then let's prove it."

He tilts his head. "Prove what?"

"That there wasn't another heir. If Ophelia was delirious, then the annals of the second queen should show no mention of birth or a child, right? What was her name again?"

Vale stares at me as if I've gone mad, but eventually says, "Queen Maeryn."

I stride to the next aisle, eyes scanning the flickering spines. The shelves narrow around me, their smell of dust and age swallowing every sound but my breath. The brass labels blur by—ledgers, taxes, inventories—until a low trunk crouches beneath a table, stenciled in faded paint: *Household Annals—Maeryn.*

I drop to a crouch, pulse thudding in my fingertips as I reach for the hasp. "This might take a minute."

Vale doesn't move closer, but his presence feels like a shadow at my back. "We're running out of time, Elara."

"I'll hurry." The latch clicks open. Hinges bark. Dust blooms, then parts like a curtain.

The trunk is tidy.

Extremely tidy.

Because it's empty, aside from dust printing around the absence where book-shapes were lifted recently. A faint smear where a thumb had slid along the bottom is the only thing left behind.

Vale peers in and makes a small, knowing sound. "If I were a suspicious man," he says lightly, "I'd say someone made certain those records couldn't trouble you."

EIGHTEEN

Elara

The spring glistens from afar.

Brine rides the air long before the stone's mouth reveals itself: an arch of rock torn open like a wound, with scrub along the ridge, brittle and dry.

In front of me, the king's lantern sputters as he picks his way down the uneven slope. The wet breath in the air dislikes flames, shivering the light down to a nub and leaving most of the half-cave in darkness.

Like the library trunk.

My toes curl in my boots. Someone wants the past

buried, its proof stripped from sight. But proof of what? An older heir? Something else entirely? And who?

Vale, perhaps? He's too composed, too careful not to let on that he knows more than he says. But then again, the king hasn't been very forthcoming, either. And Death? If the curse was his design, then who's to say he doesn't still guard its truth, keeping the rest of us chasing shadows and—

"Miss Elara." The king's voice cuts through the current of my thoughts.

I blink, almost startled.

A few paces ahead, he stands by a boulder that marks the water's edge, his gaze flicking over his shoulder. "I asked if this spot is to your satisfaction."

"It'll work." Moonlight slicks the surface of the pool in trembling silver, the water shifting with every sigh of wind that whispers past the wide mouth of the cave. "Sorry. I was just…thinking."

"Dangerous habit." His tone is softer than usual, with a thread of amusement woven through. "For most, at least."

"Then it's a miracle I'm not most."

"You most definitely are not." The words carry a warmth that doesn't belong in a cave. He looks away quickly, as if he regrets giving it. "I remember the water being pleasantly warm."

"There's sulfur in it." Pebbles grind under our boots as we wobble toward where the water laps at the white-dusted stone edge. "Not the most alluring smell, but your skin will be as new tomorrow."

"Superior to all my healers and previous caretakers."

I flick my eyes starward and make sure he sees it. A lie, and we both know it. The crown heals him faster than any salve ever could. Still, it's doing less work now that he's slowed trying to destroy himself. Flesh filling back into muscle. Straightness crawling its way into his spine.

"I can get in here." He eyes the shallower end of the spring, near a boulder slick with minerals. The air hums faintly. When he tries to step onto the ledge, his boot slides.

"Careful."

He huffs, half laughter, half frustration. "I shall regret having made this concession." His cloak goes first, folding neatly beside the boots he's now slipped out of, then his fingers go to the ties at his throat. "Least when I drown."

"Try not to," I mutter. "My good graces with Miss Hampshire are hanging by a thread already."

The shirt peels off, and despite my best efforts to look at the cave wall, my gaze snags. It drags over the cords of lean muscle drawn tight over broad planes, the faint lines of healed scars trailing down his ribs. When he rolls his shoulders back, the flex pulls shadows across his abdomen, tracing each ridge until it disappears into the narrow dip of his waist.

A waist that drops its trousers.

My breath hitches, jamming somewhere in my throat. I force my eyes to the ground, to the pebbles, to anything safe. But the image is already burned there—skin, strength, and vulnerability all mixed into a shape that is terrifyingly male.

"It *is* warm." He steps into the water until it laps his calves, then his thighs, mercifully touching linen that clings low at his hips. "Warmer than I remembered it to be. Perhaps I—" He slips, hand darting for the nearby boulder to steady himself, if barely. "That was close."

My pulse drums. He'll drown with how weak he still is.

Yet here I stand, rooted by a panic that has nothing to do with deep water and everything to do with the man standing in it. Vale's words haunt me. *His breath, close. His naked body, closer.*

I breathe down my jagged nerves.

At his next wobbling step, I finally move. "Wait."

The command comes out a bit sharp, and his head jerks at the sound. I'm already at the edge, kicking off my boots. Cold pebbles bite the soles of my feet as I step forward. The first lap of water licks my ankles, climbs, turning the hem of my dress dark and heavy.

"You will soak yourself through," he says with an arched brow. "Then you'll catch a cold on the way back, and I'll be forced to care for *you*. Wheel *you* through the gardens. Force water down *your* throat."

His jest nearly coaxes a smile, but I'm too busy gathering my courage. My apron falls to the stone behind me easily. The dress comes next, my fingers fumbling only slightly with the ties before the fabric slides from my shoulders in a whisper and puddles at my feet.

I join him in my white underdress. The water curls around my calves, my thighs, then hips, cloth wrapping its weight around me until even breathing feels deliberate.

He leans on my arm as much as I lean on his as we move together along the boulder. "There," I say, nodding at a ledge beside it. "Sit."

"And to think there were times I scaled mountains," he murmurs.

I settle behind him, the water climbing only a little higher—just above my breasts. "You still can, so long as you keep on climbing."

"And yet I seem to make no progress." He opens his eyes and stares at the cave wall where moisture glitters like trapped stars. "Seems I am merely...enduring."

I hesitate for a second, giving myself time to choose my words wisely. "Enduring is easier with company."

I let the words hang between us like bait, expecting the usual snap of teeth—his scorn, his dismissal, the quick lash that keeps me at a distance.

Instead, he remains still.

No bark. No bite.

Something about him has shifted. Softer at the edges, like the rage burned itself out in his chamber and left a man behind, raw enough to be quiet. Or maybe it isn't the outburst at all...

My pulse flickers. Is he opening because he means to, or because the door was forced and he's too tired to slam it shut?

He shifts after a while. "So I heard."

I scoot up beside him, bringing my knees up in the water. "When my brother and I were young, we used to climb an old watchtower. I would have frozen halfway up every single time if Daron hadn't been there to guide me to the next ledge. He always went first. Always made sure the stone held." I pause, watching his delicate profile, looking for any tension. "I can't imagine what it's like to grow up in a palace. Did you have friends when you were young?"

"Princes rarely have true friends," he says. "Kings have even fewer."

"What about other children to play with?"

An older brother to shove him up a ledge, perhaps?

For a long moment, he just watches the steam curl off the water. "There was the stablemaster's son," he says quietly, the memory seeming to ease the line of his shoulders. "His half-sister, too. We would hide in the haylofts solely so the guards would have to come find us."

He pauses, and the steam seems to swallow the small,

phantom smile that had touched his lips. "That ended the year I turned fifteen."

My mind drifts to the marginal note, the counsel to keep the prince under lock and key. "Why?"

"To quell my *rebellion against rites and traditions.*" He drags a hand through the water, watching the dark waves it sends across the surface. "Whatever poor king the alleys call me out as, my father would've agreed. He himself never failed to remind me that I made a miserable heir."

Something sharp twists behind my breastbone at the old pain in his voice. "Was there no one else to carry the burden?"

"No. There was not." He lets out a harsh, dry sound—a laugh stripped of all humor. "Had there been... Saints, I doubt I would have given up the opportunity to slaughter my father back then. I was angry. Young. Not fully in control of my—"

He flinches. A sudden twist seizes his shoulder, his teeth clenching around a hiss.

My spine straightens. "Pain again?"

"It's this damn shoulder," he grinds out. "The muscle keeps snatching."

"Let me." I reach out, my fingers hovering over his wet skin.

He hesitates. For a second, he looks at me with pure suspicion—why is she so eager to touch?—but the pain wins. Or maybe the loneliness does.

Either way, he nods.

I press my palms to his upper arm and begin to knead gently, working slow circles into the muscle that's hardened with tension. "It's just a knot."

His breath leaves him in a slow, disarmed exhale as I

press deeper. He leans back into my hands, sinking into the touch.

"Is that...too much?" I ask.

"No," he rasps, his head lolling to the side, exposing the line of his throat. "It feels...strange."

"Strange how?"

"Strange, because we shouldn't be this close." He reaches back, his hand finding mine under the water, covering my fingers. "Strange, because I have this damnable urge to be even closer."

He slowly turns in the water, the movement creating a current that drags my dress against my legs. His fingers lift out of the water, glide up along my arm, following the path of my touch to its source, his palm landing on my cheek, warm and sure.

Blue eyes meet mine, moonlight lifting the last of the clouds from them and bringing out their depth. "Thank you."

His voice is low, soothed into something I've never heard from him. Gentle. Intimate.

As intimate as that sweep of his thumb across my cheekbone. Back and forth it goes, slowly lighting my nerves like struck tinder.

"Of course," I whisper, and curse the way my voice thins. "Your Majesty."

His gaze drifts down to my mouth. The barest parting of his lips mirrors my own breath catching. His head tilts. Leans. Draws toward me. Hovers.

Then he lifts his eyes to mine again, stormed over with something hungry and aching. "Kael. Say it. Say my name."

A thick swallow. "Kael."

The name lands between us like a heartbeat, the warmth of his breath grazing my lower lip. The space between our mouths shrinks, thins. His thumb grazes the corner of my mouth—a question made of skin and heat, asking me to give what he would never just take.

A kiss.

My heart slams against my ribs. Instead of triumph, a sharp, cold spike of terror drives into my belly.

I picture it: the weight of him pressing me backward into the steam, wet skin sliding against wet skin, hands roaming where they shouldn't. The sheer reality of it crashes over me, stripping away the plan and leaving only the primal fear of being touched, of being taken.

His lips lower some.

The cave presses in.

The water feels like a trap, making me flinch. It's a violent, reflexive jerk, my face ripping away from his grasp as I scramble backward. Water splashes loud and harsh, shattering the moment.

He freezes.

I'm breathing hard, chest heaving, my back pressing against the cold, rough stone of the boulder. "I-I can't."

The words are a ragged whisper, but in the echo of the cave, they sound like a scream.

He rises slowly, the water cascading off his chest, the hunger in his eyes replaced by a shuttered, brittle stillness. "Elara?"

"I'm sorry." My voice shakes. I wrap my arms around myself, trying to hold the pieces of my composure together. "It's not... I just can't."

I turn away, hands shaking as I push damp hair from my face, trying to steady myself, trying to breathe, trying to be anything but the frantic mess I suddenly am.

Behind me, water ripples. "Of course," he says, but the

gentleness is gone. It sounds flat, like resignation. "You owe me no apology for my appalling constitution."

"Kael, wait." I spin around, finding his expression already closed off, all softness gone from his demeanor. "It wasn't you. I didn't mean to—"

A lift of his hand wards off my words. "I understand enough."

My mouth opens.

Nothing useful comes out.

My tongue feels thick, glued to the roof of my mouth by shame. I want to explain. I want to tell him it isn't disgust; that it isn't him, that it's the panic chewing through my ribs like a starved rat.

But he's already turning away, wading toward the edge with stiff, purposeful movements.

I am left standing there, dripping and shaking, lips closing around apologies that no longer have anywhere soft to land.

Kael gathers his cloak from the rocks, steps behind me as I emerge from the water, and drapes it over my shoulders. He tucks it gently against my ribs, his hands steady, even as the space between us ices over.

"We should return," he says, his voice devoid of the warmth he held only moments ago. "Before the cold grips you."

After I slip into my boots, we walk. Wool drinks my shivers. Our footsteps echo, the sound gnawing at the silence between us until I can't bear it anymore.

"I didn't mean to push you away," I start, voice small.

He doesn't slow. "Please stop. I beg of you."

The words aren't cruel.

They're worse...pained.

"I wasn't disgusted," I try again, desperate to salvage the trust I just shattered. "I was—"

"Do you smell that?"

"What?" My mind is too tangled by this strange question to separate scents. "Salt?"

"Pear." His voice lifts. Not in joy, but in relief. In distraction. Anything to speak of something that isn't...*us.*

He steps off the path toward a patch of wild growth. Behind a thatch of dark leaves, half-hidden, hangs a single pear. Wrinkled, misshapen, but unmistakably whole.

He plucks it with a twist of his wrist, turning it in his hand, the moon catching its curve. "Strange," he murmurs. "I thought they'd all been cut down."

"Who cuts down fruit trees?"

"My mother." He turns the fruit once more, thumb tracing the wrinkly skin. "She was allergic. Pear. Roses. Most things that flower. I was...eleven when she made my father clear them all. Perhaps twelve." A faint, humorless smile. "I didn't think they could still grow this close to the palace."

Allergic. To flowering trees. Roses.

Roses.

The greenhouse flickers in my mind, the severed shrubs clinging to life along the glass, the plaque bolted to the stone. Why would the king have gifted a greenhouse full of roses to a severely allergic Ophelia for the birth of Prince Kael?

Unless it was for a different queen...

Unless it was for the birth of a different prince...

NINETEEN

The Prince

...long ago

My governess told me to stand still, but it's so hot in Father's chamber. Why do we have to be here?

Father puts his crown on Mother's head. Everyone claps their hands; I clap, too, but my neck keeps itching. It's the stupid cravat. I quickly scratch it. Did anyone see?

No, they're looking at Father's knife. It's pretty, with a handle that shines. Why does his hand shake? His face looks all wrong, like he's angry, but also with tears. I've never seen him cry.

"You must do it," one of the priests hisses. "Your Majesty, do it!"

I don't know what Father is supposed to do.

But I don't think he's doing it.

The air goes cold, but not the normal cold, not night cold. This is winter cold, like when I stay out too long and my teeth chatter. Everyone is shouting, and then the shouting stops all at once.

My belly drops.

My skin prickles.

I look up. And I see him, the man from the fountain, so big and tall as if he turned everything to night. His eyes are black, like holes.

I make a sound, but I can't hear it. My mouth is open and empty.

He grabs me.

My throat hurts. My heart beats so heavy as my feet leave the floor. I can't breathe. I can't scream.

I kick like a stupid rabbit as my hands slap at his arms. They're not warm, and it's like grabbing cold stone. I see Father through tears that spill from my eyes.

He's shouting, but I can't hear the words, only see the shape of his mouth, wide and ugly. Then Mother's eyes find mine. My heart beats so much faster.

She's looking at me.

Really, really looking at me!

Father is shaking, but his hands are shaking worse. Somehow, he still holds the knife, and in one sweep, he rips it across Mother's throat.

She looks away from me. Why is she looking away again? What did I do?

I hit the ground. The floor bites my cheek. My throat hurts. My eyes sting. My head feels like it's full of buzzing bees.

I push up on my hands. "Mother?"

I don't know how my legs work, but they do. I run. I run so hard my feet slip on something. I stumble and catch myself with my hands, trying to get to Mother. Why did she look away?

No one stops me.

Or maybe they try, but I don't feel it.

I crash to my knees, and there's blood everywhere. "Mother." My voice comes out wrong, too high. "Mother? Mother!"

Her eyes don't look at me.

They look through me.

TWENTY

Elara

By the time I reach my chamber, the king's cloak hanging damp and heavy around my underdress, my mind is a storm I can't calm. *One of them— Queen Ophelia, I think—gave him the heir,* Mother's words whirl inside my skull. *Or maybe it was the one before her?*

But what if both birthed heirs?

How else does this make sense?

Cloak abandoned on the chair, I strip out of my soaked underdress with trembling, clumsy hands, barely noticing the chill on my skin. Stories from the palace changed like bed linens, Mother told me two nights before I left, leaving behind a people's confusion thicker even than my own.

With a greenhouse that can't possibly have been gifted to an allergic Ophelia, someone must have lied about the line of inheritance? The inscription itself never named Kael; it only said heir. Did they hide an older prince? Or bury one?

I drag on a dry shift, shove my arms into my bodice, and fasten ties with fingers that don't feel attached to me. All these questions press against my temples from the inside with such force that I don't know how to shake them. This might be a waste of my time and energy.

What if the answers change nothing?

But what if they change everything?

My shoes *thud* to the floor before I slip into them, one after another, as if they're also impatient to learn the truth. Or maybe they're just sick of tripping through shadows without knowing what casts them, same as me.

I leave my room, stepping into a corridor where the night is starting to thin, and turn toward the glow of a nearby lantern. My feet know where I'm going long before my mind catches up. I'm done begging books for help because their pages go missing. And men? Their tongues curl whichever way they please—or not at all.

But blood?

Blood has no reason to lie.

Cold, quiet corridors lead me to the abandoned royal chamber. That stain under the rug has been gnawing on me since I first found it, and I'm done being chewed up.

"Elara." Miss Hampshire's voice snaps from the corridor, her lamplight swaying nervously as she stomps away from the king's chamber toward me. "Do not bother going to the king."

I wasn't planning to. Not after what happened—or

rather, what *didn't* happen—in the spring. "What's the matter?"

"Having him return from the spring? In this state? The last time I saw him like this was after his mother's funeral!" Her brows tighten enough to pinch themselves, putting such a strain on her fat pustule I want to shift back a step in precaution. "Whatever have you done now, girl?"

My shoulders sag. That's hardly something I can confess to this woman, and another scolding is the last thing I need right now.

No. What I need is answers.

"Truly, I don't know, Miss Hampshire." That's exactly the problem: how I seem to know nothing about anything. "He found a pear and said it reminded him of his mother because she was allergic to it." I pause, watching her face. "Could it be that?"

The hand tucked into her apron stills. For a beat, her eyes drift—past me, past the corridor, as if she's turning over the past in her head and weighing its impact on the king's moods like ingredients. "Queen Ophelia suffered many ailments."

Oh, did she now?

Was a stepson one of them?

"Oh." I let the word fall like surrender, like I'm only making sense of moods and memories the way any caretaker would. My gaze drifts anywhere but her eyes, because looking too directly is how questions start to sound like accusations. "That's strange, then..." I add, lighter, as if it's an afterthought that wandered in on its own. "I thought I saw a plaque—out by the greenhouse—saying his father gifted it to his mother."

Miss Hampshire's attention returns to me, her gaze tilting, her shoulders going rigid.

Too rigid?

I swallow, careful to make it sound like confusion and not curiosity. "Maybe I misread it," I say quickly. "Or maybe it wasn't meant for her. I really don't know what else could've upset him so."

Miss Hampshire stares at me—a long, dismantling look that feels like it's peeling back my skin to find the lie etched into my bones. I said too much, didn't I? Took too much risk.

"His Majesty has locked himself in his chamber," she eventually says. "If he calls, I will fetch you. Until then, we have no choice but to leave him be."

He locked himself away.

Something in me folds, a slow collapse beneath the ribs. Appalling, he'd called himself in that cave, thinking I'd recoiled in disgust rather than this old fear braiding dread through my bones. Ugh...why am I so scared of this? Why did I act so stupid?

"Of course, Miss Hampshire." My shoulders sag at my own words. Every time I gain an inch of closeness to Kael, two steps drag me back into the muck. "I'm truly sorry."

There's no nod, no formal dismissal when she turns away. Only a brief halt, where she looks over her shoulder back at me. "And Elara?"

"Yes?"

"Some secrets never get buried properly," she says, her voice tight. "And while they may have learned to roam the palace quietly, those who are wise treat them as what they are: lies."

She moves on, her half-hand ticking an eerily calm rhythm against her apron, her footsteps fading.

But the weight on my chest doesn't fade. Her words hook into everything I started to question: missing annals, a plaque that doesn't match, recordings that distort timelines.

My eyes lift to Kael's door.

Leave him be.

Reluctantly, I turn away, toward the double doors of the abandoned royal chamber. Plenty of time to waste on the dead now that I've bungled the living, putting myself out of my caretaker's job. Maybe temporarily. Maybe forever.

The door gives under my palm with barely a protest.

The receding moonlight mingles with the first hints of dawn, washing across the wooden floor. If there truly was an older prince, why erase him? Why hide books that might mention him? Who decided that the pages of his life shouldn't be found? A king hiding his shame? A steward scheming his victory?

I walk straight to it.

The blood hides beneath the rug exactly where I left it —an ugly, dark stain peeking out from under expensive weave. My breath trembles as I drop to my knees and yank the edge back.

The smear blooms into view.

It's bigger than I remember, sunk into the wood like a wound the floor itself couldn't heal. Also incredibly neat. Barely any splatters—no violence, no struggle, no panic. Just a ritual, factual, and as clean-cut as this awful curse.

If the second queen—Queen Maeryn—died here, then Kael couldn't have been present; he wasn't even born yet. That means someone else stood in his place, someone older, someone whose memory has been stripped from the library, safe for Ophelia's *hysterics*.

A recording left behind by accident? After all, the page had been hard to spot...

I stare at the stain until first light breaches the horizon, filtering in through one of the large, undraped windows. It casts a warm, orange ray over the stain, giving it the color of rust before it crawls under the fold of the rug, revealing a splatter I hadn't noticed before.

No, not a splatter.

It's too uniform for that.

Too neat around the edges.

My breath catches as instinct takes over. I hook my fingers under the rug and shove it farther with a rough, impatient sweep of my shoe. The fabric rolls back in a graceless heap, revealing a new part of the stain that chills the air in my lungs.

Not just any stain...

A handprint.

Slowly, so slowly, I lean forward and place my hand beside it, trembling fingers splaying for scale. It's too small to belong to a king. Too small for a queen. It does, however, perfectly fit the hand of a child.

A prince.

Something inside me wilts with a silent, inward sound, like ribs curling around grief that isn't my own. "How did I miss this?"

If I'd peeled the rug back properly the first time, shoved it aside like I meant it, I would've seen this. Clear as daylight.

I stare at the small, bloody handprint until my eyes burn. But Vale came in that day. Caught me snooping. And then he sat down, making it impossible for me to find it because...because...

He sat.

Right. There.

Hiding it?

No. No, that's the sleepiness talking, the exhaustion.

He sat wherever the rug fell. That's all. I was flustered because he surprised me. Anyone's weight could've landed here.

Except...

The moment I replay it, the details return sharper than they should. How he angled his body. How close he came that night. How, for the very first time, and after dismissing my curiosity and suspicions, he gave in. Offered to take me to the library.

Helping me?

Or distracting me?

Slow, rhythmic *thud-thud-thuds* stride through my memories, like polished boots striding around secrets and lies...

If anyone in this place knows how to walk quietly, it's Vale. Dressed in silk and velvet inside a palace that runs out of thread. And wasn't it fine cloth Miss Hampshire had warned me about?

My stomach turns. What if Vale isn't just a liar? What if...what if he is the *lie*?

I clamp down on the idea before it can form a shape with a crown. No, I don't get to go down that path just because I'm desperate for answers. Not until I can be certain.

Muscles twitch along my calves, forcing me to my feet. The rug folds at my shoes as I storm toward the door. I have to find him. Have to confront him.

The corridor yawns empty against the first hints of dawn that touch it. I stride forward, jaw set, heart hammering a furious rhythm against my sternum. The palace suddenly feels too big, endless hallways stretching out like a maze built to mislead.

I turn into the first room on the left. Push the door open

with more force than needed. A chair, a cold hearth. Nothing else.

"Vale?"

No answer.

I march on, skirts snapping around my legs. Down one corridor, then another, poking my head into every room worth a glance. Sitting room: vacant. Storage chamber: empty. Linen closet: just dust and the smell of soap.

"Where are you?" I mutter, the anger in me spreading like heat under my skin, urging my feet faster, louder. Each step clacks against the stone floor. The sound ricochets along the corridors, sharp and accusing.

No guard comes.

Just sick servants who look away.

I descend a narrow set of stairs, half certain I'll find him leaning against a wall, arms crossed, nonchalance in place. But the landing is barren, lamplit and lonely, aside from the occasional staff that stare at me from small, sleep-squinting eyes. Going to the kitchens probably.

The kitchens!

I follow the staff. Pass them, trailing to the scent of charred oak and grease. Inside the kitchens, knives tap half-heartedly against wood. Thin steam rises from a single pot. A few women stand hunched over their chores, sleeves rolled, eyes shadowed from too many mornings like this one.

Vale isn't here.

Of course he isn't.

Guess it's a good thing I didn't come here to find *him*. No, I came to find *her*—the only person who has seen me with him, the only person I can ask about him without risking the noose.

She pushes through the back door with an armful of

kindling; the big-eyed girl, same slip of a thing as the night she startled at seeing me and Vale at the table. She nearly drops the bundle when she sees me blocking her path.

"Where is the steward?" I ask. "Where can I find him?"

Her brows pinch. "Who?"

"The steward, for fuck's sake!" My tone is as sharp as that rageful heat biting into my empty stomach. "Where is Vale?"

Her face pales, just like before. Pupils widen. Breath hitches. The kindling in her arms trembles—not enough to spill, but enough to show her fear. "I—I'm not allowed to—"

"Where is the steward?!"

"Miss...t-the palace..." Her voice quivers. "There is no steward. We haven't had one in years."

TWENTY-ONE

Elara

The gardens have corners I haven't discovered yet —hollows between hedges where even the wind forgets to pass. I sit tucked behind a wall of half-dead hawthorn with a view of the fountain, the lowering sun refusing to touch the statue where heavy linen carved from stone cloaks Death's face.

Of course, Vale was nowhere to be found. Not in the kitchens. Not in the galleries. Not in those hallways he always traversed with such unhurried ease, the *steward*.

Something scrapes under my breastbone. What a fool I am.

I draw my knees up to my chest and wrap my arms around them, but it does little to hide the utter embarrassment that laughs at me from beneath my ribs. *"I cannot say,"* that jerk had told me when I asked him about what happened in the royal chamber, his voice as smooth as his lies. *"I was not there."*

Oh, but he was. Wasn't he?

My next breath tastes like old dust. I should go back inside. Lie down. Rest until he finds me. Isn't that how it always goes?

God...how could I have been so stupid? How could I have brushed past the kitchen girl's terror, or how Kael called him a bastard, or the way he desperately tried to keep me from finding any proof of an older prince like the scheming cunt he is?

A step scuffs the gravel behind me.

I don't turn. My pulse remains annoyingly calm, nothing but a reminder of how foolishly at ease I was around this man who played me like a fucking pawn. But a pawn in what game? With what goal?

"I've been looking for you," he says, his tone heavier than usual. "You weren't in your chamber. Or in the corridors. Or with...His Majesty." A pause. "Not that he's receiving anyone after...well, whatever it is that happened between you two in that spring."

My ears prick at the curiosity in his tone, at the spiked heaviness riding its undercurrent, but my gaze stays fixed on the distant fountain. The king is the least of my concerns right now.

"Elara." When there's no reaction from me, Vale exhales

through his nose, a thin, tense sound. "There's something I need to tell you."

A humorless breath escapes me—half scoff, half laugh. *Oh, is there?* As if I need more of his damn lies...

I let the silence stretch for one beat longer before I say, "Bastard."

More pebbles shift, crunch, then still. "Whatever did I do now?"

"Bastard," I say again, slower this time, measured.

Only then do I turn.

Vale stands half-shadowed, half-sunlit, brushing a black curl from his forehead. His expression is politely blank: the kind of blank that means calculating.

"That's what he called you." Back when Kael upended the chess table. A word I'd taken for a simple insult spent on a steward...until the kitchens told me there was no steward to insult in the first place. "During the argument."

A single brow lifts, arching over those olive eyes with a royal elegance I'd ignored this whole damn time. "Who?"

"Kael." My voice doesn't waver. I won't give him that satisfaction. "Your...brother?"

The question is a hook.

I watch it sink.

Something flickers behind Vale's eyes—a flash of steel, though quickly shuttered. Neatly tucked away as if it had never existed. Not confession. Not denial.

Just...containment.

"Pardon me." I tilt my head the way he often does, letting the pieces arrange themselves where he can't swipe them off the table. "Half-brother, then. Correct?"

He doesn't move. He doesn't even blink. He just watches me with that infuriating stillness of his, the kind that makes you feel like your bones are being counted.

"Well?" I snap. "Say something."

"What," he offers softly, "do you think there is for me to say?"

"Oh, plenty."

His jaw shifts. "Indulge me."

I push myself to my feet so fast that the dried leaves crack beneath me like knuckles. "Fine. Let's start small." I jab a finger toward his immaculate vest. "You're not a steward because there hasn't been one in years. So, what are you, Vale?" I step closer, the anger in me sharpening my breath. "Other than a liar with good tailoring."

His jaw tightens, just a little.

"The greenhouse plaque mentions an heir, a place gifted to the child's mother," I continue, unable to stop with all this anger in my throat. "A queen who couldn't possibly have been Ophelia, because the woman was apparently allergic to anything that grows. It was a gift to Maeryn for the birth of *her* son."

Vale's nostrils flare. "Elara—"

"I'm not finished." Everything inside me shakes. "A son mentioned on the page that recorded Ophelia's *hysteria*. A boy who watched his mother get slaughtered in the royal chamber, leaving behind a bloody handprint. Prince-sized." My voice drops, and my skin prickles with the memory. "Yours?"

Finally, a reaction—a shifting of balance so subtle a blink could've erased it. But no confession.

"You're slightly older than Kael, you told me yourself. Said that, at least once, the curse went to the wrong heir. Then you sat your ass right on that handprint, keeping it under you, hiding it like you hid away those missing annals in the trunk. Presume that is why you requested five days to accomplish that task." I take a step closer without meaning to, rage pulling me like a tide until a new thought sweeps into my head. "Oh my god, tell me the scribe wasn't your doing. Did you kill him?"

My fingers go cold.

A liar is one thing.

But a killer?

Vale's nostrils flare again, harder this time. "Don't be stupid. We both know he was dying."

My guts twist. My breath turns thin. I take a step back without meaning to. Then another. The earth shifts beneath my heels until bark presses against my spine. The tree stops me where courage cannot.

That's not a *no*.

"Kael hated your father for the curse, hated him for killing his mother," I manage, breath unsteady. "But you? You hate your brother for claiming your birthright, don't you? He told me at the spring how he wouldn't have given up a chance at killing him. When Merrick passed on the curse, it was Kael who snatched the lifted crown. Who slit your father's throat before you could, costing you the throne."

Vale watches me with infuriating stillness.

"Well? Admit it!" I hiss. "Admit you're the older prince, the rightful heir Kael tried to erase."

A corner of his mouth twitches, like the prelude to a snarl he's too well-bred to show. He chews it away.

"Spare heirs turn into useless ornaments when a crown gives invincibility," he finally says, stepping toward me. One slow stride to shrink the distance. "The incident was hidden under words. Stories rewritten and birth ledgers burned."

"May the crown live long and prosper," I whisper back in his own words.

"Is it not all so very neat?" He looms over me, shadow melding into shadow. "How history denies my existence? How my brother's hatred robbed me of my birthright?"

My mouth turns dry, his confession quickly buried under a new load of questions. Why come to me? Why play this game?

"From the very beginning, you lied," I spit. "You deceived me. Used me like the stupid little puppet you needed to get...to get what? Huh? What grand scheme am I a piece of here?"

Vale tilts his head slowly.

"You tell me, Elara." His voice is silk over steel as he inches closer. Not fast. Not threatening. *Deliberate.* "What, pray tell, is my"—his warmth melds into mine until there's barely any air left between us, his breath caressing my lips, the heat of him startling against the cold in my bloodstream—"...ulterior motive?"

My breaths scrape up, shallow and thin. What is his motive? Saving the realm? No, too virtuous for Vale. Save his brother from himself? Hardly. To get what's rightfully—

Vale's eyes drop to my lips, and my pulse staggers, his nearness making my thoughts slip and skid like wet stone. Why did I ever let him kiss me? Why did I ever let him put his hands on me, taste me, breathe into me like he did in the library?

Focus.

What motive?

Why would Vale, the brother cheated out of his birthright, orchestrate a plan that leaves his usurping brother with a healed, prospering realm?

He wouldn't.

My pulse stumbles over the pieces arranging themselves in my mind, creating a mosaic of pure malice. "You never wanted Kael to slit my throat," I breathe, the words tasting like ash as the logic locks into place. "Only for him to lift his crown on my coronation. So you can snatch it, slash his throat, and make yourself king."

The air between us thickens, tightens, turns into something that crawls down my spine. I retreat on instinct, but the tree is right there, the bark biting between my shoulders. The jolt stops me with a small gasp I hate him for hearing.

Vale's mouth curves. Not up, but down. "Are you afraid of me now?"

Any smart woman would be afraid of a man who killed a scribe to hide his identity—not that I would ever let him hear that. "Merely cautious."

Another step closer, accompanied by how he lifts his arm and braces the trunk right beside me. "Nothing has changed, Elara." His eyes lower to my mouth again, the shift so slight it drags heat through every nerve in me. "You will still seduce my brother. You will still wed him. Fuck him. Get him to lift that damn crown while I wait in the shadows. The only difference is that you won't die...at least, not for him. Isn't that"—his head tilts more—"fortunate?"

My thoughts shear sideways. *Fortunate?* I came here with my death clutched like a dowry. This robs me of the only coin I had to pay!

"You promised me a chance to save my family!" I shout. "That was the deal!"

"And?"

"And now the curse won't be fed! The rot won't leave!" My voice cracks open. "I didn't mind dying for that; I never did. But like this? My brother will die!"

He reaches over. Slow, certain. His thumb brushes my lower lip, letting stupid heat jolt through me. He watches the way breath shivers out of me before dragging his thumb back, the pad gleaming faintly in the half-light. His tongue touches it as if tasting the truth from my skin.

"I could solve that." The words purr, low and dangerous. "Once I've killed my brother and crowned myself king, I'll take pity on his widow." He leans in, close enough that the warmth of his mouth brushes mine without touching. "I will wed you myself." A beat. "Fuck you." Another beat. "And then I shall crown...you...dead."

My breath doesn't just stutter; it fractures, splitting down the center of me like a bone giving under too much strain. Everything I've held together with spit and stubbornness threatens to spill out of my ribs.

"There's one problem with this, Vale." I lift my chin, the words gathering sharp enough on my tongue to cut. "Once you put that blade to my throat, your heart is supposed to ache."

His answer is low, almost a growl. "And what if I tell you that it will?"

The meaning of those words pours over me like a heated murmur—full of something that hits my chest with a violent thud, a pulse that puts a tremble on my lips before I can choke it down.

No.

I shove it away. Crush it. Deny it breath. What is it other than more of his lies? More scheming?

"As far as I can tell, Vale—" I slap his hand away from his mouth so hard the sound cracks like a whip. His fingers jolt aside, leaving a smear of spit and heat on the air between us as fury erupts straight up my throat like fire. "You have no heart."

His jaw goes still.

His knuckles flex around nothing.

For one breath, Vale stands there—silent, rigid, breathing too slowly to be calm and too deeply to be unaffected. Then he exhales a long, controlled, surgically even breath that wipes the rawness right off his face. His expression resets into that infuriating mask he wears so well: bored, detached, unbothered.

Without warning, he leans in again. Fast, harsh. Close enough that I flinch back against the bark as if he were a blade himself.

"There was something I meant to tell you," he says, and his voice is no longer soft. It's a bite. "News...from the city."

Everything inside me recoils. Tightens.

"No..." My pulse surges, crawling up my throat in a wave of nausea. "Daron?"

Vale watches me for a long moment. Long enough to torture. Long enough that I feel every second carve itself into my guts.

"Your father." He pushes himself off the tree with a smooth, dismissive motion, turning away as he fixes the lapels of his impeccable vest. "He died in the early morning hours," he says, tone flat as he walks back toward the palace. "Choked on his rotten blood."

TWENTY-TWO

Elara

Morning kneels me in the herb plot behind the kitchens, but grief seems to be the only thing that thrives out here. The earth is cold enough to bite, damp seeping through my skirt until it finds bone, while my knife scrapes at dry rosemary that breaks with the small sound of a neck snapping.

When the bushes in front of me blur all over again, I wipe my sap-sticky wrist over my stupid eyes. Daron is best with the eyes, but I was supposed to wire Father's jaws. Put marigolds around him. Cut a hole in the ground.

My bottom lip quivers.

I wasn't there.

Another tear trembles loose, landing on a winding stem of dry thyme, but I ignore it. Mist clings to the herb garden like a shawl someone forgot to shake loose, settling heavily over frostbitten grass. The sun crawls slowly toward the palace, as if reluctant to touch the rot inside, the curse it holds, or the many secrets it hides.

When the yellow-stained envelope pokes from the pocket of my apron, I shove my final wages deeper into the cotton once more. *Take what you need, child,* Miss Hampshire told me when I handed her my notice, pointing her nubs at the herbs in a last extension of kindness before I take the carriage home.

What else was left here for me?

There's no more goal. Nothing left to try. No hope. And Vale's plan? Well, it benefits nobody but himself—the lying snake of a bastard.

Memories shove forward unbidden: the library's dust, his breath heavy against my mouth, fingers curling into my flesh with trembling restraint. The way he kissed me patiently, gently...and then hard.

And what if I tell you that it will?

Heat licks up my sternum, stupid and treacherous. God, look at me, being a fool all over again. For all I know, that kiss might've been another of his attempts to distract me. Get me out of the library, away from the truth. Away from the fact that Vale can't be trusted.

I shake my head, eyes climbing to the dark windows at the corner of the palace, draped until the light dies at the seams, a mausoleum stitched shut. For days, Kael has kept the door barred, refusing Miss Hampshire, refusing maids, refusing food.

Refusing me.

The basket digs into the crook of my arm as I rise from the dirt. No. Even if Vale had true affection for me—which he doesn't, the filthy liar—his brother has shut himself away from me so completely, so irrefutably, that there's nothing left here to salvage.

I turn toward the hedges leading back to the kitchens, the basket clutched to my chest, the herbs inside trembling with each step. It'll take all day, the ride in the carriage. Maybe longer if—

"Elara…"

It's merely the breath of my name, carried on the cold air like a fragile thing not meant for mornings, yet it halts my steps.

That's not possible…

I turn.

Kael stands halfway down a path, one arm braced against his ribs, breathing like each inhale claws him raw. The sun slices across his face, and he squints, grimacing at the sting of light.

What on earth is he doing here?

"You shouldn't be out here." The words feel strange, as timid as those slow steps I take toward him. "It's much too bright."

"I am aware," he says with a slit-eyed flinch. Then softer. "But I had to come."

My heart beats faster, the rhythm as tangled as my thoughts as I take him in. He's dressed—*actually* dressed—in a fresh shirt, fresh trousers. Damp golden hair is combed around his crown, a few strands curling down along freshly-shaven cheeks.

God, he *combed* himself.

He takes a step closer, blinking hard as the daylight

needles at his eyes. "I heard..." His jaw works, the muscle in his cheek fluttering. "Some maid at my door. She mentioned...your father."

Everything in me pulls tight, twisting in on itself like a rope yanked too hard. The basket sags on my arm the way Father's bucket used to before emptying—heavy and uneven. I don't know what to say.

Why is he here?

Outside?

In the sun?

"I meant to find you sooner." He swallows, breath fogging between us. "To see if you were...alright."

If I'm alright.

The words scrape something open inside me. I clamp my jaw shut, swallow it back down. I will not fall apart again. I've already cried myself raw. I'm hollow enough to rattle.

He steps closer, and his shadow folds gently over my feet. "You cried," he says quietly.

My spine stiffens. "It's nothing," I manage, swiping at my cheek in a useless, frantic gesture. "Truly, it's—"

"Hush." His voice doesn't command; it offers. Soft. Careful. His hand rises. Pauses midair. Then touches a tear I missed beneath my eye, brushing it with a tenderness that makes something inside my ribs quake. "Cry if you must, Elara."

No, not again.

Not here. Not in front of him.

I grit my teeth against the swell rising in my throat and shake my head. "I'm alright."

But he doesn't step back, doesn't retreat into the shadows the way he used to. He just stands there in the painful sunlight, blinking through it, eyes watering from the brightness.

Hurting...for me.

And something inside me gives.

The next breath I take collapses instead of fills. A choke breaks loose from somewhere too deep to swallow again. My vision blurs, blurs more, until his chest is nothing but contour and color, until the herbs in my basket double and triple, until the ache inside can't be forced back down.

A sound I hate tears out of me—small, broken, child-like. The basket slips, herbs scattering around my boots.

Kael catches my arms before I fall to my knees, pulling me into him with a care so gentle it undoes me entirely. His chest is warm beneath my cheek, steady in a way nothing else in this cursed world seems to be.

"Shh..." He wraps one arm around my back, the other coming up to hold the back of my head, fingers threading through dampening strands. "Let it out."

Somehow, that makes it worse.

I sob into his shirt, shaking so hard my ribs throb with each breath. He doesn't stiffen, doesn't pull away from snot or tears. There's just the slow weight of his palm between my shoulders, the steady stroke of my spine as if he's teaching my breath how to move again.

When the sobs burn down to something smaller, he lowers his mouth to my hair. "Stay," he says, quiet as a prayer lost in my strands. "Please."

The plea knocks my breath sideways. I thought that whatever fragile closeness I'd scraped together with him had snapped clean in the cave, and now he's asking me to stay? Why?

But it doesn't matter why.

None of this is mine to choose anymore, never was. Whatever fragile thread I had spun between Kael and me,

Vale never intended for it to reach its end. He will never allow it.

"I can't." My voice tears as I retreat from the warmth of his chest. "I have to go. Mother...Daron. I need to be with them."

He nods against the top of my head. There's no argument in it, no rejected king. Only understanding.

That, and... "Then I shall bring them here."

"What?"

He eases back enough to see my face; the light bites his eyes till they gloss, and still he looks. "Your mother. Your brother. Allow me to bring them here."

I blink up at him, sure I've misheard, until the words settle. "Here? To the...palace?"

"Rot is everywhere, even in the palace." He glances at the draped windows and back to me, the deep orange of the morning sun giving his face a warm glow. "Here, rations are slim, but still regular. Linens are clean. Water, fresh from the spring."

"You would do that?"

His eyes search my face for a moment. For what, I can't say. "Yes."

Three letters, simple and unadorned, yet they cause a flurry at my core. "Why?"

The question hangs between us in the stillness of the morning, as heavy as the moisture clinging to the chilled air. Guilt is a cruel friend, and shame even crueler. Is he trying to buy himself penance? For the suffering he knows he caused? What if this intimacy between us didn't erode after all?

My lungs stall for a moment. What if it grew deeper than I thought?

"Perhaps it is as simple as wanting," he confesses at

last, voice roughened at the edges. "Wanting to repay your kindness, your patience." A small breath. "Not to mention your utter rudeness and annoying tenacity when I need it most."

A sound snags in my throat, tries to be a sob and decides to be a chuckle instead—crooked, wet, painful as a stitch in my side. I clamp a palm to my mouth, but it leaks out anyway.

A faint smile curves his lips, if only until his blue eyes narrow once more when the sun shifts out from a small cloud. "Yes?"

I study him through the leftover blur in my vision. How he blinks against the sun. How he draws his breath slowly, as if trying to warm the air before it stabs his lungs. What if this situation isn't doomed after all? What if not all is lost?

On instinct, my eyes wander down along his throat, and for once, not to check on the rash there. No, to look exactly at the place where his esophagus bobs—where Vale might slit his brother's throat the moment he lifts his crown.

Unless I prevent it.

I can hardly warn him of his brother's plan without implicating myself. And my family? Is bringing them closer to this mess wise? I'm not sure, but Kael has a point. The palace is in bad condition, yes, but still much better than the city.

Against the tension in my arm, the subtle dread tingling my fingers, I lift my hand to rest on the side of his neck. Then I nod. "Bring them."

If Vale's scheming means Daron dies, then I guess it's time I do some scheming of my own.

TWENTY-THREE

Elara

It takes longer than any of us guessed.

Daron can't sit the jostling anymore, a messenger came to tell me earlier. The roads have turned violent, forcing them to lay him flat on boards padded with blankets, stopping every mile when the breath won't come, stopping when the pain overwhelms his senses.

The waiting is a physical weight, heavy and suffocating. It'll take days...

Ignoring the restless whirl at my core, I turn to my hearth

where it sulks in the corner. I kneel, my skirt catching ash, and coax a structure out of kindling the way Miss Hampshire had shown me works best inside these walls: cross, cross, patience.

I crack the flint. Sparks fly. One catches, threatens to die under a wobbly string of smoke, then takes—thin and stingy, but alive.

Kindling and wood are still plentiful at the palace. It'll help Daron rest once they finally—

Knuckles rap on the oak.

Three times. Even. Unhurried.

The last of the kindling slips from my palm and taps the bricks, a cold roil raking through my belly. There's only one person in this place who knocks like that—the nonchalant cadence in it more insult than decency.

I watch the flame flare and settle. Count one breath, then two. Steeling my nerves for what I must do.

Turn from pawn to queen.

With Kael pleading me to stay, the only thing keeping me from having my throat slit by him is Vale slitting his brother's throat first. The only way to reduce that risk? Play Vale exactly the way he wants to play me.

Another knock.

Same measured cadence.

"It's unlocked," I call out.

The latch turns, and Vale steps in—shadow first, then embroidered silk and clean lines, the quiet arrogance of a man who never arrives anywhere by accident.

I rise from the hearth, wiping ash from my hands. "What do you want?"

He doesn't answer right away, the silence echoing with what had been said between us in the garden—the low, venom-soft promise to kill me himself, my knife of a reply about his lack of a heart, the news that Father had choked on his rotten blood.

The little fire snaps.

Vale looks at it, then at the curtains I've drawn against the night before he pulls his gaze back on me. "What do I want?" he repeats at last, mild as a razor laid flat. The corner of his mouth almost tilts. Not amusement, but in habit. "To see whether you intend to finish what you started."

Heat crawls up my throat, ugly and familiar. "What I started..." I echo. "You mean the plan you never meant to let me finish?"

His eyes don't move from me, but something hardens behind them. He steps farther in and closes the door, the latch clicking with a finality that shrinks the room. "Let's not waste either of our evenings pretending we don't know why I'm here."

Oh, I know exactly why he's here. As much as my goal seemed out of reach mere hours ago, so does his. Without me, Vale is no closer to getting his brother to lift the crown than he was when he first appeared between my graves.

"Because you need me."

"Precisely," he says with the same enthusiasm as though he stated the temperature of the room. "His Majesty himself left the palace this morning, or so the waitstaff says. Remarkable." He folds his arms over his chest, leaning back slightly, casual only in the way a sword is inside its sheath. "Whatever it is that is happening between you two..." A pause. "It appears that his heart is softening toward you. Exactly as we hoped."

I scoff. "*We.*"

His lips press together for a moment. "You will gain his heart. You will get him to lift his crown."

"And then you'll slit his throat," I say. "Yes. I understood your poetry in the garden."

"The realm needs a king who will act."

"The realm needs a fed crown," I snap. "Which your little fratricide doesn't accomplish for me. Or for Daron. Or for anyone outside your vanity."

"Vanity," he spits. "I have every intention of feeding the curse as soon as possible. I'm not my useless half-brother, letting the realm rot itself thin because of his whiny, soft heart."

That word... *Heart.*

His mouth tightens the instant it leaves him, as if he's realized he's just put his wrist beneath the very knife I handed him in the garden. Why did it upset him so?

I look him dead in the eyes and say, "At least he has one."

"Oh yes, such a heart." Vale's laugh is vicious, a sharp sound that scrapes the walls. "Sparing one woman and forsaking an entire realm to rot. He feeds his conscience while the rats feed on the dead in the streets. Is that what my brother made you believe, hmm?" His lips twist around the venom in his voice. "Has he started to look like the golden-haired hero to you?"

"You're twisting it."

"I'm setting it straight!"

His shout sends a flinch through me. I never heard him shout like that before...

"You love to paint me as the villain, Elara," he bites out, "but how precisely am I the monster when I'm the only one willing to claim what is mine and fix what he refuses to touch?"

My stomach clenches. Vale's goal isn't fueled by an urge to help, or empathy, or compassion. It thrives on entitlement and pride. And yet…does the sin matter if it leads to salvation?

"I never said you're a monster." And perhaps he's only *my* personal villain. "It's the way you used me that I despise. How you lied, *Prince Vale*."

His head throws itself back, releasing a subdued laugh toward the ceiling that seems to twist with humor and hate in equal measures. Then it snaps forward again.

"There is…no…Prince…Vale," he grinds out, each word a hinge ripped off its pin. "I wear silk my brother shoved into my hands so I don't shame his halls. He dismissed most of the old staff the moment he crowned himself king. I'm nothing but a rumor, but ask the current servants why I'm here—who I am to the king—and watch their mouths stall." His voice roughens, heat rising under each word. "To the priests, I'm a smudge in the margin. To the scribes, a line they skip. To the rabble? The king's right-hand one day, envoy the next—ghost by morning, haunting some godforsaken tower nobody bothers to visit."

"Vale, I—"

"Do you have any idea what it is to be raised for a crown, Elara? Hmm?" His mouth contorts, lips curling in nothing short of aggression. "Only to stand at your father's funeral with…*nothing?!*"

I take two small steps back. I've never seen him like this —every ounce of practiced ease stripped clean, leaving only the anger that cords his neck and feeds the veins at his temples.

"I. Am. Nothing." His voice trembles with the growl in it. "A shadow. A tale. A man without a title, who was gifted his own damn silk in charity, so he may walk these forsaken corridors with no position. No purpose. No"—the breath leaves him rough—"existence."

His jaw locks, his shoulders set. The careful tilt of his head is gone; it's just raw, masculine force now, poured into each stride as if he's teaching the floor who owns it. He keeps coming. Not fast, not loud.

Just unstoppable.

"Yes, I want to kill him for what he took from me. Yes, I want to cut his throat." The tip of his boot stops inches from my naked toes. "Is it such a sin to want revenge when the blade also brings back harvests? When wells stop tasting of iron? When gravediggers have a season where they can put down the shovel and rest?"

"Like I said, I don't hate your aim," I say, and the admission costs me. "I hate the way you manipulated me."

"Like you're manipulating him?" His eyes keep mine hostage, and his head angles slowly, each degree adding a pound to the weight of his question. "Like how you lied your way into his chamber? Around his defenses?" His scoff scathes me. "And here she stands, the righteous one."

My molars grind down on my cheeks. "Don't call me that."

"Why? It fits your mouth." He leans his shoulder against the mantle, his gaze sharpening as it drops to my lips. "Do my brother's lips fit it better?" Those words drip acid. "Tell me, did he win you with his suffering in the spring? With his shakes and his sighs and his groans and his sad, sad stories?"

My pulse is thrumming too fast, too frantic. "Stop."

"Oh, how he endured our father's cruelty," he whimpers out in jest. "Oh, the curse is so heavy, the suffering so—"

"I said, stop."

"Tell me, Elara, did his pain make a lover of you where mine doesn't? Are you under the impression that I did not...

suffer?" He lifts his hand—slowly, carefully—and sets his palm against my cheek, letting the warmth of his touch seep into my skin. It burns. "Did I not put these fingers to my mother's gushing throat and kneel beside her twitching, jerking body? Do you think I did not call her name? Did not cry? Did not grieve? Do you think I didn't have nightmares my entire damn childhood, showing me how my father slit my mother's throat?"

The image slams up from the back of my skull—the small hand stamped in rust on old boards—and my breath goes thin.

Vale is that boy.

Only all grown up now. Taller, angrier, his old hurt rolling off him with a heat that matches the flames near my calves.

His thumb finds the seam of my mouth and drags once, light as breath, only for him to dig into my bottom lip, forcing it open. "Did you kiss him in the spring, hmm? Did my brother get to taste that mouth of yours?"

His voice is a whisper, as if his anger has simmered down to coals, but what's left is worse. I feel it on my face—in the steady weight of his hand, in the way his thumb traps my bottom lip with a possessiveness that makes a spark catch low in my belly, tinder and traitorous.

I shake my head. "He tried," I whisper against his thumb. "I...retreated."

A muscle ticks in his jaw. He leans in, letting the distance collapse as his breath skims my cheek, then the hinge of my jaw. He drops his mouth to the crook of my neck without touching, hovering there, heat and the faint rasp of his breath dragging over my sensitive skin.

"You didn't retreat with me in the library." The roughened words vibrate against the place where my pulse won't slow. He inhales shamelessly, the scrape of his lower lip almost-kissing the tendon on my neck. "You stayed."

A tingle blooms low and cruel. He's right, and I hate him for it. Hate myself even more for the way my body stands its ground now, heat licking the space between us.

"We can still finish this," he breathes, the words warm against the thin skin under my ear. His mouth ghosts lower, a slow, deliberate press that isn't quite a kiss until it is, feather-light. "You and I."

His hand slides from my cheek to the back of my head, fingers threading into my hair, holding me steady without forcing. "You get him to lift the crown, and I will do the rest," he murmurs, lips shaping the vow against my neck. "I will make sure you get what you came for, Elara. Your brother breathing, your mother safe." Another kiss, a fraction higher, a fraction deeper. "Together."

My pulse drops between my legs, flooding warmth there in a way I never felt before. Annoyance, too. "I hate you."

His lips curve. "Then it's a good thing the curse isn't reversed." He faintly chuckles against the shell of my ear. "The crown will be pleased because I happen to find you quite...enthralling. So practical, so cynical. So at ease around death."

A lick of his tongue at my lobe, along my cheek, toward my mouth—patient as a thief at a lock. He tastes the edge of me, slow, testing, and when I don't bolt, patience turns into pressure. His mouth covers mine, warm and deliberate, claiming in a way that makes my breath hitch, misbehave, start anew...only to falter again.

Heat rises. Anger follows.

Fine.

If he wants a willing accomplice, I can wear the shape of

one. I can be soft in his arms. Let him mistake it for surrender. Let him think I'm the puppet of his performance. It serves both of us.

So, I kiss him back.

For a split second, he freezes—just the tiniest arrest of motion, a stutter in his assault. Then the grip on the back of my head tightens, fingers tangling brutally in my hair as he angles my face, refusing to let me pull back even an inch.

Vale groans, a dark, rough sound vibrating against my lips. He deepens the kiss, drowning out the world, the room, and the struggling fire until there's only the wet, hot slide of his tongue sweeping against mine, claiming everything I offer and demanding more.

His other arm snakes around my waist, banding like iron, hauling me into him until every inch of my softness is flattened against the unyielding wall of his chest. Beneath the courtly silk, he's terrifyingly solid: a landscape of hard muscle and rigid tension I've never been close enough to map until now.

Vale grinds his hips forward, the distinct, heavy ridge of him pressing against my stomach, undeniable even through the layers of our clothes. The shock of it—the sheer, physical proof of what I've done to him—sends a jolt of liquid heat straight to my core, wringing a low, needy moan from my throat that vibrates against his tongue.

His low chuckle trembles against my lips. "No retreat with me, not even an inch."

"Don't be pleased with yourself," I manage, but it comes out on a gasp I don't mean to give.

"Oh, I couldn't possibly. Not with how I'm currently so very pleased with *you*." His hand moves again, impatient now. It sweeps around to my front, finding the heavy fabric of my skirt and bunching it upward. "How you lean into my touch. How your body writhes in demand for more." His fingers graze the bare skin of my thigh, scorching a path higher. "Let me oblige you."

When his fingers reach for the heat between my legs, a hint of white finally flares, sharp and sudden, piercing the haze of lust. It's one thing to offer a mouth to keep a monster distracted, but it's another entirely to let him inside me like this.

My fingers dig into the silk at his biceps, bracing, my muscles locking up as I struggle to shift his touch. "No."

"No?"

His hand slows, but doesn't withdraw. Instead, he flattens his palm, letting his fingertips graze my soft down of hair, letting tingles spread over my mound.

"Did my brother manage to make you feel like this? Did his hands make you grind your body for more? Did his fingers make you burn like this?" He slowly shakes his head on my behalf. "He didn't; he couldn't." His voice drops to a rough murmur. "But I can. I can take the fear away, Elara..." His thumb works a maddening, feather-light circle just against the sensitive slickness I'm trying to hide. "Let me take it away."

I can't. I have to stop him. To give him this is to give this liar a piece I can never take back, a part of me that can't be renegotiated.

Yet, as his thumb brushes the sensitive, silken skin of my lower lips, the protest dies in my throat, tangled in a web of curiosity and a terrible, traitorous want. "Vale..."

"Why aren't you freezing up, Elara, hmm?"

My bottom lip trembles.

I don't know.

"Why aren't you running off?" With a slow, reverent

slide that steals the breath from my lungs, he slips one finger past the slick barrier.

My knees buckle when he sinks into my tight, wet heat. Vale catches me, holding me upright against him while his finger falls into a rhythm that is devastating in its gentleness. The shock melts into a pleasure so warm I have to bury my face in his neck to stifle another moan.

"You have no idea how much I want you," he rasps against the shell of my ear, his voice thick with a wretched hunger that mirrors my own. "It wasn't part of my plan, you know, to *crave* you so. I held back in the library. Told myself that I couldn't compromise my plan by tasting you." He twists his hand, hitting a spot that makes my vision blur, and he inhales the scent of my arousal rising between us like it's oxygen. "Now, there's no more reason for me to hide it. On the contrary..."

My head presses against his shoulder when he retreats and circles my overly sensitive bundle of nerves. His touch is maddening, causing my breath to come in short, ragged hitches.

I thought I was steering the moment. I'm not. It doesn't matter...

I'm still controlling the plan.

I am.

His free hand drops from my waist to the front of his trousers. He undoes his buckle with a metallic *clink* while his fingers keep up that ruinous tempo inside me, dragging me closer to a crest, putting my mind into a haze while he works the buttons on his trousers.

"Let me take you to bed. I won't hurt you," he promises, lips moving against my jaw, hot and wet, eager. "You will enjoy it."

The drag of leather and linen gives way. I feel the blunt,

searing heat of him, pressing slick and hard against the naked skin of my inner thigh.

It's that sensation—the slipperiness of it—that finally cuts through the fog, making my hips stutter in their lewd rhythm. As much as my blood is screaming to let him finish what he started, a cold shard of clarity drops into my stomach.

This is going too far.

I shift, subtly at first, angling my pelvis away from that threatening hardness, even as I chase the pleasure of his hand. "We can't."

"Shh..." he hushes. "Let me see if reality matches the torture of my imagination."

When he tries to shift his stance, to guide himself toward the entrance he's prepared so thoroughly, I clamp my thighs tight against his wrist, physically blocking the path. "Not inside."

"Elara..." he groans as his slick head prods against my bundle of nerves. "I want your smell on my skin for days. I want to feel every part of you tighten around me."

I can't give him this.

It belongs to the only sliver of dignity I have left.

"No!" The word tears from my throat, ragged and desperate. I wrench myself away, twisting out of his grip with a strength born of frantic panic.

I don't get far.

Vale catches my waist, spinning me around until my chest presses against the mantle. His arm comes around my stomach from behind, holding me pinned against the oak while his other hand dives back between my legs. He finds the swollen, aching pearl of my desire and abandons all gentleness.

"You're so terribly difficult sometimes," he growls

against my ear, his breath hot, his hard cock pressing against the ruffles of cotton around my buttocks. But he isn't shifting, isn't trying to enter. "Hold still."

His hand works me with ruthless, terrifying precision. His fingers are a blur of motion, circling, pressing, rubbing the sensitive nub until white speckles my vision. It's too much sensation, too fast, brighter than anything I've ever known. I throw my head back against his chest at the coil tightening in my belly, the pressure mounting higher and higher until it becomes a desperate, blinding need.

"That's it," he whispers against my damp nape. "So close..."

I'm there. I'm standing on the precipice, toes curled, my body arching like a drawn bowstring. The release is right there, a heartbeat away, a scream waiting to happen.

And then his hand vanishes.

I stumble forward, deprived of my anchor. My body gives a violent, involuntary twitch, searching for the friction that was just there, screaming at the sudden, brutal absence of it. I grab the edge of the mantelpiece to keep from falling, my knees trembling so hard they knock together.

"What...?" My voice is a broken croak as I turn, bracing myself against the stone, wild-eyed and gasping.

Vale is standing a few feet away, tucking himself back into his trousers, his face composed, though his pupils are blown wide, dark with unspent lust. He looks at me, watching the flush stain my chest, the way my legs shake, the humiliation wrecking my face.

And he smiles. Not kindly.

"If you want to save it for my golden-haired brother," he says, his voice gaining its icy, smooth veneer, "then by all means, save it."

He fastens his belt.

The click echoes.

"But should you change your mind," he says, opening the door and looking back, "I'll be in the eastern tower room, ready to oblige."

He steps out, the door slamming shut.

I'm alone again—wrecked, wet, and aching with a need so sharp it feels like a wound.

TWENTY-FOUR

Elara

"Now!"

At my command, Kael pulls the edge of the curtain as I lean my weight into the rod above, the two of us tugging in a graceless duet. The heavy cloth heaves, groans...

...then gives all at once.

Sunlight pours through the first unbarred window like a wave, drowning the gloom of Kael's chamber with a flood of gold that illuminates the swirling dust, finally washing away this damned darkness.

We both flinch.

Kael does so with a hiss and a hard blink. I do it with a laugh, sensing the muscles in my cheeks tense from how hard I grin at the sight before me. Red-spotted oaks. Deep green pines. A sheen on the far horizon. Maybe the sea?

"The view is beautiful." I head to the next window, rubbing my palm over my itchy face with how the dust tickles my nostrils. "Next one."

Kael squints at how I'm maneuvering the wooden ladder to the next spot and take the first rung. "One would think I'm still employing help for these types of things."

"Where's the fun in that?" A couple more rungs bring me up to the next rod, where I fumble the iron ring from its hook. "It's free. Pull!"

"I am pulling," Kael grunts from the floor, his boots braced against the stone wall, his white shirt straining across his shoulders.

"You're tugging," I correct as I wipe sweat from my forehead with my wrist, the air as thick up here as fifty-year-old breath. "Let me give the rings a little shove. That should—"

Iron clinks. Thick velvet drops from the air, and not even the way Kael lifts his arm can fight off the fabric. It spills over his head, his boot catching in a heap of velvet before he stumbles blindly, arms flailing for balance.

"Oh for—hold still." I quickly step down, grab the velvet, and give a hard yank.

"Do not"—the muffled protest wafts through the fabric, breath hitching when the cloth tugs at the crown— "pull."

"I'm not pulling; I'm rescuing." I lift the stubborn fabric free of one of the crown's points, but it only commits more fondly to another. "It likes your crown."

"It has poor taste," he mutters.

With both hands, I bunch the heavy maroon folds and lift them up and over, a slow unmasking that feels less like housekeeping and more like peeling back a shroud to find a miracle beneath.

The sunlight catches it first, getting tangled in hair that has grown quite a bit since I arrived—thick, honey-gold waves, clearly intent on softening the sharp, noble angles of his high cheekbones. Now his face is flushed with life and exertion, stretching smooth over a jaw broad enough to command armies.

Kael blinks down at me when the velvet drops to his feet. "You found me."

For a heartbeat, I forget to breathe.

His eyes aren't just blue. They're the color of that deep sea he refuses to visit, clear and startlingly alive, crinkling at the corners as he fights a grimace that digs deep enough to reveal a faint, boyish dimple on his left cheek.

"I guess I did." Never would I have thought that all this darkness and gauze hid the true sight of a young king from me: tall, well-built, gaining more virility with each day. Aside from that blond lock tangled around a point of his crown, he's truly good-looking. "You have a...a..." My fingers lift to the strand, trying to untangle it from the metal. "You have a knot there."

"I have many knots," he says softly as he holds so very still, each rise of his chest scenting the air with soap and sun-warmed linen. "You seem determined to undo them all."

My fingers pause on the crown.

I look up at him.

His face is inches from mine. The humor has drained away, replaced by a quiet, heavy intensity that pulls the air from my lungs. His eyes are searching my face, dropping to my lips, then flicking back up to my eyes with a hesitation that is both sweet and agonizing.

My heart gives a traitorous thud against my ribs, then another when his hand lifts to my waist, warm and large, resting there lightly. He could pull me in. He could close the distance. I can see the want in the flare of his nostrils, in the way his gaze drops to my mouth again.

Eager to kiss me.

And if he kisses me now, I won't turn. Won't retreat or run. For once, I have to stay put and let this blossom into the salvation my brother needs.

He clears his throat. His hand slides from my waist as he takes a step back, ducking his head to free the crown from a thread I hadn't seen.

"Apologies," he mutters, turning his profile to me, feigning interest in the dust floating in the sunbeam. "I... encroached."

My hand sinks along with the mood in the room. The spring. My panic. My retreat.

He thinks I don't want this kiss, doesn't he?

Something in my chest tightens and loosens in the same breath. I had built a physical wall between us that night in the spring that he's too well-bred to ignore. And if I don't tear it down? Well, then we might as well stay on opposite sides forever.

Daron doesn't have forever.

I take a breath, stealing courage from the air, and step into the space Kael just vacated. "You didn't encroach," I say, my voice steady where my knees feel like water, ready to give and make me plunge. "The night at the spring, I wasn't appalled, or disgusted, or any of those things. I was just...nervous."

He glances at me, wary. "Nervous..."

My hand trembles as I reach out, but I force it to land on his chest, right over his heart. Beneath the linen, the beat is strong, steady.

"I've never been with…a man."

He goes still under my palm. "I see."

"Nothing about you is appalling." Whatever rashes and scrapes the rot left behind here and there aren't even worth the thought. "I did want that kiss."

And yet my stomach clenches into a cold, hard knot at the prospect of it. A startling contrast to the heat Vale so expertly ran through me two nights ago with the slide of his tongue, his fingers digging into my flesh as if—

Stop it!

The mental command scalds me, sharp with shame and confusion, bringing me back to what truly matters. If Kael won't bridge this gap with his noble hesitation, then *I* have to be the one to drag us both across it.

"Do I have permission to kiss you then?" Kael's voice is a rough whisper as he stares down at me.

I don't answer.

Instead, I rise onto my tiptoes.

I press my body against his, soft curves meeting hard lines that appear to broaden more with each day. When our noses brush, I tip my chin. Then, I do the thing that the woman I was last week would never have done, and the woman I am today cannot afford not to.

I kiss him.

I put my mouth to his like a stitch to a seam, and he goes very still the way frightened animals do. The first shift of his lips is so careful it could be a mistake; the second less so.

With a low groan that vibrates against my mouth, he sweeps his arms around me. He gathers me close, not with the crushing force Vale used, but with a desperate sort of reverence. His mouth finally moves against mine, gentle, tasting, sweet.

It's pleasant, I guess.

It's...easy.

Emboldened by that fact, I part my lips a fraction more, just as Vale had done, offering access. Then I send the tip of my tongue out to trace the seam of his lower lip.

The reaction is instant.

Kael shudders against me, a full-body tremor that travels from his chest straight into mine. His hand, hovering respectfully at my waist, suddenly tightens, fingers digging into the fabric of my apron as he pulls me flush against him.

My belly flutters.

It works. God, it works!

I mimic the slide of Vale's tongue—a shy sweep that turns bolder when Kael answers it with a groan that rumbles between us. He tastes of nothing but himself now, clean and fragrant, devouring the kiss I'm feeding him like a starving man offered a banquet.

He walks me backward, blindly, eagerly, until my shoulders hit the stone wall beside the window. The impact is solid, jarring a gasp from me that he swallows whole. And then I feel it—the distinct hardness pressing against my stomach through his trousers.

A spike shoots through my veins, sharp and cold.

No, it's fine. No different than two nights ago. I can handle this.

But then Kael shifts. He doesn't grind with the arrogant, rhythmic precision of his brother. He presses into me with a chaotic, overwhelming need, his hips canting forward as if he wants to bury himself in me right through our clothes.

He pulls his mouth from mine to dive his face into the crook of my neck, his breath hot and ragged. "I want inside you. God, I'm burning with need."

The panic I hoped I'd smothered wakes up, clawing at the back of my throat. What do I do next?

Undo the buttons on his trousers?

Retreat and play coy? No, he'd feel rejected.

Touch him...*there?*

My throat ties up.

I don't know how to do that.

Vale stopped before...before *this.* I don't know how to touch a man. I don't know how to move my legs or where to put my hands. What if it hurts? What if I freeze? What if I disappoint him?

A thick swallow.

What if I ruin this?

The pressure of the plan descends on me like a collapsing roof. If I fail here, Daron dies. If I stop this, Kael retreats, and Daron dies. But I have to be the queen. I have to die. I have to...have to...

Dammit, I can't breathe.

The walls of the chamber seem to lurch inward. The sunlight feels too hot, too exposing. Too much. I have to get out. I have to—

No!

I can't reject him, not again. For if I pull away in fear, he'll retreat into his shell forever. He'll think he's a monster, just like Vale said.

I force a swallow past the lump of terror in my throat, praying my voice doesn't crack when I lay my forehead against his chest, hiding my face. "The sun," I gasp, letting my knees buckle just enough to seem faint rather than frigid. "It's... I'm dizzy. The heat..."

Kael is moving before I even finish the sentence.

He steps back, putting a foot of blessed, cold space between us. The pressure against my stomach vanishes as air rushes back into my lungs.

"The sun." He sounds frantic, guilt instantly washing away the desire on his face. "Of course. We've been working in the glare, and you haven't eaten since dawn. I...I am an idiot." He reaches out to steady me, but keeps his touch light, supportive. "Here. Sit."

I let him guide me to sit on the nearby chair, but it does nothing to calm the confusion whirling in my mind. Why am I like this? Why with him?

Or rather...why *not* with Vale?

I fan myself a little just to play the part of the fainting maid. The kiss I just gave Kael worked. But it worked because I had a map. Vale had shown me the way, and I had followed it—right up until Kael pressed his hips against mine.

That's where the map ends.

A sharp rap echoes from the door.

Kael's spine snaps straight, the lover vanishing, the king returning in a blink. "Enter."

The door swings open, and a man in travel-stained leathers stumbles in—a messenger, by the looks of it—clutching a scroll case with a white-knuckled grip, sweat shining on his thick brow. He looks frantic, eyes darting around the room until they land on Kael.

"Your Majesty!" The man bows hastily, nearly tripping over his own boots. "We think we have her! We already sent a new carriage, but—"

His eyes land on me.

The messenger's mouth snaps shut with an audible *click*. He looks from me to Kael, sheer panic flaring in his gaze as if he's walked in on a murder. Why?

Kael moves with a speed that would be graceless in another man. He crosses the room in three long strides, grabs the man by the shoulder—rather roughly—and yanks him into the corridor.

The door slams shut.

What's that all about? Have who? Who is *her?* Mother? It has to be. Kael promised to bring her here. He sent a carriage. Why would the messenger say they sent a new carriage... Unless something happened to the old one?

A cold prickle of dread races down my spine.

What if the old carriage broke down on a road? Or worse, got attacked. The city is starving, and desperate men look for anything that might hold bread or coin. If they stopped my family, if they opened the door and found only an old woman and a dying boy...

Righteous fear propels me out of the chair. *I need to know.* I stare at the heavy oak door, straining my ears, but the wood is too thick, the stone too dense. What are they saying? Where is my brother?

Eavesdropping is wrong, but if Kael is hiding a tragedy from me to spare my feelings—or worse, to manage me—then I need to know it now.

I look down at my boots.

Heavy. Loud.

Without a second thought, I toe them off, leaving one abandoned by the chair. The other skids across the boards and stills near the door. In stocking feet, I creep across the room, silent as the dust motes dancing in the sun, and press my ear against the door's cold, unforgiving wood.

"...village," comes muffled and torn through the oak. The messenger's voice. "Not a doubt...heritage...original translation." Some distorted words I can't make out follow, and then, "…curse."

"He must not find out." Kael's voice is low, vibrating through the wood, but there's an undercurrent in it I've never heard before—not in his rage, not in his self-pity, certainly not in his gentle moments. It's cold. Chilling enough that it sends the fine hairs on my arms straight up. But they tingle at the roots when he growls, "The bastard is scheming."

My breath hitches, freezing in my throat like a shard of glass. The bastard. There's no doubt who he means. A jolt of pure, cold adrenaline floods my veins, making the floor beneath my stocking feet feel miles away.

Kael knows… He knows Vale is moving pieces in the dark. Does he know that I am one of them?

A wave of nausea rolls through me. If he suspects I'm a trap set by his brother, then that kiss, his hesitation, was all a test. A way to see if the weapon would strike?

No. I felt his heart hammer against my palm, felt the raw, shaking need in his body. You can't fake a tremble like that.

So he knows Vale is scheming, but perhaps he doesn't know the shape of the blade? Or maybe he knows something about Vale's plan that I don't—another layer of rot hidden beneath the floorboards of this cursed palace.

A heavy thud of boots.

He's coming back!

Scrambling backwards, I turn and flurry-step across the floorboards, practically throwing myself into the chair just as the iron latch clicks. I grab a nearby water cup, my hand shaking so badly water sloshes over the rim onto my wrist, and bring it to my lips just as the door swings open.

Kael enters. The cold mask is gone, replaced by a

strained, visible effort to reassemble the gentle lover he was moments ago. His shoulders are tight, jaw clenched, but when he sees me still sitting where he left me, he forces a breath out through his nose and softens.

"Forgive the interruption," he says, his voice a little too careful.

"He mentioned a carriage." Unlikely to be about Mother and Daron, given the other context, but I have to be certain. "My family?"

"No. God, no. Your family should arrive tomorrow. Midday, if your brother can keep his resilience up." He walks toward me, keeping that respectful distance. "How do you feel? Has the dizziness passed?"

"Yes." I set the cup down with a clatter I can't quite prevent. "Much better. The water helped."

He manages a smile. It's a weary thing, but it reaches his eyes. "Good. I would not want you to end in a faint."

"What was it about?" I ask, forcing my voice to sound casual, bored even. "The messenger seemed almost frightened."

Kael's smile doesn't falter, but his gaze drops. It slides from my face, down my dress, and lands on my stocking feet.

He stills.

I don't have to look to know where his gaze travels next. My boot, sitting a bit incriminating near the door, so very far from the other by the chair.

Silence stretches.

Thick. Suffocating.

He stares at it for a long, terrible moment. Then, slowly —so slowly it feels like the turning of a heavy wheel—he lifts his gaze back to mine.

The blue of his eyes is flat, unreadable.

"M-my feet got hot," I say.

"Of course." He smiles again, but this time, the dimple doesn't show. The skin around his eyes remains tight, the expression pulled taut by invisible strings. "I apologize if the messenger caused you a scare." He leans down, his lips pressing a kiss just behind my ear. It should be warm, but it sends a shiver down my neck as he whispers, "Trust me, it is nothing you should concern yourself with."

CHAPTER
TWENTY-FIVE

Elara

S eventy-six. Seventy-seven.
We think we have her.
Heritage. Original translation.
Curse.

Wax drips from the candlestick onto my thumb, hot and stinging. Maybe Kael isn't the golden-haired, pitiful hero he paints himself to be, still hunting an angle to break this curse while letting the crown mend him. What does that mean for me?

I pause, leaning against the damp curve of the wall, the

stone weeping old fog and last night's rain. The flame judders against my ragged breath, and my mind goes back to how he found my boot near the door. How he looked at me...and said *nothing*.

Instead, he gave me a kiss that should've felt warm, but felt more like a warning...

If he wasn't suspicious before, he might be now. If I'm going to defeat this stupid fear of mine once and for all, it has to be now, before Kael posts someone to watch me more closely.

A cold sweat prickles my skin. How can these brothers be so different, yet alike in the worst of ways? Vale lies blatantly. And Kael? I'm starting to fear he might be lying beautifully.

I can't tell which one is worse between the two. Vale is a scheming cunt, but apparently, so is his brother. Not that I can hold it against them. After all, I am one, too.

I push off the wall and lift my tired leg. *Seventy-eight.*

These stairs eat breath for breakfast. They wind up the eastern tower in a mean, narrow spiral, each step a shallow grave for ankles that I step into gladly. Getting distracted by whispers I wasn't meant to hear won't change my goal. Worrying about hidden agendas won't bring it to fruition any faster.

I tilt my head back, looking up into the gloom where the stairs twist out of sight. My stomach twists right along with it, but I keep on climbing. I'm not here for the memory of his thumb bruising my lip...nor the heavy, dark heat of his breath. No, I'm here to take what he offered.

The rest of the map.

I reach the landing with a swallow that scratches on the way down, the corridor smelling faintly of dust and...yes, carnations. "Vale?"

I lower my candlestick onto a nearby chest and tap my knuckles on the scarred wood of the door. It eases open under the force of my hand, unlocked. Uncared for.

When I step inside, the room beyond is less a chamber and more a forgotten storage closet that found a bed. A place where the castle keeps its unwanted things—like a leftover prince who has no purpose.

Stacks of books teeter like drunken soldiers against the walls, climbing halfway to the ceiling, while an armoire leans crooked on three legs. In lieu of a proper hearth, a squat iron stove chugs in the center of the room, radiating a dry, fierce heat.

It shouldn't, but the sight amplifies Vale's insignificance so loudly it almost hurts to look at. To go from heir to...to this? I'd be angry, too.

"Well..." That word is a long drawl, coming from where Vale leans one shoulder against the window jamb, as if he'd been poured into the morning's dim, a book in hand which he holds angled toward the sparse gray light. He closes the cover with a snap that sounds like thunder in the quiet room, turning to face me with a slow, predatory curl of his lips. "If it isn't the little saint."

Molars grinding together, I let the door click shut behind me. "I'm no saint."

"You don't say." Book tossed onto a nearby table, he pushes off the wall, stalking toward me. The space is so small that two strides bring him into my personal orbit. He stops just shy of touching, looming over me, darker and larger than memory served. He tilts his head, eyes gleaming. "Did the golden boy scare you?"

Heat crawls up my throat and doesn't even have the decency to feed me a quick or convenient lie. "You know the answer to that."

Vale hums, a sound of dark amusement. "And you think I won't?"

That question only sharpens the scathe in my lungs. It sounds like a taunt, a challenge. And damn him for knowing full well that I would never shrink from that. Not when coming from *him.*

I lift my chin. "I'm counting on it."

"Brave words." He steps closer until his thighs bracket my own and trails his knuckles down the side of my neck—cold, like a blade. "Let's see if you can back them up."

He doesn't hesitate. His mouth moves over mine with a drugging intensity, coaxing my lips apart. When I yield, his tongue sweeps inside, reclaiming the territory he marked days ago.

Heat returns to my lower belly with a vengeance that scares me. It makes no sense. I should be repulsed by the taste of him—sharp with arrogance and the bitter tang of his lies—but instead, my body melts under his roaming hands.

They slide down my back, heavy and sure, over the curve of my waist, cupping my rear through the thick fabric of my dress. He pulls me into him, grinding his arousal against my belly. How can he be this hard this fast?

He grabs my wrists, his fingers wrapping around them like iron manacles, and drags my hands to the hem of his tunic—an invitation, a request, and a demand all at once.

My fingers tremble as they curl into the rough fabric. I pull the garment up to the lift of his arms, the motion clumsy and hasty. The moment his head clears the neckline, he tosses the tunic aside, leaving nothing but skin and air between us.

God, he is beautiful.

In a severe, ruinous way.

I've seen men before—laborers in the fields, builders on rooftops—but this...this is different. Vale is carved from smooth skin laid over lean muscle, a trail of hair leading down his stomach, disappearing into the waistband of his trousers.

He catches my hands again, pressing my palms flat against his chest. His heart thuds hard and heavy beneath my fingertips, a rhythmic drum of war. "I need your hands on me."

He drags them down, making them trace the hard planes of his pectorals, the taut ridges of his abdomen, along the dark dusting of hair. Every inch I descend, the tension in him ratchets tighter, stomach muscles clenching under my touch, his hips twitching forward. Seeking. Wanting.

Then my nails brush the cold metal of his belt.

My fingers lock up. The heat radiating from below bites into my skin.

What if Kael finds me like this? Did anybody see me climb the tower? What will—

"Shh..." Vale releases my hands to capture my jaw instead, forcing my gaze to the green burn of his. "Watch."

His eyes never leave mine as his hands go to his belt. The heavy buckle comes undone with a dull *clank*. Then the laces, the leather snapping loud enough to make me flinch. But when he shoves the trousers and linen down his hips in one sharp, ruthless motion?

I squeeze my eyes shut as cold fear floods me. I've bitten off more than I can chew. I'm going to choke on this.

"Look at me, Elara." Vale's voice drops, a command wrapped in silk. His warm palm frames my face, thumb digging into my cheekbone hard enough to bruise. "Open your eyes."

When his hand retreats, I force my lids to part, bracing to find him looming over me. But he hasn't moved closer.

He has stepped away.

He stands naked in the center of the room, unashamed, a fallen prince illuminated by the hellish glow of the iron stove. Veins wind like blue rivers along his forearms, pulsing beneath fair skin. He is terrifyingly substantial, from the powerful sweep of his thighs to the calves that look carved from rock. And there, at the junction of those powerful legs, a thicket of black curls frames the heavy, swollen reality of his desire.

He turns his profile to me, unbothered, bending to pick up a piece of firewood. With a rusted squeal of hinges, he opens the stove door and feeds the fire. Slowly.

Giving me time to observe...

Breath shaking, I do just that, drinking in the threat. The muscles in his shoulders ripple and bunch as he moves. The firelight licks at his skin, gilding the hard muscle of his ass and the long, powerful lines of his legs.

He straightens and turns back to the window, casually leaning against the stone wall, ankles crossed, arms loose. He looks bored, as if we were discussing cloud patterns and not standing on the precipice of my ruin. But his body betrays the lie. His cock stands out from his body in a thick, angry curve, obscenely hard, jerking upward with a heartbeat of its own. A single, clear bead of fluid wells at the dark slit of the head, glistening there.

Vale slowly lifts his arm, palm up.

Then, three curls of his fingers.

Come here.

I swallow hard, the sound loud in the quiet room. My instinct screams at me to bolt, to run back down those stairs until my lungs burn, like prey fleeing the trap.

But he doesn't move.

He doesn't stalk.

He doesn't use his strength to pin me against the wall or force my knees apart. He's letting me walk into the fire myself in a twisted sort of kindness—like a predator leaving the door to the cage open—but it gives me enough air to breathe.

This is what I came for.

I force the air into my chest and unlock my knees. One step, then another. The floorboards creak beneath my shoes, ticking off the seconds of my surrender until I stop in front of him.

"Touch me," he rasps. "Explore me."

My hands lift. They shake, just a little. I place my fingertips on his shoulders. The skin is scorching, the muscle beneath hard as iron. I trace the lines of his collarbone, pulse hammering violently in the hollow of his throat. Down the plane of his chest, over the clenching muscles on his stomach...until my hands hover over his navel.

Vale watches me, his eyes dark pools of starving patience. He doesn't push. He doesn't grab. He just burns.

With trembling breath, I lower my hand. My fingers brush the dense hair, the heavy weight of his sac, the granite length of him until I reach the weeping, velvet head.

Vale groans, a low rumble that vibrates fear through my bones, making me pull my hand back. But his hand shoots out, catching my wrist. He doesn't hurt me, but his grip is a shackle as he guides my hand back, closing my fingers around the thick, pulsing shaft.

"Grab me like this," he commands hoarsely, his hips bucking disjointedly into my grip. "Don't stop."

His hand covers mine, his palm rough and warm, forcing the rhythm. Gently up. Down again, tighter. It isn't a frantic motion, but a deliberate, milking drag that pulls a hissed breath through his clenched teeth.

"That's it," he grinds out, his hips snapping forward to meet my stroke. "Just like that."

With each of his broken noises, my terror melts into a heady, intoxicating sense of power. This man is unraveling at the mercy of my hand, clear fluid slicking the head of his cock, spreading down the shaft as I squeeze tighter, mapping the veins that throb beneath his skin.

He releases my hand and nods.

Keep going.

I do, boldly so. I watch the way his head falls back against the stone wall, his throat corded and exposed, his eyes sliding shut as I work him faster, the sound of wet friction filling the silence.

"Fuck," he breathes, the word a prayer and a curse.

His hands reach for me. They're deft, impatient fingers that make short work of my laces. There's no fumble, no hesitation. Only a peel of cotton, the chill from the window biting my skin for a second before his hot palms replace it. He shoves the dress and my shift down over my hips, bunching the fabric until it falls in a puddle around my ankles.

I step out of it without stopping my rhythm. Naked now, exposed in the gray light, and for the first time in my life, unable to hide.

And I don't think I want to.

Vale opens his eyes. They're dilated, swallowed by black lust, devouring me whole. He reaches out, cupping my breasts, his thumbs rough over nipples that ache for attention. He leans down, kissing the sensitive slope of my shoulder.

"You are so..." His murmur fades against my neck, the

vibration going straight to my core. "You walk like the world owes you nothing."

He kisses his way down my sternum, over my stomach. As he descends, the angle becomes impossible, and his cock slips from my slick grip. I make a sound of protest at the loss of heat, but he ignores it, dropping to his knees before me.

He grips my hip with one hand, and with the other, he lifts my foot, placing it squarely on his broad shoulder.

My breath hitches. The position leaves me entirely open, ruinously displayed.

"Vale—"

"Easy..." His breath ghosts over my clit. "Let me try this."

My knees buckle when his tongue swipes hot and wet against me. If he wasn't holding me up, anchoring me with his iron grip, I would collapse. He doesn't tease. No, he feasts, his tongue broad and skilled, finding the sensitive nub and swirling around it with relentless, maddening pressure.

I throw my head back, a ragged moan tearing from my throat. My fingers tangle in his black curls, not to push him away, but to hold him there. To drown him in it. It's too much sensation—the wet slap of his tongue, the suction of his mouth, the finger he slides inside me to curl and pump in time with his licking.

Pressure builds in my belly, a tightening coil of dark energy. It climbs, higher and higher, the air thinning. So close...

"Please," I gasp, my hips bucking against his face. "Vale, please."

He stops.

The loss is sudden, violent. I whimper, opening my eyes

to find him looking up at me, his chin slick with my arousal, his expression feral.

"Not like this," he growls. "You'll come apart on my cock, with me, or not at all."

Before I can curse him, he stands, sweeping me into his arms effortlessly. He carries me the three steps to the narrow bed, lowers me onto the mattress, and positions himself between my spread legs.

I reach for him, desperate, needing the friction back, but he catches my hands and pins them above my head with one hand. He looms over me, his chest heaving.

"Look at me, Elara." When I do, he uses his other hand to position the tip of his cock at my entrance. It is swollen, weeping fluid, lewdly spread. "If there is pain, you will say. Yes?"

I lock eyes with him. There's no deception here, only concern carved between his brows with a sincerity that stalls by the next inhale.

I nod.

He leans forward, a shift of weight so subtle it's barely a movement. Pressure builds against my entrance, stretching the sensitive skin, demanding space where there is none. I suck in a breath, my body tightening instinctively against the invasion, bracing for a pain I'm sure is coming.

He stills instantly.

"Don't close up," he roughs out, his voice deeper than ever before. "I'll go slow. I promise."

When my muscles ease, he enters me not by the inch, but by smaller fractions. He presses forward until the ring of muscle stretches, until I feel the absolute limit of what I can take—and then he stops. He squeezes his eyes shut, a hiss escaping through his teeth as his arms tremble violently, fighting the strain of holding his massive weight in check.

"Fuck..." The word is wrecked, stripped of all arrogance. "Vale?"

He opens his eyes, pupils blown so wide they swallow the green. "You..." he grinds out, looking down at me with something bordering on accusation. "You're gripping me like a vise."

It sounds like he's blaming me for his lack of control, but the flush staining his neck betrays him. He waits for my body to accept the width of him. Waits for the tightness to slacken, for my hips to lift in a silent, unconscious plea for more. Only then does he move: a careful, shaking slide forward that parts me. Parts me more.

He buries inside me, filling me with a tingling pressure that borders on pleasure and pain. Instinct takes over and I lift my hips, rocking them to the rhythm of his in a slow, gentle glide that synchronizes so perfectly.

Time loses its meaning.

Retreats feels like hours.

Thrusts feel like seconds.

Until his hand snaps down to my hip, pinning me to the mattress with bruising force. "Stop. Don't move."

"Why?" I gasp, dazed.

"Because if you grind into me one more time, this ends right now." He glares down at me, looking furious at his body's betrayal. "And I refuse to spill myself on the threshold after all this waiting. Be so still, Elara."

Power, sudden and intoxicating, floods my veins. He isn't just holding back for my sake, isn't he?

He's hanging on by a thread.

One I desperately want to undo. I slide my heel up the back of his thigh, the friction of skin against skin deliberate and slow, hooking my calf around his waist. Like that, I pull, urging him deeper inside me.

He groans, fighting the leverage. He tries to hold back, his hips locking, but the lure is too strong. He gives in with a guttural groan, sliding another inch deeper, the thickest part of him stretching me wide.

"Fuck, Elara... I can't..."

He stops dead again. His head drops to my shoulder, his breathing ragged, sounding like a man drowning. And then I feel it—the rhythmic throb of his cock deep inside me, the pulsing of his flesh against mine.

That sensation undoes me.

The feeling of him twitching inside me sparks a fire that runs straight through my core, making me pulse my hips in time with it, faster, harder. It pushes me right to the very edge, where I teeter.

Crying out in frustration, I dig my heel into the small of his back and pull with everything I have, forcing his hips down, pulling him deep into me. "Move!"

The sensation of him bottoming out, hitting the deepest, most secret part of me, shocks a gasp from my lips. Vale tosses his head back and unleashes an animalistic growl that shakes the walls.

His control snaps.

There's no more patience, no more gentle siege. He withdraws almost fully and slams back into me with a wet, heavy smack of skin against skin, burying himself to the hilt.

"Saints," he snarls against my ear, thrusting so hard the bed hits the wall with a crack. "I can't hold back."

Neither can I.

The force of that thrust, the sudden, violent claiming, shatters me. My climax hits instantly, a white-hot explosion that clamps my body down around him in tight, rhythmic spasms.

Vale roars, burying his face in the crook of my neck as he, too, erupts inside me. I feel every pulse of his release, hot and torrential, flooding me, coating me deep inside where no one else has ever been.

Then he collapses, his weight pressing down on me for a second before he shifts it to the side. Like that, we lie tangled in the cooling aftermath, the silence of the room crashing down on me louder than any scream.

Slowly, the golden haze begins to lift from my mind, replaced by the sharp, cold edges of reality. The ceiling comes back into focus. The smell of dust and carnations return.

It's done. This was it.

I should feel triumphant.

Instead, I just feel...empty.

The intimacy—stripped of the driving madness of lust—suffocates my lungs. The stickiness between my thighs, the sweat drying on my skin, the sheer proximity of his heart beating against my ribs...I don't know what to do with that.

I look beside me, where his hard breaths into his pillow return to something more even. I should go. I should gather my clothes and my scattered wits before I do something foolish.

Like trail my fingers through his damp curls...

I wiggle, trying to shift his bulk off me. He grumbles low in his chest, a sleepy, satisfied sound, but he rolls onto his side, releasing me from the cage of his limbs. But before I can sit up, his warm palm settles down on the back of my hand.

He squeezes it ever so slightly before he rasps, "Stay."

TWENTY-SIX

Elara

S*tay.*

The word hangs in the dusty air, heavier than the stone blocks of the tower. It hooks into my ribs, a command wrapped in a plea, or perhaps a plea disguised as a command. I stare at our joined hands—his large one swallowing mine.

He wants me to...stay? Why? For what purpose?

My first instinct is to wrench away. Away from this sense of emptiness at my core, the awkwardness of this moment. I finally got this part over with, so what's left here for me?

Nothing.

I pull my hand from beneath his and sit up. "I should go. If your brother finds me here—"

"Nobody comes here," he mumbles. "It's storage for useless things nobody ever needs."

Again, useless hurt at how he's been reduced to a mere ghost, but it doesn't replace the restlessness that's seeping into my core. "My family will arrive in a few hours. I want to be there when they do."

"Not before afternoon." Fabric flaps behind me. Then, his warm arm comes slinging around me to the sensation of his lips pressing a kiss to my spine. "Last night's rain turned the roads into pig shit. A carriage won't make it up the incline until the sun dries the mud." His fingers curl into my belly, and the slightest pressure urges me back. "Stay. Just a while."

Reluctantly, I surrender.

I sink back onto the mattress, what for, I have no idea. Certainly not for how he shifts, pulling me into him until my back presses against his chest, curving me against the shape of his body. He drapes a heavy arm over my waist, locking me in place, and buries his face in the crook of my neck.

Then, he begins to stroke my hair.

It is a rhythmic, hypnotic motion. His fingers catch in the tangles, smoothing them out with ardent patience. It's...strange, this closeness between us. Even stranger is how it makes me meld into him, my muscles easing one by one, each caress filling that hollow, howling emptiness at my core with a languid warmth I have no name for.

My eyes drift through the room, to the stacks of books

leaning against the empty walls. "Am I going to find your mother's missing annals over there?"

He chuckles into my hair. "Is this the moment you start prying into my sad childhood? Where I weep into your hair about my family tragedies, and you pretend to care until the sun dries the roads?"

"I do care."

I mean it. But god, I don't want to hear about curses, or blood, or crowns, or any of the grim realities of this place. Here, tangled in his heat, the world has stopped...and I'm not ready to start it up again.

"You seemed to know what you were doing just now," I say, mostly to the ceiling.

"Did I." It isn't a question, and the flatness of it makes me turn my head just enough to look at him. "A praise to my meticulous observation."

"What does that mean?"

A long exhale moves through his chest and into mine. "Nothing."

I frown at him, but only for a second. "Do you actually know the story of how the king fooled Death? The one you mentioned at the grave?"

Another tingling caress along strands, but this one extends down my arm. "Every prince knows. It's a story handed down in the royal bloodline ever since it began."

"Will you tell me?"

Vale says nothing for a moment, his hand slowing in my hair until his voice rumbles against my shoulder blade. "The legend goes that, centuries ago, Death met a ferry-man. An old man named Eamon, with a bad back and a boat, who asked Death for help to retrieve an oar from the river. In return, he said, he would share a story."

I shift slightly, trying to imagine the looming figure

from the fountain entertaining a simple ferryman. "And did he share a story?"

"Daily. For years." Vale's hand picks up its gentle strokes again. "Through the ferryman, Death learned things he had never understood about mortals. Why mothers keep baby teeth in a box. Why widows smell their dead husband's coat for months." He pauses, his voice dropping to a hush. "Eamon became his friend—the only one he ever had. The one mortal who treated him like a man with a heart, with flaws, with dreams, with fears."

"He sounds kind," I whisper.

A beat of silence. "One day, Eamon brought a board to the riverbank, saying that he would teach Death a game. Chess."

I can't help but chuckle at that. "Did the ferryman fool Death into losing and gained the crown?"

"Not at all," he says. "As the story goes, Eamon told him that the queen was the fiercest piece on the board, but ultimately, she was expendable. That she existed to be sacrificed if it ensured the king's survival."

"Oh..." My stomach squeezes. "Is that what gave Death the idea of demanding a queen's blood? Because he thought them expendable?"

"On the contrary, it was the one lesson Death could never grasp." Vale shakes his head against the pillow. "Death didn't understand it. Why would you sacrifice your companion? How could the victory be worth the loneliness that followed?"

The question hangs in the dusty air, striking a chord deep within me. A soft, aching pressure blooms behind my ribs.

"How the first king found out about all this, nobody knows for certain," Vale continues. "But one evening, Death arrived at the river, only to find a soldier's blade set at the ferryman's throat. The king present demanded a game of chess. If Death won, Eamon would remain unharmed. If he lost...Death would grant the king a wish."

I shiver, the cold of the story seeping into the warm bed. "Why didn't Death just kill them?"

Vale shakes his head, the tip of his nose nuzzling my nape. "Death can't just take a life before its time. His interference with the mortal world is...limited."

"Death lost."

"It is what happens when you don't play with your head, but your heart," he whispers. "The king baited him into a position where sacrificing his queen was the only move to win. Death couldn't do it. So, the king sacrificed his queen without a moment's hesitation and checked the board."

Something shifts at my core. Unfeeling, Kael had called Death, but being unable to fathom bartering your companion for victory doesn't fit the shape of that word. But maybe that was before he tore at his heart?

"Death fashioned the crown currently sitting on Kael's head, with powers as demanded," Vale goes on, "but warned that he would weave a curse into the gold for the trickery. The king was furious; called Death a cheat. And in his fury"—his fingers in my hair slow, almost stiffen—"the king drew his sword and beheaded Eamon. Clean off."

"He lost a dear friend," I whisper, my throat tight.

"I would like to think that..." Vale hesitates for a moment. "I think Death might've lost something like a father."

My breath hitches. *A father.* That's an ache I recognize. That is a hole in the world that cannot be filled, no matter how much soil you shovel into it.

"The grief tore through him," Vale says, his voice devoid of all emotion, terrifyingly flat. "He had never felt such pain. In his agony, the legend says he reached into his own chest..." Behind me, Vale mimes the motion over his sternum—a clawed hand digging into ribs. "He slashed at his heartstrings to make it stop hurting. With the one he tore out completely, he wove the curse into the crown."

He falls silent, leaving us suspended in the tragedy.

"Maybe I should have asked for your sad childhood story after all." I turn and gently cover his hand with mine, pressing it flat against his beating heart. "The king was a fool, thinking he could kill a father and not face the wrath of the son."

Vale doesn't answer. Slowly, he pulls his hand from beneath mine and reaches up, his palm cupping my cheek.

His eyes find mine, like moss saturated from rain. They're damp, glistening with unnamed sorrow as his thumb traces the line of my jaw, then softly drags over my bottom lip. It isn't the hungry touch from before; it is reverent, apologetic.

"It's a story, a lesson, passed down to every prince." His thumb stills on my mouth. "Whatever we love...we eventually have to lose."

Seeing him like this, with his usual nonchalance not just slipped but shattered, hits me with the force of a physical blow.

It hurts.

And in that pain, a dangerous seed is planted. It burrows into my core, a dozen questions spreading through me like vines. What if the sadness in his gaze isn't just manipulation? What if his words were true? What if he truly *is* growing love for me?

My breath hitches.

What if I could love him back?

I reach up, my fingers trembling as I brush the dampness from the corner of one eye. He leans into it, closing his eyes, and a single tear escapes, tracking hot and silent down his cheek to wet my thumb. Then he kisses the heel of my palm with an ardency fit for a fairytale.

But the reality is far grimmer, isn't it?

Even if he kills his brother, even if he takes over the crown and curse, it needs feeding. He would still have to drag me to the altar. Would still have to drag a knife across my throat. The ending would be the same, and it might come too late for Daron.

And for what? Love that won't survive? No, it's a luxury for the living.

I'm already half dead.

And yet, as his mouth continues up along my arm, his lips leaving a trail toward mine, I cannot bring myself to pull away. Not yet. I want to stay in this delusion for just a moment longer—where he kisses me, where he pulls me tighter against him, letting the warmth of our bodies meld into one.

When our mouths part, I force a smile onto my lips and lightness into my tone. "Well, guess it's a good thing you're not king then."

Vale rolls his eyes a little—a flicker of domesticity that feels dangerously intimate in this moment. Then he sighs. "The realm is dying, and I can't figure out what feeds my brother's deluded hope to break this curse. If he doesn't feed the crown soon…"

I sense it in my calves first, that stiffness that comes as the messenger's words echo in my mind. *Heritage. Original translation. Curse.*

My tongue presses against the roof of my mouth. I don't

think Kael is just hoping. I think he's thinking, plotting, scheming.

Should I tell Vale?

I bite my lip. Knowledge is power, and I'm not sure if handing it to Vale is in my best interest. But then again, what if telling him will help us both figure out the answer? Isn't swaying Kael away from breaking the curse in my best interest?

I hate giving him power, but ignorance kills.

"A messenger came to his door," I say, sensing the way his chest goes still against mine. "The wood is thick, and the king kept his voice low, but...I heard some."

Vale stills, then pushes his body up on one elbow. "What?"

"Something about a village. Heritage. Original translation. Curse—yes, the messenger definitely said curse." I sit up slightly, clutching the sheet to my breasts against the sudden chill of the room. "He said he thinks they have her."

"Her?" Vale frowns. "You?"

"I don't know. No, not me—that doesn't make any sense," I say, shaking my head. "At first, I thought they were talking about my mother, but that wasn't it, either. It can't be."

Vale stares at me, his mind clearly dissecting the information as the damp sparkle fades from his eyes, replaced by a predator's focus. "Who is *her*?"

I just shrug. "That's what I wondered, too."

"Heritage." Vale pushes off the bed, pacing the small room naked, oblivious to the cold. He grabs a book from a stack, flips it open, snaps it shut, and throws it down in frustration. Then he looks at me, eyes blazing. "Original translation? Are you sure that is what was said?"

Wrapping my arms around myself to ward off the chill, I nod. "I'm sure."

Vale's jaw tightens. He grabs my discarded shift from the ground, walks over to the bed, and hands it to me. "I don't want you to get cold."

"What does it mean?" I ask as I take the linen and slip it on. "About the translation."

He runs a hand through his curls, muscles shifting in his abdomen. It's a motion of concern—maybe even confusion—that's so unlike him.

"I assume that's for you to find out since he barely tolerates me as of late, and the curse recordings in the chapel are...inaccessible to me," he eventually says as he kneels before me, takes my hands into his, and gazes up at me. "Can you find out?"

I look down at him. "I guess I can try."

"Do more than try, Elara." He presses a kiss to my knuckles. "Go. Before the household bustles."

I pull away, dressing quickly, my mind a churning sea. As I descend the spiraling stone steps, leaving the heavy air of the tower for the drafty corridors of the halls, the task he gave me feels heavy. Is digging for more secrets truly worth my time? Instead of focusing on my connection with Kael? Intimacy? On the—

"Miss Elara!"

I jolt back, breath catching. Miss Hampshire stands there, clutching a stack of fresh linen to her chest. Her pustuled face is flushed, her bonnet slightly askew.

"Miss Hampshire," I breathe, trying to smooth my skirts. "I was just—"

"I have been looking for you," she interrupts, her voice shrill. Her eyes narrow, scanning me, eyes traveling from my disheveled hair down to my wrinkled bodice.

Then, her gaze stops.

I follow her line of sight, and my heart hammers a frantic rhythm against my ribs. There, on the darker fabric of my skirt, near the upper thigh, is a damp patch. It's unmistakable.

Miss Hampshire's lips thin into a razor line. She looks up at me.

"Rot or not, Miss Elara," she hisses, her voice dropping to a scandalized whisper, "this is still a decent household. We do not prowl the palace looking like...that."

I flinch. "There was a leak in the roof—"

"His Majesty sent me," she cuts over me, unwilling to even hear the lie. She steps back, putting distance between us as if my impropriety is contagious. "He is waiting for you by the main gate. The carriage has been spotted on the rise."

"My family?" The blood rushes from my face. "Now?"

"Yes. They made better time than expected." Her eyes flick to the damp spot one last time, filled with judgment and a dangerous sort of calculation. "I suggest you run. Though I fear you may already be too late to make a good impression."

I don't wait for her to dismiss me; I nod, clutching my skirts, and hurry past her toward the daylight at the end of the hall. My shoes slap against the stone, fast and desperate.

I have to get to Daron. But most of all, I have to get to Kael faster than what Miss Hampshire can report.

CHAPTER

TWENTY-SEVEN

Elara

Lungs burning, I sprint toward the massive iron-banded gates. The morning mist hasn't yet lifted from the cobblestones of the lower courtyard. It clings to the stone, a creeping white tide that smells of wet earth and moss and the faint metallic tang of the portcullis.

Kael stands in the midst of it, a dark shape carved out of gray. Charcoal wool, silver embroidery that steals what little light the sky offers. He glances back at me as I skid to a halt at his side.

217

"I looked for you in your chamber," he says. "You weren't there."

There isn't enough air left in my lungs to breathe a lie, so I just nod once, sharp. "They're early."

His gaze travels over me with a slow, meticulous weight. From my hair—likely knotted and tangled—to my wrinkled dress and down to the hem of my skirt. I feel acutely aware of what I just did, as if his brother's touch is still on me, fingerprints rising from my skin like steam.

"The rain did not wash out the Oakhaven bridge the way it often does," he answers.

"That explains it..." My voice comes out thinner than I'd like.

I resist the urge to claw my dress straight, to scrub at the damp stain, to sniff if Vale's scent is stitched into the cotton. But I force my hands to smooth down the fabric with agonizing care instead, as if all I'm brushing away is dust and not a tower's worth of sin.

"Do not worry yourself, Elara." Kael's hand settles warm and steady at the small of my back, rubbing up and down in the same rhythm he used when I wept against his chest. "I had Miss Hampshire prepare the best rooms in the west wing. Your family will be looked after."

I lean into his touch before I can stop myself. Maybe my body remembers its comfort, even as my mind cautions me not to trust it fully. Not with what I heard behind that door. Not with how he'd looked at my boot.

I stare down the winding road that disappears into the fog-choked tree line. Somewhere beyond that veil, a carriage rattles toward us.

Mother. Daron.

"Thank you, Kael."

It sounds small. Pathetic, even. Too thin a word, given how I held his brother mere moments ago. Too flimsy for a king who stepped into the pain of daylight to hold my grief.

I flinch at my own confliction.

How did this all get so...tangled?

"Do not thank me for decency," he murmurs, his hand stilling at the base of my spine. "It makes it sound rare."

"Perhaps because it is," I answer. "You didn't have to do this."

He turns fully then, and the silver thread at his cuffs pulls a glint out of the gray air. There's something kingly in that, how he commands grace without trying. But when he wraps his arms around me? There's nothing regal in how he inches me into the warmth of his body.

"I wanted to," he says into my hair. A beat, then softer. "For you."

My throat tightens like a knot tugged from both ends. His warmth crawls under my skin, turning it hot. It makes my nerves prickle, like an itch under my flesh, as if I'm being held by the wrong man, in the wrong place, at the wrong—

No. That's nonsense.

It's just my stupid head scrambling even stupider delusions. This is the *right* man. The one whose love I need. The one who has to put a crown on my head and hold a knife to my throat.

Not his brother.

I shove the confusion down. What if he wasn't even suspicious about my boot? What if that was just in my head? And what if I'm making progress here, and whatever I heard between him and that messenger was nothing but the frail leftovers of a plan he is slowly abandoning? Didn't he hint at that in the spring? Is he not here to receive my family with me?

"Elara..." His hand, still resting at the base of my spine, presses just a fraction more firmly. Not pushing, just...holding, anchoring. "I need you to stop worrying. This was my choice, and you owe me nothing for it in return."

His eyes flicker down to my mouth, then back up. A question, a hesitation. Giving me room to pull away.

I don't. I bridge the last bit of distance and press my lips to his with a determination that makes his breath catch.

When it returns, it does so with fire. His hand slides up my back, splaying between my shoulder blades, pulling me closer in a way that feels urgent. His lips move against mine with desire, faster as if—

A throat clears. Loudly.

We both jolt.

But only I move, breaking the kiss, pulling back to find Miss Hampshire standing a few paces away: jaws tight, lips thin, wrinkles carved between her brows. Maybe she suspected, but she's never seen us intimate until now—and after she caught me coming down the tower. Will she tell?

Kael's hand doesn't leave me. If anything, it tightens as he turns toward his head of staff. "The linens are laid out? The hearths started?"

His tone is calm, as if being caught kissing a gravedigger in a king's courtyard is nothing more than an item on his morning agenda. His hand strokes once down my side, soothing, entirely unconcerned with how her eyes flick to me, heavy with what looks like judgment. Maybe concern.

"Yes, Your Majesty." She curtsies, then her gaze drifts to the gate. "The carriage is coming over the rise."

My heart hammers against my ribs, echoing loudly enough between my ears it almost drowns out the rhythmic crunch of gravel, the jingle of harness bells, the heavy creak of wood under strain.

They're here!

The carriage cuts through the fog, its shape slowly resolving out of the gray: black wood, iron-rimmed wheels, two horses slick with dried mud. The driver hauls back on the reins. The horses snort, tossing their heads. The whole contraption shudders to an uneven halt.

For a breath, nothing moves—no door opens, no curtain parts. Then, the latch lifts with a *click.*

Mother steps out. She's...smaller, somehow. Her dress hangs looser at the shoulders, and there are new lines etched around her mouth in a way that makes my stomach knot. What if I made it all worse by leaving?

"Elara," she breathes.

I run. My shoes skid on the damp stone, and my arms fling themselves around her, whether she's ready or not. I bury my face in the familiar hollow of her shoulder, where she smells faintly of soap, potatoes, and...iron?

I turn my head, spotting dark purple veins webbing up the side of her neck, each one like rope tightening around my chest. *No. Not her too...*

"Mother..."

Her arms come up tight around me, fiercer than her body looks capable of. "Let me see you." She pulls back, her rough fingers cradling my face, turning it this way and that. "You look like you've been worrying yourself into the ground. Are you—"

Her gaze flicks past me.

Up.

Over my shoulder.

"Your Majesty," she says, and I hear the tiny adjustment

in her tone. Less loving, more formal. "Thank you. Thank you for bringing us."

"Of course." Kael inclines his head. His voice is perfectly even, but I feel the brief, reassuring press of his hand at my back again. "Welcome to the palace. I am sorry the circumstances are what they are."

"A roof that doesn't leak and bread that isn't green already improves them," she answers bluntly.

"Ma'am." The driver shifts on the box, glancing toward the still-open carriage door. "The boy…"

Daron. I move before anyone, elbowing past one of the approaching footmen to peer inside the carriage—and still.

A shudder rakes my spine.

What happened to him?

Laid out on a makeshift pallet of wood and layered blankets, his long limbs look like kindling atop the wool. The rot that started at his nails has crept further, climbing up his hands, mottling his wrists, licking at his forearms like frost. His cheeks are hollow, eyes too big in his gaunt face, but when he sees me, they brighten with a sick little spark.

"Hello, broom queen," he croaks, trying to push himself up on his elbows. The effort makes him wheeze.

"Don't you dare move." I crawl inside, sweeping stray brown curls away from his clammy forehead. "Look at you, trying to leap out of your deathbed. You'll have me out of work."

He grins, or tries to. It comes out lopsided, but it's there. "Wouldn't want that. World needs its gravediggers."

Something tight and hot squeezes behind my eyes. "Idiot."

One of the footmen clears his throat. "If we may—"

"We'll carry him up." Kael appears at the carriage door,

his presence filling the space like he's pushed the fog back. "Slowly. Hands under the wood, not him. No jolting."

Kael ducks inside—never mind the mud, never mind the cramped space, never mind the stink of rot—and takes one end of the board himself. Another footman takes the opposite side.

"On my count," Kael says. "One. Two. Three."

Daron groans as three men maneuver him through the narrow carriage door, but the sound is less pain than effort. I jump back, then scramble alongside as they carry him through the arch and into the shadowed cool of the palace interior.

Miss Hampshire follows, as does Mother, right to my side, but with a brittle kind of silence. The corridors feel different with Daron in them. The rot is more present, somehow. More personal. Every dark spot on the wall, every faint smell of damp and sickness feels like it's leaning in to listen.

Kael leads us not to some cramped servants' nook, but to the west wing he promised. Up one flight—slowly, with pauses for Daron's wheezing—then down a broad corridor lined with faded tapestries.

The room he opens is...nice.

There's a large bed, piled high with clean linens. A small hearth already crackles with welcoming heat. A jug of water, a basin, folded cloths. A chair by the window, another by a table.

"Oh, this is much nicer than the city," Mother says, and there's a catch in her voice that almost sounds like awe.

Kael nods, then jerks his chin at the bed. "Gently."

They lower Daron onto the mattress, blankets and all. He sinks with a soft grunt, hands curling into the sheets.

I rush to his side. "Here, let me—"

I grab a pillow, intending to wedge it under his head, but the moment I lift his neck, his back arches off the bed. A sound claws its way out of his chest—half cough, half scream. And with that sound comes a streak of gray. It bubbles out his mouth before it runs down the corner and onto the clean linen, seeping into it like frothy tar.

I drop the pillow. I step back.

My feet freeze two paces away, useless as the sound rattles through him. His knuckles whiten. His toes curl. Another dark, viscous strand dribbles from the corner of his mouth. How did it get this bad, this fast? How can I possibly still save him?

Kael pushes past me.

"Easy," he says, one knee on the mattress, one foot on the floor to brace himself. He slips a hand behind Daron's head with a careful steadiness that speaks of practice and lowers his head back down. "Miss Hampshire! More pillows. Large ones, so we can elevate his entire upper body."

"Yes, Your Majesty," she answers with a curtsy before she spins around, leaving with the footmen.

"Least I can do is make myself useful carrying it all," Mother says before she hurries after them.

The room goes quiet, save for the crackling fire and the wet rattle of Daron's breathing. Kael moves to the window, where his entire posture seems to collapse, a slow, heavy sway that drags his chin down to his chest, tumbling his golden curls forward in a curtain that shrouds his profile and swallows the gleam of his crown.

I look back at Daron.

He is unrecognizable. Gone is the boy who hid his sickness to spare us the worry, who kept joking and laughing to keep death away. In his place is a skeleton wrapped in skin the color of wet clay.

His eyelids flutter, battling weight I can't imagine, until they drag open. They roam the unfamiliar ceiling before locking onto me. His lips part. "El..." The rest of my name dies in a wet rasp.

I'm there before he can try again.

My knees hit the floorboards beside the bed, ignoring the impact. Carefully, so very carefully, I slide my hand into his. "I'm here."

He blinks, forcing a focus that makes his brow furrow. Then, a ghost of a smirk pulls at the corner of his cracked mouth. "You look..."—a wheeze—"...like you let a drunk goat...do your hair."

A wet laugh bubbles out of me, burning my nose. "Stop wasting your breath on nonsense."

His thumb brushes my hand, a flutter of pressure. "If I die...in this palace...I'm haunting you..."

That burn climbs my sinuses, creeping and crawling behind my eyes until my vision blurs. "You're not dying."

He smiles that same lopsided, boyish thing he's always flung in the face of bad news—only now it trembles at the edges. His eyes slick over, wet gathering in the corners with each slow blink. He holds my gaze for as long as he can, like he's trying to make this lie I'm telling true by sheer stubbornness alone.

Then his lashes drag shut and don't lift again. A single tear escapes, slipping down the grayish hollow of his temple, and in that tiny, shining trail is the truth neither of us can outrun:

My little brother is dying.

A sob claws its way up my throat, a jagged, sharp thing

that I have to crush behind my teeth until the taste of iron floods my mouth.

Lies. Messengers. Plots and schemes. Fuck all of it!

I look over at Kael. Tonight, I'll go to his chamber. If I can bring out his guilt, I'll use it. If I can bring out his desire, I'll use that, too. Whatever it takes—tonight, I'll bring myself one step closer to queen.

To coronation.

To death.

TWENTY-EIGHT

Elara

Night in the palace is quieter than the graveyard ever was.

At least in the graveyard, something always moved. Worms under the soil. Wind through leaves. The soft scuttle of rats between headstones. Here, the halls hold their breath while the flames in the wall torches make the shadows stretch across the floor, grasping like fingers at the hem of my gown.

I pull the silk tighter around myself. It's a flimsy thing,

pale blue and shivering-thin, chosen from a trunk in one of the many abandoned rooms. It offers no warmth, but it isn't meant to.

It's a costume for a play.

My shoes click gently against the stone as I hurry toward Kael's chamber. There's no more time to waste on mysteries. I have to make tonight count.

For Daron.

When I reach the oaken door, I knock. Once. Twice. A pause.

"Enter," Kael's voice comes muffled through the wood.

I push the door open just enough to slip inside, bringing the draft from the hallway with me.

His chamber isn't the mausoleum he used to rot in, not anymore. The curtains on two windows are open, letting in pale moonlight that washes the floorboards in silver. The hearth burns low, banked down for the night. The air is cleaner. Fragrant, even.

"Elara?" He looks over from where he sits at his desk, quill in hand, candlelight pooling gold across parchment. Frown lines cut between his eyes, and tension cords his forearms as he sets the quill down, his shirt sleeves rolled to his elbows. "Are you alright?"

The sorrow choking my voice is the easiest part of the play. "No."

He stands immediately. In three large strides, he's in front of me, cupping my face between his warm palms before he tugs my gaze up to his. "Is it Daron?"

"He's sleeping, but I just couldn't stay there." My arms lift, fingers anchoring around his wrists, the tremble in them not studied but real. "The sound of his breathing... It bubbles, Kael. He sounds like he's drowning on dry land."

"Oh, Elara..." He lets out a breath, shoulders dropping an inch as his blue eyes stare deeper into mine. "Come here." He wraps his arms around me and pulls me into the solid warmth of his chest. "I'm so sorry. You have to believe how sorry I am."

I lean into his embrace, my eyes swimming with tears as honest as the burn in my throat when I whimper, "He's dying."

"No," he murmurs into my hair. "Daron still has time."

"No, he doesn't." Not much anyway. "Kael, please do something."

He tenses, only a little, but it's there. Until his arm sweeps around my waist, crushing me deeper against the quickening beat of his heart. "I'm trying, Elara. I swear to you, I *am* trying."

Coldness rakes my skin.

Trying isn't enough.

"I'm losing him." My own words split me. The way my legs give out underneath me? How I grapple at his shirt? That ugly sound hiccuping from my throat? It's all real, making my weight drag toward the cold floor in the same way death drags corpses into their graves. "Oh my god, I can't lose him, too..."

His other arm sweeps around my waist, stopping how my body sinks along with my grief. "I've got you."

He holds me there for a long time. Everything is silence, the crackle of the hearth, and stuttering sobs. Eventually, they ebb into shuddering breaths that I draw against his skin where a button has popped open on his shirt. The beat of his heart rises—thudding hard, thudding fast.

His hand, which had been rubbing soothing circles between my shoulder blades, stills. Then slides lower.

I lift my head.

Kael is looking down at me, his face inches from mine. His eyes are dark, the blue swirling with a concern that is slowly being crowded out by something else. The air between us thickens, heavy with the scent of wax and sudden, sharp awareness.

When his gaze drops to my mouth and lingers there, I tilt my chin up. It's enough for him to close the tiny distance until our noses brush, until our breaths mingle in the small, charged space between our lips.

"I'm so sorry," he whispers, the words vibrating against my mouth.

Good. I need him sorry.

I lean in, brushing my lips against his—softly at first, a ghost of a touch seeking comfort. He shudders against me, a low sound rumbling in his throat, and his hands tighten on my waist.

Our lips finally touch.

All softness shatters.

A groan tears out of his chest, vibrating against my ribs as his mouth opens against mine, hot and desperate. His tongue sweeps past my lips, tasting of wine and berries. His hands are everywhere. They tangle in my hair, slide down my back to grip my hips, haul me closer until there's no air left in the room, until my toes barely brush the floor.

He lifts me.

I gasp against his mouth as he backs me up and sits me on the edge of a heavy table near the hearth and steps between my knees. My silk gown rides up, baring my legs to the firelight and his touch. His hands slide up my thighs, thumbs pressing into the soft skin, leaving brands of heat.

I wrap my legs around his waist, pulling him flush against me. Not with hunger, but with intention.

I need this.

He needs it, too. I can tell from how his hard cock strains desperately behind leather, rocking against the junction of my legs with an urgency that feels frantic rather than right. It's a heavy, insistent pressure that creates friction but no spark—a clumsy heat that sits on top of my skin instead of singing through my blood.

I ignore the subtle way my body stiffens and force my hips to meet his. It doesn't have to feel right...it just has to work.

"Kael," I breathe his name against the damp salt of his skin. "Kael, please."

The plea snaps the last fraying thread of his control. His hand slides higher, rough and urgent, rucking the silk of my gown up to my waist. He hooks a finger beneath the lace of my smallclothes, dragging the fabric aside to stroke through my folds.

"So fucking long..." he growls as his hands drop to his waist, tearing at the fastenings of his breeches until he frees himself.

His cock springs loose—heavy, thick, and demanding. He steps back between my knees, gripping my hips to anchor me, and presses the broad head of his length straight against my entrance.

The pressure is immense, a blunt weight dragging against my sensitive skin, threatening to stretch me open. I force my thighs to relax, opening wider for the invasion.

One step closer.

I *need* this to happen.

But he doesn't push inside.

He freezes, his hips trembling with the effort of holding back. He looks down at where our bodies meet, where his cock is poised to breach me. Then he looks up at me, his chest heaving, his expression fracturing into something angry.

"Fuck!" The curse tears out of him, harsh and loud. He rips himself away from me, stumbling back a step. His hands fly to his waist, shoving his heavy cock back into his breeches with shaking fingers. "I cannot do this."

My stomach drops. Rises...

...then drops all over again

"What?" My voice comes out sharp. "Kael—"

"I cannot do this," he repeats, his tone gaining a hard, brittle edge. He turns away from me, gripping the mantel of the fireplace. "If I take you, then I start down my father's road. This cannot happen. Not ever."

My stomach tilts.

Not ever?

The confusion bubbling in my gut instantly turns to acid. "What do you mean by *not ever?*" I slide off the table, my legs shaking as they hit the floor. I fix my gown, worry warring with humiliation. "Because...because I'm a servant?"

"Don't be foolish," he snaps, glancing back at me. "You know that is not the reason."

"Then what is it?" I step toward him. "You want me...I felt it. You want me, Kael."

He spins around, and the anguish on his face stops me cold. "What I want does not matter!"

His shout silences even the fire until the flames crackle again, a mocking cheerfulness in the tension.

My mind races in too many directions at once, making me dizzy, making me sick. He won't sleep with me. And if he won't sleep with me, then he won't marry me. And if he won't marry me, then I cannot be queen. And I cannot be queen, then I cannot die.

A-and if I don't die...

Daron does.

The thought is a guillotine blade dropping in my mind. It severs the remaining threads of my pride, my hesitation, and my shame. There's no room for dignity in a graveyard. If he won't walk willingly into the trap, then I have to drag him. I have to make the hunger outweigh his conscience.

I step forward, ignoring the warning in his eyes. "Don't say that," I whisper, my voice rough with a panic I don't bother to hide. "Don't tell me it doesn't matter when your body is screaming that it does."

"Elara, stop."

I close the distance between us in a heartbeat. "I want you."

I don't give him time to retreat, don't give him time to think. I grab his hand, pressing it to my waist, and with my other hand, I claw at the fragile silk of my gown. I yank the fabric down, baring my breast to the firelight and to him.

Kael's breath hitches, a harsh, ragged sound that scrapes against the silence. His gaze drops, snagging on my exposed skin, his pupils blowing wide until the blue is swallowed by black. He wavers, the rigid line of his shoulders crumbling.

"Look at me," I beg, pressing my body flush against his. "We want each other."

I reach down, finding the bulge in his breeches, hot and hard as stone. I cup him through the leather, my fingers digging in, kneading his thick length.

Kael throws his head back, a guttural groan tearing from his throat. His hips jerk forward, instinctively seeking my touch, betraying his will. His hands come up, tangling in my hair, gripping tight, not pushing me away, but holding me there.

"Elara… Fuck…"

"Take me, please," I hiss, emboldened by the tremor in his body.

His entire body shudders against mine. "No…"

"I want you inside me." I stroke him harder, rubbing the sensitive ridge, feeling him twitch and throb against my palm. "Take me. Please, Kael. Just take—"

"I said no!"

He tears my hands away from him, his grip so tight it burns, and shoves me back. It isn't a strike, but a desperate, frantic need to put space between us. The force of it sends me reeling. My heel catches in the trailing hem of my silk gown, and with nothing to grab, gravity takes me.

I crash hard onto the stone floor.

The impact jars my teeth and knocks the wind from my lungs, leaving me gasping at his feet. Pain radiates up my spine from where my hip struck the stone, but it's instantly eclipsed by a humiliation so profound it feels like he poured boiling oil over me. I offered him everything—my body, my pride, my life—and he cast me aside as if I were the sin itself.

Kael stands over me, chest heaving, his hands trembling violently as he hastily fixes his breeches. He looks horror-struck—not just at me, but at himself.

My shock cracks open, and what spills out isn't tears; it's blistering fury. I scramble to my feet, ignoring the throb in my hip, my shame incinerated by the sudden, violent need to hurt him as badly as he's hurting me.

"My brother is dying!" I scream. "He's rotting from the inside out because of *you*!"

"I did not cast this pestilence!" The anger in his voice matches mine, defensive and raw. "I'm a victim of it as much as your brother!"

I step toward him. "You're standing there, talking about adoration while Daron coughs up his own lungs a hundred feet away!"

"I'm doing what I can!" Kael yells, yet he backs up until his hips hit the edge of the heavy desk. "I have given him the best quarters in the palace. I'm ensuring him every comfort that—"

"Comfort is no substitute for a cure!" The words tear up my throat. "I don't want soft pillows for his coffin, Kael! I want him to live!"

"There is no cure that does not require a price I am unwilling to pay."

"Then you're useless!" I charge forward, slamming my fists into his hard chest. A sob follows, sorrow grinding my voice down to a whisper. "If you adore me so much, then save him for me. Please..."

Kael stares at me, his chest heaving, his blue eyes swirling with a torture that mirrors my own. "You seem to know a great deal more about this crown of mine than you ought to..."

His words hit me cold and hard, but only for a second. Let him be suspicious. Let him worry that I'm part of his brother's scheme. What does it even matter? Might as well be blunt.

"People are dying, Kael." I swallow past a knot in my throat. "Please, just...feed the curse. Save this realm."

I see the temptation flare there—the desperate urge to say yes, to take the offering, to trade my life for the salvation of his conscience.

Until he closes his eyes, a muscle feathering in his jaw with a terrible resolve. "No," he whispers, the word heavy as a tombstone. He grips my shoulders, not to pull me close, but to hold me steady. "I will not feed it, Elara. I will not watch another innocent woman bleed out. This curse ends with me. I will make it end."

The nobility of it makes me want to scream. "How?" I demand, breaking his grip. "How will you end it? With what plan? With what power?"

Kael opens his mouth. Closes it. Opens it again.

He stands there, helpless and empty-handed, and I realize with a jolt of horror that he has absolutely no idea, no plan. It's just a fairytale to him, isn't it? A wish cast into a well with no bottom so he can sleep at night while my brother suffocates.

"You have nothing," I whisper, the realization heavier than the rejection, dragging my gaze down along with my shoulders. "You have nothing but hope, and hope is going to—"

My eyes snap to the desk. To the parchment, the ink still glistening in the candlelight, the script jagged and rushed —*hide her, and hide her well. Prepare the rite. He cannot find her, or—*

Kael snatches the letter from the desk, crumpling the parchment in his fist. He advances on me, his exhaustion replaced by a fury so pure, so hostile, that I instinctively scramble away from him.

"You will forget what you saw," he snarls, looming over me, his shadow swallowing the light. "Do you hear me?!"

"Hide whom?" I look up at him, breathless, clinging to this sudden, violent raft in the storm. "Who is *she?* Prepare what? What—"

"If you so much as whisper a word of this..." he hisses, leaning down until his face is inches from mine, his eyes burning with a terrifying promise. "If you tell *anyone* a single syllable of what was on that desk, I'll hang you and your entire family from the portcullis. Do you understand me, Elara?"

I stare at him, trembling, seeing a violence in him that shakes me to the marrow in my bones. "Y-yes..."

"Get out of here," he barks. "Run!"

TWENTY-NINE

Elara

The next morning feels like a throat after a scream —raw and swollen. The chill of the stone seeps through the soles of my shoes, biting into the skin of my heels, but I'm too numb to care. My legs move of their own accord as I turn toward Daron's room.

Run, Kael had said.

And I did run. I ran until my lungs burned and the silk of my stolen gown clung to my sweat-dampened skin. I ran until the heavy oak door of my chamber thudded shut, sealing me in with one brutal truth:

There's nowhere left to run to.

It's fucking over.

I wipe remnants of tears from my cheeks while Kael's threat echoes between my ears. *I will hang you and your entire family from the portcullis.*

My temples ache. I can't decide what frightens me more: Kael's willingness to say such a thing, or how easily those words came. Like they'd been waiting under his tongue the whole time, patient as rot. Should I be shocked?

There have been tells, scattered like bones in the grass. The way he could roar and fling a table. In the gardens, when he spoke of his father, the brutality not an accident of rage, but calculated precision. When I tried to peer through a crack in his secrecy, his warmth turned to stone-cold warning.

So, no, maybe I shouldn't be shocked. Maybe I should be furious with myself for thinking I could outwit a curse, a prince, and his king all at once.

Well, it's over now.

All of it.

I reach the door to Daron's room. At least Kael hasn't chased us off the grounds yet. How long he'll keep up that kindness, I don't know, but I'll take it. I'd rather have Daron die on a comfortable pillow than out there in a wet ditch, with—

Why is his door ajar?

A frown touches my brows. I always close it. To keep the drafts out, to keep the sound of his dying in.

I push the door open, the hinges giving a soft, familiar groan.

The room is still dim, lit only by a single tallow candle sputtering on the bedside table. The shadows it casts are long and jumping, distorted shapes that dance across the walls. But one shadow barely moves.

It hunches over the bed—tall, lean, still. One palm resting on my brother's chest, five fingers splayed with a precision that gnaws a strange hollow into my belly.

My voice is a croak, raspy from the screaming match with Kael. "What are you doing here?"

Vale doesn't jump, doesn't snatch his hand away like a thief caught in a larder. He lifts it slowly, deliberately, his fingers trailing off the linen sheet covering Daron's heaving chest. He turns to me, his face a mask of smooth, pale indifference in the candlelight.

"Checking on him," he says softly.

For a breath, I can't move. Probably because the sight doesn't make sense. Vale has never been the type to check on anyone who isn't useful. Vale is a man who counts outcomes, not heartbeats.

"Since when?" I ask, and I hate that my voice trembles on the edge of the question. "Why would you care?"

"Always so suspicious of me." He sighs as if I'm being difficult over the weather. "Yesterday, you curled into me like you belonged there. Now, you're acting as if I'm your enemy all over again."

The words hit a place in me that's already scraped, making my distrust lose its teeth. Because it's true. I *did* curl into him. I *did* enjoy his fingers comb through my hair until the world stopped spinning.

I swallow hard. What if I've been wrong about him this whole time? Vale is cruel, yes—scheming, selfish, sharp as a blade—but he never threatened to hang my family.

Kael did.

"If anyone saw you coming to this room, they'd wonder, you know. As if things aren't bad enough already." I step fully into the room, the floorboards creaking under my weight as I nod at Daron. "He's asleep?"

"Passed out," Vale corrects. He tilts his head, studying me. "Forgive me for saying, but you look terrible."

I shift my jaw, forcing the words into shape...but courage dies in my throat. How much do I tell Vale? Is there even still anything to gain by saying anything at all? Considering that, if I say too much, my family might full well lose their lives.

My teeth dig into my upper lip until it throbs, but I eventually say, "Kael won't lift his crown."

Vale's expression stills.

Then he blinks. "Pardon me?"

"I went to his chamber," I say, each word dragged out under strain. "I tried to...make him."

Vale's jaw tightens so subtly I almost miss it, the muscle jumping once beneath his cheekbone. "Make...him?"

"Sleep with me." I don't know why my gaze flicks to Daron's ribs rising and falling as if I'm confessing disloyalty here. As if that hadn't been the plan all along. "He wanted it. He had me on the table by the hearth, hands everywhere, ready to—"

"Uh-huh." Vale's gaze drifts to the floor, jaw shifting once, as though he's chewing something he'd rather spit out. "I don't recall asking for details."

I look at him for a breath too long, considering there's no room here for the jealousy of a man who eagerly plots me toward my death, however it may come. "He stopped. And... and he got angry."

Vale's eyes find my face again, but something in them sharpens—green going darker, colder. "Angry."

"Furious. We argued. I...I was desperate, and I just..." Heat crawls up my neck, ugly with shame. "When he realized I knew more than I should—when I begged him to feed the curse—he..." My throat tries to close, but I force it open. "He said the curse will end with him."

Vale goes very still. Then he gives a soft, humorless laugh that contains no amusement at all. "How? How will it end with him?"

"I don't know." My mind goes back to when I asked Kael that very thing. How he looked at me. How his mouth opened and closed, but no explanation came out. No hope. "I saw it in his eyes, the helplessness. But..."

But the letter.

If he truly has nothing—if it's all just stubbornness dressed up as nobility—then why snatch the page like that? Why the secrecy? Why the threat? Is that the behavior of a man with no plan?

My stomach tightens.

I just... I don't know.

"But what?" Vale's gaze drops to my mouth, like he's scanning it for bruises that aren't there. When he looks back up, his voice is almost mild. "What else was said? Did you find out anything about the situation with the messenger? What they spoke of?"

The bruise on my hip pulses like a second heartbeat to the cadence of Kael's threat. If I tell Vale about the letter, then Kael could make good on his threat. I stare at Daron's slack face, at the shallow, rattling rise of his chest, and something in me goes cold.

We're dead either way, aren't we?

"I found out something." I swallow, because there's no un-saying it once it's loose. "He was writing a letter. I saw a few lines before he snatched it."

Vale's gaze narrows slightly. "Saying what?"

My molars clench together once. Twice. "Hide her, and hide her well. Prepare the rite. He cannot find her, or—"

"Or what?"

"That's it. It's as far as I got." Before he crumpled it as if his life depended on it. "It's meaningful enough for him that he threatened to hang me and my family if I told anyone."

His jaw works once, hard. He takes a step, then another, the room suddenly too small to hold him. He paces once along the foot of the bed, boots whispering over the boards.

The stove crackles.

The candle flickers.

Vale's fingers flex and relax at his sides as if searching for a hilt that isn't there. "Hide her," he repeats, quieter now, tasting the words like poison. "Prepare the rite. He cannot find her. Heritage..." He stops. His head tilts, eyes unfocusing as something slots into place behind them. "Original...translation."

"Vale?" My voice cracks on his name. "What is it? What does it mean?"

His eyes widen—just a fraction, but enough to turn my stomach. Not anger, not shock, but in recognition. The kind that arrives with a cost. He looks at me, and for the first time since I met him, his composure slips into something like urgency.

"Stay here," he says, too sharp. "Do not do *anything*, do you understand?"

"What—"

He yanks the door open, cold corridor air rushing in, and strides out as if chased. "I have to go."

I lunge after him, skidding on the boards, the hem of my dress snapping around my ankles. "Vale!" I hiss, stumbling into the hallway. "Tell me what you—"

A sound cuts through my words—wet, strangled, wrong.

I whip around.

Daron.

He's convulsing on the bed, shoulders jerking, mouth open as if trying to pull air through mud. A gray-black blob slides from the corner of his lips, thick as paste, and dribbles down onto the sheet in a slow, obscene rope. He makes a sound like a choke half-swallowed, fingers clawing weakly at the blanket.

"No—Daron!" I sprint back, dropping to the bedside, shoving pillows up behind him with shaking hands. "Breathe, you idiot. *Breathe.*"

I lift his head, careful, keeping him angled so whatever is in his throat can spill out instead of drown him. The smell hits—rot and iron and something sour that makes my eyes sting.

Behind me, the corridor stays empty. Footsteps don't return.

The only sound left is my brother's wet rattle. My hands are slick with gray filth, the stain spreading across clean sheets as if the palace itself is bleeding him out.

CHAPTER

THIRTY

Elara

Two days bleed into one another, gray and suffocating.

They're long, dull stretches where the sun doesn't quite rise and the clocks in the palace seem to tick slower, as if the rot in the walls has infected time itself. I move in a daze between Daron's room, Mother's, and my own, a ghost haunting a corridor of dying things.

Two days of not seeing either man.

My nerves are frayed ropes, snapping with every

shadow that shifts. The pot I brought Daron earlier is empty—eaten or spilled, I don't know. So I go back down.

I carry the empty pot through the twilight of the lower hallways. The servants I pass keep their heads down, eyes averted. They know. Everyone knows that something is wrong—a tension that has all our spines straightened.

I push open the heavy oak door leading to the kitchens, but the usual clamor of pots and pans is gone. It's late, the fires are banked. I get the broth, ladle it out, head back.

My path takes me past the greenhouse. The glass structure looms in the gathering dark, condensation weeping down the panes, blurring the twisted shapes of shadows.

I grip the pot tighter, the ceramic hot against my palms, and quicken my pace. I just want to get back to Daron. I just want—

Metal clanks somewhere.

I jolt, nearly dropping the soup as a figure stumbles out of the humid dark, silhouetted against the moonlight. He sways, catches himself on the frame, and then lurches forward. Toward me.

"You!" The roar is slurry, thick with rage and liquor.

He looks like a ruin all over again, his white shirt unbuttoned halfway down his chest, stained dark with wine or dirt. His hair is a tangled golden mess, and his eyes...his eyes are bloodshot pits of fury, burning with a frantic, unhinged light.

"Kael?" I take a step back, fear prickling up my spine. "Your Majesty, you're—"

"You ruined it!" He lunges at me, closing the distance with terrifying speed for a man who sways.

I gasp, stumbling backward.

He's faster.

Kael grabs my upper arm, his fingers digging into my

flesh. The pot slips from my hands, hitting the stone with a wet, heavy crack. Pottery shatters. Hot broth splashes over my boots and the hem of my dress, but Kael doesn't even flinch.

"You ruined *everything!*" he bellows, shaking me. His breath hits my face, a noxious cloud of sour wine. "Everything I laid out. Everything I held in place. Everything I was about to—"

"Let go of me!" I struggle, clawing at his hand, but his grip is iron. "Kael, you're drunk!"

"Drunk?" He laughs, a harsh, jagged sound that scrapes against the glass walls. "You stupid harlot!"

He shoves me backward.

I stumble, my back slamming against the metal frame of the greenhouse so hard the glass panes rattle in their casings. Pain flares in my shoulder, but fear eclipses it instantly. I've seen him angry before, but this is different. This isn't the rage of a king; this is the flailing violence of a drunk.

"I don't know what you're talking about!" I cry, pressing myself against the glass.

"Liar!" He slams a hand against the pane beside my head. "I know where you've been. I know what you've been doing." He leans in, his nose inches from mine, his eyes swimming with a toxic mix of hatred and tears. "Under the sheets with that...that bastard!"

The blood drains from my face.

I don't understand. Is he accusing me of plotting with Vale? That's high treason. Or did Miss Hampshire report what she saw at the bottom of the tower? That's disloyalty. I don't know which one it is. Between the two, I'd rather defend myself for the latter.

"It...it wasn't like that," I stammer, my heart

hammering against my ribs. I have to fix this. I have to talk him down, or this will end badly. "Kael, please, listen to me. I went to him, yes, but—"

"So you admit it?" He looks at me with wide, horrified eyes, as if I just confessed to murder. "You admit you let that bastard...corrupt you?"

"I didn't let him corrupt anything!" I cry out, desperate to calm him. "I went to his tower to ask him about the curse!"

Kael stares at me. He blinks once, twice, the information processing slowly through the haze of alcohol. "Tower?"

"Y-yes," I stammer. "He...he kissed me, but I pulled away! Kael, I swear to you, nothing else happened."

His expression twists. The horror deepens, liquefying into a nausea so profound he looks ready to retch. "Repeat that."

"Nothing else happened! I swear—"

"Not that!" he roars, his voice trembling. "He kissed you!?"

"Just once!" I plead, the lie spilling out, desperate to save my skin. "I swear, Kael, nothing more happened! I wouldn't betray you like that. I pushed him away immediately!"

Silence stretches thin and taut.

Then he starts to laugh.

It starts low in his chest, a rumble of disbelief, before erupting into a full-blown, hysterical cackle. He throws his head back, laughing at the dark sky, at the glass, at me.

It's a chilling, broken sound.

Loud. Unhinged.

The fine hairs on my arms stand up. "I swear, I rejected him immediately."

He laughs even harder. His head tips back again, throat

exposed, crown glinting cruelly in the moonlight. Then he drops his chin and looks at me again, and whatever is in his eyes makes my blood freeze over.

"You...told...him." His face contorts, rage snapping his features tight. "You told him about the letter!"

"I didn't!" The denial flies out before I can think.

"Liar!"

He lunges. This time, there's no clumsy stumble. He slams me back against the greenhouse glass with a force that squeezes my lungs, one pane cracking. His hands clamp onto my shoulders, fingers digging past the cotton, bruising the muscle.

"Where is she?" he bellows, his face twisting into jagged lines of pure aggression. He shoves me again, my head thudding painfully against the metal frame. "Where did he take her, huh? Tell me!"

"Take who?" I'm sobbing now, terror replacing confusion. "I don't know who you're talking about!"

"Don't play the fool!" He releases one shoulder, only to grab my jaw, forcing my head up, his thumb digging into my cheekbone hard enough to bring tears to my eyes. "Did he hurt her?" His voice cracks, fracturing on nothing short of panic. "Answer me! Is she dead?"

"I don't even know who she is!" I shriek, my hands flailing uselessly against his madness. "Kael, stop! You're hurting me!"

He draws back his other hand, looking like he might strike me, but instead he slams his fist into the glass beside my ear. *Crash!* Shards rain down on us, glittering and sharp as he screams, "Where is she?!"

I scream, cowering away, covering my head. "I don't know. Your brother never said!"

Kael freezes. "My what?"

"He told me everything," I whimper, the words tumbling out of me as my mind claws for the nearest rope. "That Maeryn was his mother. How you stole his crown—and I don't blame you! I don't!" My voice cracks, a sob threatening to spill, and I seize it, turn it into something sharper. "That's how he got to me, alright? He made me pity him, but I swear, the kiss meant nothing!"

Kael just stares. His mouth hangs open slightly, releasing a single scoff before he gives a slow shake of his head. "The audacity of that bastard."

Then he starts laughing again. But this isn't the hysterical laughter of before; this is darker, sharper. It sounds like bones snapping.

"He stole my misery!" Kael spits, voice shaking with rage. "He took *my* mother's blood, *my* childhood, *my* nightmares—just so you'd open your goddamn mouth for him!"

His last shout has me jump all over again. "What?"

"I have no brother!" Kael steps closer, eyes blazing, blue turned almost black in torchlight. "My father had one son. Me!"

"But...Maeryn..." No. None of this makes any sense. "He told me that the curse went to the wrong person, that the bloodline was no longer intact. He told me that Maeryn was his mother."

"Maeryn was *my* mother!" Kael strikes his chest, the sound hollow and hard. "She never held me, never kissed me. Never even fucking looked at me, but yes, that bitch birthed me."

My breath hitches. "No...that's—"

"I watched her die!" His voice shatters on the last word, then hardens again. "I watched as my father cut her throat in the royal chamber. Ran to her. Tried to make her look at me. And then..." He shakes his head, laugh turning ragged. "Then my *true* mother came to the palace."

My veins freeze over. Not the one who birthed him—the one who finally showed him love.

"Ophelia," I whisper, voice snagging on that name like cloth on a nail.

"They brought me to the painter's chamber." His voice is soft, nothing but a whisper. "Told me to sit still. Told me to smile. Told me to take her hand so we'd look...like a family." He drags the back of his hand across his mouth like he can wipe the memory off. He can't. "I wouldn't. I didn't know her. I didn't want her touching me. I thought—" Kael's gaze goes unfocused, like he's seeing that sunlit room again: dust in the air, paint on cloth, the smell of oils and old wood. "She reached into her sleeve," he says, and his mouth trembles. "And she pulled out a stupid little toy —boxwood, carved into a horse. Blue thread at its mane." His breath breaks on a sound that might have been a laugh in another life. "A ridiculous thing. A child's thing. She held it out like it was treasure."

The memory of that diary entry slams into my chest, heart cracking clean down the middle. "Kael..."

"She smiled at me. Not a polite smile for court, not a painted one. A real one." He squeezes his eyes shut, and when he opens them again, they're drowning. "And she looked at me—really looked. So, I stole a rose," he says. "From the greenhouse. Thorns bit me, and I didn't care. I carried it to her room like I was bringing her a treasure, too." His eyes squeeze shut again, tears spilling faster now. "And when I held it out...she sneezed. God, she sneezed so damn hard I thought she'd shake the walls down." A wet laugh slips through the sob and dies immediately. "She thanked me, and she put that stupid rose in a vase in her room and just…kept sneezing."

The pieces of the puzzle clash together in my mind, pressing into alignment. The painting. How he refused to take Ophelia's hand at first. How could I have missed this?

"I tried to save her. I interfered. I begged. I threatened." Kael looks back at me then, and the devastation in his gaze is so naked it feels like a wound. "And after I watched her die, too, I erased Maeryn from my lineage and put Ophelia in the place she deserved." Kael steps in close again, breath hot and bitter. "And I swore I would break this curse."

Kael's face twists, the softness of memory snapping. The tears on his lashes don't dry; they sharpen, turning into something that looks too much like hate.

"And I was close." He jabs a finger at my chest, hard enough that it thumps my ribs through the fabric. "Until you ruined *everything!*"

My chest curls in on itself. "I don't know what I did."

"Oh, I know." Kael steps closer, breath sour with drink and fury, eyes bright with a manic, terrible clarity. "From the beginning, I suspected that he sent you, albeit a bit more delicately than how he tried to shove that kitchen girl into my bed. I let him think I'm smitten with you…and perhaps I am." The cold tip of his nose presses against my temple, letting a shudder pebble my skin with how he's inhaling me. "I needed him sure that his plan was working. I needed him distracted. Because I had it laid out!" His voice fractures into a shout so violent, it makes the torches tremble. "And then you—" He grabs my shoulders and shakes once, hard enough my teeth click. "What did he do with her?!"

My stomach drops through the floorboards. "Kael, I don't know who you're talking about. I don't know what he did with—" My voice breaks on a shake of breath I can't control. "I swear, I thought Vale was your brother. Who is *he?*"

"Vale? Is that what he calls himself?" His chuckle vibrates through those fingers he still clamps around my shoulders with bruising strength. "Oh, you stupid, stupid girl." The whites of his eyes gleam in the torchlight, red-rimmed and wild. Then he leans in, his sharp breath scraping my skin as he whispers, "There is a place every soul goes to eventually, the low ground where gold means nothing and blood means everything. He owns that place; he rules it. And he waits for us there, in the valley of death."

For a heartbeat, I don't understand those words. They're nonsense. Noise. They slide past my ears like water past stone. Until the last one lands.

Death.

The air leaves my lungs in a thin, useless pull. My stomach turns as if the floor dropped out from under me, and for a moment, I swear I can feel the imprint of Vale's hands all over again—warm on my waist, fingers in my hair, his mouth at my throat—only now the memory curdles, wrong in a way I can't name.

"No." No, that's impossible. "You're...you're drunk. You're angry, and you're drunk, and you're trying to scare me."

But then why is my skin prickling everywhere? Why is cold sweat licking my spine? Why does my throat tighten until swallowing hurts? And didn't the entry of Ophelia's coronation mention Death? If he appeared in his *divine* form...doesn't that indicate there's another?

No. It can't be.

"It's not true." My knees threaten to fold, so I brace a

hand against the greenhouse frame, fingers trembling so hard they scrape glass. "He's a man. He... he cried."

Kael's grip doesn't loosen. If anything, it steadies, like he's holding me up just to watch me break. "Did he?" he murmurs, and the softness in it is cruelty. "Or did he show you water, and you called it tears?"

My vision blurs. I blink hard, but it doesn't clear. It only makes the torchlight smear into streaks, like blood on stone. I shake my head because that's all I have. Denial. Stubbornness. The desperate need for this not to be true.

Because if it is...

If it is, then I didn't just make a mistake. I didn't just betray Kael. Didn't just ruin whatever plan he had.

I opened my body to Death.

"He *is* a bastard," Kael spits. "But not of blood. He's a bastard because he feels no love. No guilt, no sorrow. He feels nothing at all because he...has...no...heart." Scoffing, his fingers finally ease their grip, arms falling uselessly by his sides. "Lure him into the moonlight."

My breath stumbles. "What?"

"Your...*lover*." He smiles too wide, a grotesque stretch on a mouth that twists from amusement to rage and back again. "Let moonlight touch him and show you what he really is."

He looks down at me. The drunkenness seems to settle over him again, a heavy blanket weighing down his limbs. He blinks, his eyes glazing over. Then he drops hard against the greenhouse frame and slides down, hair falling across his face.

"You ruined it," he mumbles again, softer now, almost like a child repeating a grievance into a pillow as I step back.

Step back further.
Turn. Run.

255

THIRTY-ONE

Elara

I don't look back.

Not at the king slumped against glass and iron. Not at the shards glittering on the stone like teeth. Instead, I run.

I run until my lungs burn, past a startled guard, past the dark windows, and I don't stop until I crash into my chamber. My hands shake violently as I throw the heavy bolt, locking the door.

Leaning against the wood, I slide down until my knees

hit the floor. My breath comes in jagged, tearing gasps that sound too loud in the silence.

A silence interrupted by a voice coming from the dark, low and smooth, scraping down my spine like a cold knife. "There you are."

I scream, scrambling up and spinning around. "Who—"

Vale is sitting in my wingback chair by the dying fire, one leg crossed over the other, his black riding boots gleaming in the low light. He holds a book in one hand, his finger marking the page as if I've interrupted a quiet evening of reading.

The firelight kisses his cheekbones and leaves his eyes half-shadowed—moss-green, unreadable, calm. "Did I startle you?"

"How—" My voice is a wreck. I can't breathe. "When did you get back? What did you do?"

He closes the book with a soft *thud* and places it on the side table. His gaze drifts over me—the broth on my skirt, the trembling in my hands. "Why do you look panicked? What happened?"

"Answer me."

"Very well." He rises in one smooth motion that makes my pulse trip, arms clasped behind his back as he slowly walks toward me. "I returned only now and came straight to see you. As for what I did..." He stops a few paces away. "I'm afraid my brother has been fooling both of us all along, feigning that he's coming to his senses, only to keep me distracted from his own scheme."

When he takes another step toward me, my finger digs into the bolt behind my back. "Scheme?"

"That foolishness he calls a plan to break the curse." His lip curls slightly. "Kael has convinced himself that there's a loophole—a secret back door to the curse that involves dragging a distant relative into this mess, a cousin a million times removed."

My throat goes dry. "The infamous *her*."

"Yes, her," he says. "I found a farm girl with no idea of the anvil Kael wanted to drop on her head, no understanding of his delusions about how Death could be outwitted if one only"—his mouth twists—"...arranged the proper theatrics. So I dealt with it."

My pulse thuds in my throat. "Did you kill her?"

"Why would I kill an innocent girl over my brother's madness?" His eyes narrow. "I found her at the place where he hid her and simply relocated the girl to somewhere far from Kael's nonsensical delusion. Perhaps now he will come to his senses."

I look at Vale.

He stands there, solid and composed, his breathing even, his expression one of mild, weary annoyance at his brother's antics. He sounds so reasonable. So terribly, seductively logical compared to the raving, broken man who just passed out drunk at the greenhouse. What if Kael is the one lying? What if the king, drunk on desperation and wine, invented a nightmare to hurt me? To punish me for ruining his foolish plan?

My gaze drifts past Vale's shoulder, seeking the windows, seeking the moonlight that Kael claims will bring out the truth. Where's the outside?

My breath hitches in my throat. Heavy cotton curtains draw across the windows, the threadbare tassels motionless.

I didn't close them. I left with them open earlier and hurried to Daron right as the sun set, its stark spills of purple and orange still vivid in my mind. But the curtains are shut now.

He closed them.

Vale's gaze slides over his shoulder to a window, to a narrow strip of moonlight cutting the floor where the curtains don't quite meet. Something tightens at the corner of his mouth. Then he looks at me again as though the sight merely bored him.

"Why are you like this tonight? Tense. Trembling." He creeps toward me, slow enough it pretends to be harmless while the air seems to thin, growing sharp and cold. "Don't let this get under your skin, Elara. Kael's little...farce is over. Even he will realize it." He lifts his hand, tucking a strand of hair behind my ear, fingers hovering a breath from my cheek. "One way or another, we can still somehow feed the crown."

My shoulders stay pinned to the door, bolt biting into my spine. I can't tell which madness to believe. My eyes flick to the curtains again. Only a lunatic would put such a ridiculous thing to the test—and that I want to might make my madness the worst of them all.

"We can use his desperation." Vale strokes his fingers down my side until they reach my waist. He pulls me into him, burying his face in the crook of my neck, where his breath ghosts over my pulse. "With the girl gone, he has no other moves to make. He'll come around now. It's not a defeat, my love. It's barely even a delay."

My love. The words land warm at first, soft as a blanket pulled up over shaking shoulders, so familiar in his mouth that my body tries to melt into it before my mind can protest.

And then the echo twists. It crawls backward through my skull and catches on Kael's voice, raw and furious in the greenhouse. *That bastard doesn't have a heart!*

Does he not?

My hand lifts of its own accord and lands on his chest—flat palm to warm skin through linen, right over the steady thud beneath.

A heartbeat. Relentless. Real.

But what if it's not?

My gaze slides past his shoulder again. I have to know. Have to open those curtains somehow and let the moon show me just where the madness lands.

"I missed you." Vale's mouth finds mine.

He kisses me slowly, with patient pressure that turns into certainty the moment my lips part. His hand cups the back of my head, fingers threading into my hair, and the warmth of him presses against me. His other arm bands around my waist, drawing me off the bolt and into his chest until I'm no longer braced for flight.

"There," he murmurs against my mouth. "That's better."

I should shove him away.

Instead, my hands lift and settle against his shoulders like they belong there. Like they remember him. Like they don't care what he is, only that his closeness makes my panic soften at the edges.

He tilts my chin and kisses along the hinge of my jaw, down to my throat, mouth warm at my pulse. "Take me to your bed."

I swallow hard, gaze flicking to the window. There's one beside the bed, but there has to be a better way.

It's not difficult to make my voice sound strained when I whisper, "It's...hot in here."

Vale hums against my throat. "Mm-hmm."

"I need air." I make it light, casual. Nothing but discomfort. "Let me open the window."

I start to turn my head toward it, shifting my shoulders

as if I'm about to step away. My fingers slide from his chest, reaching—

Vale catches my wrist.

Not painful, but firm enough that my bones feel held. He draws my hand back to his body and pins it there as if it never belonged anywhere else. "The wind is biting."

My breath stutters. "Is it?"

He answers by kissing me harder. His hand leaves my wrist and slides under my dress, palm pressing to the bare skin at my waist. The contact is a tingling shock. He drags his hand up, slow and sure, as if he's taking his time to teach my body where to respond.

I hate that it responds. Hate that my breath catches and my hips press forward without permission.

Vale feels it and makes a soft, pleased sound against my mouth. His other hand finds the tie of my dress and tugs it loose with maddening patience. The flimsy thing parts and falls to my hips, baring skin to his gaze.

"Vale..." My voice is thin, half protest, half surrender. "It's stifling in here."

His hands slide down my sides, pushing the dress to the floor, letting it expose my body to the firelight. He leans down, warm lips closing over a nipple with a slow pull that snaps a sound out of me before I can stop it.

My head tips back. My fingers clutch at his hair, and I force myself to keep my eyes open, to keep looking past him.

Window. Bed.

It's the only option.

I pull back just enough to lift my hands to the collar of his shirt. My fingers tremble as I work the first button, then the others, before I shove it down his arms. I undo the buckle on his breeches with frantic haste, working the leather down until he slips out of his boots and kicks it all away.

I close my hand around his cock, the flesh hard, warm, and weeping in my grip. "I want you inside me."

Vale's breath grows heavier as he lifts me, hands sure under my thighs, and carries me toward the bed. He lowers me onto the mattress, climbs over me, and the weight of him pins my breath in my chest in a way that feels like safety and a threat tangled together.

He settles between my thighs, the heavy wool of his trousers rough against my sensitive skin, but the heat of him is searing. There's no muscle-trembling patience this time. He simply lines himself up, thick and heavy against my entrance, and pushes forward.

I gasp, my back arching off the mattress as he fills me. He's massive, stretching me to the limit, a blunt, over-whelming invasion that feels agonizingly good. He sinks in to the hilt in one slow, relentless slide, reclaiming every inch of space inside me until there's no room left for air, for thought, for fear.

Vale groans, a ragged, broken sound dropped against my neck. "Saints…Elara. I needed this. Needed to feel you around me again. It's been on my mind for days."

He withdraws and snaps his hips forward, burying himself deep again, and a shudder rakes through his heavy frame that vibrates straight into my bones. He moves with a predator's grace—efficient, powerful, deeper than any man has a right to reach. Each thrust is a calculated collision, hitting a spot deep inside me that makes my toes curl and my vision blur.

"So perfect," he grits out, his voice thick with pleasure. He catches my lip between his teeth, biting down just hard enough to sting, grounding me in the sensation. "You feel... there are no words."

I whimper, my hands clutching his shoulders, my nails digging in. My body is singing under him, melting around him, treacherous and eager. But my mind is still screaming.

The curtain!

Through the haze of lust, I spot it. The heavy panel hangs just to the right of the bed. I reach out. If I can just snag the fabric...if I can just pull it back...a...few—

Vale thrusts.

Hard.

The impact shatters my efforts like glass. A moan punches out of my throat, and my hand falls uselessly back to the sheets, my grip failing as pleasure blinds me white. He grinds against me, his hips rolling, hitting that nerve with merciless precision until I'm utterly wrecked beneath him.

I can't do this. His weight is a mountain pressing me down, pinning me into the sheets. As long as I'm beneath him, I'm powerless.

I need leverage.

"Vale..." I gasp, my hands finding his chest and pushing, shoving against the solid wall of him. "Let me."

He freezes mid-thrust, his breathing choked. He looks down at me, hair falling into his eyes, his pupils blown wide so the green is merely a thin, burning rim. "Let you what?"

"I want to be on top," I whisper, the lie sliding over my tongue with terrified ease.

Surprise flickers across his face, followed by a flare of dark, possessive heat. He withdraws slowly, agonizingly, leaving me empty and aching for a split second before he shifts. He falls back against the pillows, spreading his arms wide in invitation, looking up at me like a man about to be devoured.

"By all means," he rasps. "Take *exactly* what you need and want."

I scramble over him, straddling his hips. The change in dynamic is instantaneous. Beneath me, he looks devastating—throat bared, slick chest heaving, his body a sprawling landscape of muscle and shadow.

I sink down onto him.

He hisses through his teeth, his head tipping back into the pillows, his neck arching. "*Yes...*"

I begin to move.

At first, it's just to find the rhythm, to keep him distracted, but the sensation is overwhelming. He's so big, so hard, filling me so completely that I forget to breathe. I ride him, grinding down, and his hands come up to grip my hips.

Not to control me.

But to anchor himself.

He watches me for a moment, his gaze dark and heavy with adoration, before his lashes flutter shut. The sight of him unraveling is intoxicating—the sheen of sweat on his skin, the flushed heat of his throat, the way his lips part on a silent groan as I pick up the pace.

I lean forward, bracing my hands on his chest, dropping my head so my hair curtains us both. I ride him harder, faster, chasing the friction, chasing the way his hips snap up to meet mine.

I'm close. To the edge.

To the truth.

"Elara," he groans, his voice ruined. He reaches blindly for me, his hands sliding up my ribs.

Now.

My hand shoots out. My fingers tangle in the heavy fabric of the curtain. I grip it tight. I look down at him one last time—at the beautiful man beneath me.

Then I yank. Hard.

The curtain rings shriek against the rod, letting the heavy fabric fly open. And the moon, sharp and brilliant as a blade, slashes across skin more pallid than a corpse. It stretches across exposed ribs in some places; in others, only sinew, wet and ropey, banding across a frame where strings of flesh cling.

Shoulders broaden with a deep, cracking roll. Limbs lengthen beneath me, joints stretching, bones clicking into new angles as if the shape of a man was never more than a cramped garment he finally shrugged off.

I freeze, perched on Death, my thighs braced against something that is no longer soft flesh, but unyielding bone —mandible, sternum, ribs, and tendons that don't give.

A scream rips out of me—raw, too big for the size of my throat. It's just air shredded into pure terror.

He's a monster!

I scramble off him. My feet find air where floor should be, and I tumble, hips slamming down onto the boards, the impact jolting through my spine and knocking another sharp cry from my mouth.

The bed lurches under the sudden shift as he jumps out. The rafters shrink around him.

"Elara…" His voice is bone and wind and something ancient dragging itself through a throat, coming from a skull where a man's features should be: cheekbones hollowed on one side, nasal cavity a shadowed notch, pale skin draping in patches over sinew exposed and shifting at the jaw. "Do not—"

"No!" I scoot backward on my hands, frantic, breath

coming in ragged, choking bursts. "Don't come near me. Don't…d-don't touch me!"

His eyes take me in.

Not green.

Not even eyes.

Just black, endless pits that swallow the moonlight instead of reflecting it. Long fingers unfurl, bone and tendon moving under strain, and the motion alone detonates my panic.

"No!" I scramble on hands and knees, nails scraping wood, and throw myself under the table by the hearth like it's a sanctuary. "Don't touch me!" The words tear out of me ragged and shapeless, more sound than language. "Don't—get away, get away, get away—" My own voice is unrecognizable, pitched too high and climbing higher, the kind of sound that fills a room and bounces back wrong. I press myself into the corner where the table leg meets the wall and pull my knees to my chest. "Go away, go away. *Go away!*"

A bare heel bone grinds against the wooden floorboards. Darkness bleeds together, weaving into black cloth. An exposed knuckle clicks as he turns away. A skeletal hand reaches for the door.

The latch lifts.

Cold air rushes in.

The door slams shut, the terror that screamed through my blood pitching down, dropping from panic into a heavy, suffocating shock.

I curl my knees to my chest and rock, back and forth, hands clawing at my arms, fingers digging into dead-cold skin. The room blurs, the shadows beneath the table stretching up to pull me down.

THIRTY-TWO

Elara

Something clamps around my wrist.

I jolt awake with a scream, jerking so hard my elbow cracks the underside of the table. Pain flashes bright as I scramble backward, knees scraping over the floorboards, pressing my spine into the corner of the wall.

The hand grips my wrist tighter. "Don't!"

Not bone and wind.

Human. Hoarse. Frantic.

My eyes drag open. I blink, my chest heaving, my vision

swimming in the gray, watery light of dawn. Did I fall to sleep?

"Did Death tell you that the bloodline is already compromised?" Kael crouches on the floor, peering under the table, his hair tangled around the crown and his face drained of all color. "Last night by the greenhouse. Is that something you told me? That the curse once went to the wrong person?"

The terror of that memory clashes over me like a wave. "What?"

I stare at him, my heart hammering loud enough to drown out the morning birdsong, the cold air biting where my skin is bare. Bare. Everywhere.

My breath catches. I'm naked, my dress left somewhere in the wreck of my chamber. I instinctively curl tighter, thighs clenching, free arm crossing my breasts as if my hands can hide what the table's shadow cannot.

"Elara!" Kael shouts, glancing over his shoulder at the door for a second before his blue gaze finds mine again. "What did Death tell you?!"

I flinch so hard my shoulder scrapes the wall, breath fluttering out of me in a thin, panicked gasp. "Don't come closer!"

Kael freezes.

He drops my wrist and holds both hands up, palms open, fingers splayed. "I'm sorry." Then, just as quickly, his eyes jerk away from the rest of me, as if decency can be restored by not looking. "I didn't mean to shout. I'm not—" A shaky breath. "On all that's dear to me, I'm not here to hurt you."

He inches back from the table, giving me space, lowering himself onto his shins like he's trying to make himself smaller. "Look at me," he says, quieter, stealing a sideways glance at my face. "I am ashamed of how I acted last night. I was drunk. Utterly hopeless." His jaw tightens. "But I need you now, and I have no time to be gentle about it, but I won't hurt you." He extends a hand into the shadows beneath the table. Palm up, trembling slightly. "Elara, if you ever saw any decency in me at all, hold on to it now. I beg you."

I'm disoriented, in pain from who knows how many hours of sleeping curled under the table, and yet I see the quiver in his fingers. I don't know what's happening. But between a drunk madman and a lying monster, there's no true choice, is there? Might as well...

I reach out and grip his hand. "What do you want?"

Kael grips me back, his fingers interlocking with mine, solid and warm as he carefully guides me out from under the table. "What did Death tell you about the curse having transferred to the wrong person?"

"Only that and no more." I try to scramble out. "He said that—"

My legs buckle. Cramps shoot through my calves, seizing up my muscles until I pitch forward in a cry of pain.

Kael catches me.

He sweeps me up into his arms, holding me high against his chest—careful to angle his gaze away—then stands, stumbling slightly under the weight before correcting his balance. "He said what?"

He pivots and snatches the nearest blanket from the foot of the bed with one swift yank, the wool unfurling in a heavy rush. It drapes over my naked body like a shield, tucking in tight around my shoulders and hips by brisk, practiced hands.

"That...that the royal family is no longer pure," I say. "Or intact. Something like that, I don't remember."

"I knew it! God, I knew it." He spins us toward the door. "We don't have time. We have to get to the knife before he senses that something's amiss."

"Knife?" I gasp, clutching the blanket as he strides through the door into the cold corridor. "Where are we going?"

"The throne room."

I stare at him, terrified and confused. "Why? What is happening?"

He rushes through the hallway almost at a run, his boots thudding heavily on the carpet. "Did you fuck?"

I stiffen in his arms. "What?"

"Elara, this is no time for modesty or propriety or any of that nonsense." He looks down at me, his expression intense, uncomfortably sharp, searching my face with desperate urgency. "Did you only kiss Death? Or did you lie with him?"

I open my mouth to deny it, to defend the shred of dignity I have left. But the lie dies in my throat, letting the terrible truth echo in my silence.

Kael lets out a sound very similar to his hysterical laugh last night and finishes with a scoff. "That is...unheard of. Never, in all the histories, in all the journals of my ancestors, did Death take a lover." He picks up speed, his strides gaining a manic, overwhelming energy. "This couldn't be more perfect."

"I don't understand."

"I figured it out," he breathes, his shoulders tightening occasionally from the strain of carrying me. "I figured out how to break the curse. It isn't about paying the debt, Elara. It's about ending it at the source."

"What does that even—"

A side door to our left flies open. A figure rushes out,

skirts flying, hair pinned back in a severe bun. Miss Hampshire.

"Is it ready?" Kael demands without stopping, continuing to rush along a vast gallery. "Did you prepare everything for the rite?"

My stomach bottoms out. "Rite?"

"Yes, Your Majesty." Miss Hampshire falls into step beside Kael, her face pale as parchment but set in grim, terrifying determination. "The knife is prepared. But the priest—I couldn't find Father Thomas. His room was empty. I think...I think he—"

"We need no priest." Kael's words echo off the ceiling that vaults higher with each quick stride. "We must hurry. He'll likely sense his heartstring aching in the crown the moment I grab the knife."

"To do what?" Pure fear floods my muscles, locking them up for a fraction of a second before they snap free, legs kicking, arms scrambling, my entire body thrashing in Kael's arms. "Put me down. Kael, put me down! What is happening? You said you would break the curse!"

"I cannot break this curse." A shove of his shoulders, then he bursts through a set of tall double doors with a violence that cracks the wood near the hinges. Behind it, a red runner guides his wavering steps deeper into the throne room, the echo of a million hurried steps bouncing off the high vaulted ceiling. "No king can."

The words land like a slab of stone dropped onto my chest. My struggles cease. For a heartbeat, I'm nothing but wool and terror in his arms, the realization hitting, slicing through me like a blade.

I'm going to die in here. Now.

Kael reaches the dais—the raised platform where the

throne sits—and finally sets me on my feet. "Stand right here. Don't move. Miss Hampshire!"

She rushes past us to a small table near the throne. There, she unwraps a velvet bundle, the object inside glinting in the pale dawn light filtering through the stained glass. Hilt crusted in gold filigree, steel dark and thirsty.

Miss Hampshire's hands shake so badly she nearly drops the knife before she presses the hilt into Kael's hand. She looks at me once—not with pity, but with a hard, sorrowful respect.

My knees wobble as I clutch the woolen blanket to my body, the stone floor freezing against my bare soles, paralyzing me. Why, I don't know. This is what I came for, isn't it? Dying? To save my family? Daron.

It sounded so noble.

Almost poetic.

But now, the reality of the moment rushes through my veins in a messy, terrified panic. I didn't even get to hug Mother. Didn't tell Daron that I love him. They won't know. They won't even understand.

"Kael, please..." I step back, trembling. "I'm not ready."

Gold-filigreed hilt in hand, Kael positions himself across from me with the knife. "Whatever happens, Elara, I cannot interfere. You can't hesitate. You have to—"

Bang!

The double doors at the end don't just open; they explode inward, torn from their hinges as if hit by a battering ram of invisible force. Wood splinters rain down across the stone floor.

My head jerks around.

Vale stands in the doorway.

But the illusion is thin, frantic, tearing at the seams. Skin too pale. Eyes too dark. Shadows bleed off his coat like smoke, tendrils of darkness reaching out to grip the stone floor, searching for purchase.

"Kael!" The shout isn't a voice; it's the sound of a heavy crypt door growling shut, vibrating into my quivering lungs. "You foolish, notoriously *difficult* boy."

Frost skitters over the ground as his boot touches the floor of the throne room. The temperature plummets. Stained glass squeaks, strains, then shatters, shards clanking the ground to frame his fast strides.

"You cannot break the curse!" Vale roars, his voice doubling, tripling, trembling with the echo of the monster beneath the skin. "It is woven into the crown! It is written in *my* blood!"

"I know I can't!" Kael yells back, tears churning in his eyes like an oncoming storm. *"I know I can't!"*

Kael's hand trembles as he raises the knife between us. The steel catches the light, a flash of silver. He steps in close. Too close. His arm draws back, muscles bunching under his shirt. The blade rotates in his grip, the sharp edge angling at my throat.

My breath catches in a sob. Closing my eyes, I brace for the cut.

"I cannot break the curse..." Kael's whisper shifts the air between us to the sensation of something solid pushing into my trembling palm. "But she can."

My eyes snap open, gaze going to the golden hilt of the knife resting in my clasp. But it's the way Kael closes my fingers over it, forcing my grip, that sends a flood of shivers across my body.

I look up at him. "What? I don't understand."

"A messenger will seek you out. He'll explain everything, Elara, but—" With his free hand, he reaches up, yanks the crown off his head, then slams it down on mine. "Cut. Now."

"What?" I try to pull back in horror, but the weight of the crown crushes down on me, heavy as a tombstone, the cold metal pulsing against my aching scalp. "No!"

Panic seizes my lungs. I came to die.

Not to kill.

"Cut!" Kael screams, grabbing my wrist and yanking it up. He presses the tip of the blade against his throat. "I cannot help further! Do it, Elara! Cut!" Kael roars, his spit flying, his eyes flooded with tears, tapping the skin over his jugular, right where his pulse beats a frantic rhythm. "Take the crown and the curse." Tears spill over his lashes. "Do it for me. Do it for all the mothers I lost!"

"Don't you dare!" Vale bellows, frost racing up the steps of the dais as his strides turn to sprints. "Elara!"

"Elara..." Kael begs, his voice cracking into a sob. He stares into my eyes, the chaos clearing for a single, heart-breaking second—and all I see is a boy who witnessed too much grief. "Kill. Me."

Time slows to a crawl. I look at the knife in my hand. I look at the desperate king with tears streaming down his face. I look at the monster lunging to stop us.

I don't understand.

And yet, somehow...I know.

I grip the handle. I lift the blade.

Then I slash.

The sound is wet and tearing. Hot crimson sprays my face, blinding me for a second. The pressure on the knife gives way to a sickening slide. *Clank.*

Kael gurgles, blue eyes rolling back. His knees hit the stone dais with a crack, and he collapses sideways, heavy and twitching.

"Elara!" Vale's shout rumbles through the ground, the walls, the very pillars holding the room.

Silence crashes into the room, louder than his scream. The frost stops inches from my feet, Kael's blood pooling, soaking into the hem of the wool blanket.

I turn toward Vale.

He stands frozen at the base of the dais, his chest heaving, looking at Kael's body, then up at me. "What did you do?"

One of my hands flies to the crown, to a golden point that pulses in time with my frantic heart. My hand is shaking. My throat is raw.

A surreal giggle slips past my lips. Maybe because I'm mad. Or maybe because Death won't have the last laugh in my life.

"Crown me dead."

This concludes *Crown Me Dead.* If you have a moment, please consider leaving my story a review.

What an ending, huh? Wanna talk about it? Join me in my Facebook Reading Group for free group therapy as we prepare for *Crown Me Yours.*

CONNECT WITH ME! (NO REALLY, PLEASE DO!)

Join my mailing list and get access to my VIP Lounge, exclusive illustrations, bonus chapters, and news about my stories.
Email Sign Up

9 781955 871150